Praise for JT LeRoy an[d]
Is Deceitful Above [A]

"I can't think of any other presence in lit like JT LeRoy, one who upon mere appearance completely redrew the lines between author and art, persona and myth. Even better is rediscovering years later how boldly and bewitchingly these words trace out their somehow ghostly landscapes of desire and debris, and therein, in their essential beauty, how alive the mystery actually still is."

—Blake Butler, author of *There Is No Year*

"One of the unfortunate casualties of the JT LeRoy saga was the career of Laura Albert, a tremendously gifted and empathetic writer who found herself overshadowed by her own creation. But long after the media frenzy died down, the stories endure—harrowing, haunting and heartfelt tales that speak with the sort of raw, devastating honesty that can seem almost impossible to muster without a pseudonym. It's thrilling to finally have Laura's stories liberated from JT's story, and to have Laura and her words back together again."

—Adam Langer, author of *Crossing California*

"An eyewitness's imagination burns in his language, which is not lyrical but as vivid as a match held close to the face."

—*New York Times*

"LeRoy manages to write simply about the most tangled of emotions—and to describe, without hatred or self-pity, the most monstrous of deeds."   —*Newsweek*

"[LeRoy is] a hungry writer with the instincts of a person who fishes to eat. Once he hooks the reader he doesn't let go."   —*Bookforum*

The Heart
Is Deceitful
Above All Things

The Heart
Is Deceitful
Above All Things

Stories

JT LeRoy

HARPER ⬤ PERENNIAL

NEW YORK • LONDON • TORONTO • SYDNEY • NEW DELHI • AUCKLAND

HARPER ● PERENNIAL

Originally published in 2001 by Bloomsbury. Reprinted here by permission.

HarperCollins books may be purchased for educational, business, or sales promotional use. For information please email the Special Markets Department at SPsales@harpercollins.com.

First HarperPerennial paperback published 2016.

Designed by Joy O'Meara

Library of Congress Cataloging-in-Publication Data has been applied for.

ISBN 978-0-06-264127-4

16 17 18 19 20 RRD 10 9 8 7 6 5 4 3 2

The things I've written about are happening to people all the time.

And when they happen to you,
you believe nobody knows and nobody cares.

But I know and I care, and I've written this book for you.

Contents

Foreword

In May of 2010, it had been almost five years since the *New York Times* revealed that cause célèbre international best-selling West Virginian, former heroin-addicted, cross-dressing, truckstop-prostitute, and transgressive gay-lit "It Boy," author Jeremiah "Terminator" LeRoy, was in fact Laura Albert, a middle-aged former punk rocker and mother from Brooklyn. The radioactive fallout from this discovery was swift and savage. The media labeled her a pariah. She was condemned and excommunicated by the literary community and found guilty of fraud in New York Supreme Court for signing the name "JT LeRoy"—a fictitious person—on the contract for a movie option of her novel *Sarah*.

When a journalist buddy of mine brought this story of what was being called "The Greatest Literary Hoax Of All Time" to my attention, I was only familiar with the name JT LeRoy as a byline on entertaining, over-the-top celebrity pieces in *The New York Press*, an alternative weekly that had its heyday in late '90's New York City. But my interest was piqued, and I quickly devoured the onslaught of JT-centric articles in *Vanity Fair*, *New York Magazine*, *Rolling Stone*, *Salon*, and beyond.

After ruminating on these well-researched accounts, I had a gut feeling that there was *way* more to the story than we were be-

ing told. One voice was glaringly missing, that of Laura Albert—
the person who befriended numerous literati, music, fashion, art
world and film celebs over a decade of lengthy intimate, often
salacious phone calls in the voice of JT LeRoy. Laura appeared
in public as Speedie, the raven-haired, pushy British-voiced han-
dler of JT LeRoy, who himself was played flawlessly, in wig and
sunglasses, by her androgynous lesbian sister in law, Savannah
Knoop. Most importantly, it was Laura who put pen to paper
and actually *wrote* the glowingly-reviewed books: the novel *Sarah*
and the collection of short stories *The Heart Is Deceitful Above
All Things*. "This," I said to myself, "is the voice *I* want to hear."

So I reached out to Laura Albert via email. After a few un-
successful attempts, due to dead JT LeRoy email addresses—
a metaphor for the author's current status—we connected, and
I expressed my interest in having her tell *her* story of the JT Le-
Roy saga to me in a New Journalism–inspired feature length
nonfiction film.

From: Laura Albert ◁ ▯▯▯▯▯▯▯▯▯▯ ▷
Date: February 3, 2011 11:17:51 AM PST
To: Jeff Feuerzeig ◁ ▯▯▯▯▯▯▯▯▯▯ ▷
Subject: Re: JT Leroy—Feature Documentary

I've had so many frogs to kiss—folks coming around—to
make a film or whatever . . . and I am like the street kid suspect of any one coming around that seems too perfect. You
check out with folks I know for what it's worth. :) In a way I feel
angry—How dare you offer me hope? I've felt the right person
to work with would appear—when we were both made ready.

It can be painful to have hope. I have to do the next indicated thing every moment. And often that is just finding a
reason to stay alive. It sounds so dramatic and I can exist in

both—the commentary and the powerlessness of my crazy thoughts. I do believe I have the capacity to be honest and G-d made me ready. Not the devil. I'm a Jew. Satan is what happens when there is no more dark chocolate in the house. I do love SARAH. And I will tell you something spooky. Everything that happens in that book has come true. You'll see. Well, with my help. LOL!

Take care,
LA

PS if we do decide to do this—you have funding? I mean—you can move on this?

I then sent her *The Devil and Daniel Johnston,* my Sundance award-winning documentary from 2005 chronicling the inconceivable life of the bipolar singer-songwriter/outsider artist—with its themes of madness and creativity vividly explored, without judgment, front and center.

Laura Albert ◁ ▮▮▮▮▮▮▮▮▮▮▮▮ ▷ **wrote:**

Jeff, watched movie. Finished it this morning. It's very very beautifully made. I have a complex reaction—which has little to do with the filmmaking and more to do with the subject. Which speaks to the organic seamlessness of your creation. That the viewer can just float within the dreamscape. I cried after—it is painful. Too painful to put down why.

So even if it does not work out—with us, I am glad I saw the film. It's as if you painted it with a feather. I always thought I would see the film but was scared to. Just knew it would stir it up within me. He's a bloodline relation in the non-reality living artist kin. We're different species, but we got the same makeup. I feel envious of how clear-cut his jazz is. It's always easier when it is clear. B&W. Crazy? Yes or No. "Do I contradict myself? Very well, I contradict myself, I am large I contain multitudes." That does not go down very well for women in our culture.

Anywayz, I try to keep my craziness compartmentalized. When it comes out full force it is frightening to everyone around me and myself. I think my whole life has been about trying to find ways to function with the impediment of distortion of reality and normalize it, for everyone else. The problem was I lived in both lands. Unlike Daniel—I knew, but could not stop it. Knowing—OK this is not normal, and the same time being absolutely powerless to change it. The only option was to have the world see what I saw & felt. In a form that I could tolerate. Ahh, it's very complex. You really are lovely at getting out of the way—being Casper. Are you in SARAH? There's another good story you might read—it's in THE BEST AMERICAN NONREQUIRED READING 2003 By Dave Eggers, Zadie Smith—JT's story is called STUFF. You can probably find it used.

Take care,

LA

And now it was my turn. If I was going to spend the years it would take to unravel this massively complex, Byzantine narrative and try to understand why this unique case of fiction took place so far off the page—I would have to love the writing.

So, with great trepidation I cracked open *Sarah*. Immediately, I was in. The critics' hosannas for *"Alice In Wonderland on acid"* were not overstated. This often hilarious, surreal world of truck stop "lot lizards," a Christ-like libido-enhancing empowered Jackalope, the oddly poignant competitive yearnings of this young boy-girl to win the love and attention of his drug-addled hooker mom, revolving around a gay West Virginia diner serving out-of-place James Beard award-winning foodie-cuisine, culminating in a nail-biting 18-wheeler truck chase that easily rivals *Smokey and the Bandit* was, simply, a joy to read.

In college I went through a period where I became a big fan of Southern Gothic literature, particularly Flannery O'Connor, Harry Crews and Tennessee Williams. The writing of JT LeRoy, to me, fell neatly into that darkly comic, world-weary and wild-ass tradition.

And then I read *The Heart Is Deceitful Above All Things*. It chronicled this fictional character's much darker sexual and physical abuse-laden coming-of-age. I was equally impressed. The striking, poetic metaphors, the unflinching portrayal of psycho-sexual relationships, and the surprising empathy for the abusers of this young boy-girl, born without choice into this sad and hidden underworld, were evidence that I was in the presence of a truly great and original writer. And I decided to move forward.

In making *AUTHOR: The JT LeRoy Story* I felt it was important for the audience to feel the power of this writing. Needless to say, in the medium of film it is simply not possible to read the audience an entire short story, let alone a full-length novel. So I came up with an idea: edit a few of my favorite JT LeRoy passages into short sound-bites, to be read in a voice-over by Jeremiah "Terminator" LeRoy himself, little animations of Laura Albert's own hand-written words and primitive blue-ink-doodles-come-to-life, a parade of fantasy boy-girls found in the margins of her aging coffee-stained lined notebooks.

The first voice-over we recorded together was *Balloons*, the first of the new short stories in this expanded edition of *The Heart Is Deceitful Above All Things*. This is fitting as this was the first piece that Terminator faxed to Dr. Terrence Owens. It was

Owens who suggested that Terminator write down his thoughts, as a form of therapy, after three long years of daily one-hour suicide help-line conversations. With its theme of nihilistic, heroin-addicted punk rock-style redemption, *Balloons* unintentionally launched the soaring writing career that JT LeRoy rode into the sun, before that same sun burned him.

Laura Albert nervously entered the recording booth and approached the large microphone and music stand holding her script. Before her spread the words she had written almost two decades ago. Around her neck she wore a silver raccoon penis bone and a tiny typewriter pendant with a legend that read "Write Hard, Die Free." After a bite of the Green & Black's dark 85% cocoa chocolate bar she requested, Laura indicated that she was ready. We dimmed the lights. She took a breath, cleared her throat and, from deep within, came this boyish Southern drawl, *"It was something I always knew. Heroin, coming in balloons, was a special message to me . . ."* And suddenly, for the first time since I'd met her, Laura Albert was free. She was relaxed. She was who she was, once again conjuring the voice of JT LeRoy, inhabiting the fictional character who inhabited her as she wrote the stories in this collection.

Jeff Feuerzeig
Director/Writer/Producer
Author: The JT LeRoy Story

The Heart
Is Deceitful
Above All Things

Disappearances

His long white buck teeth hang out from a smile, like a wolf dog. His eyes have a vacant, excited, mad look. The lady holding it, crouched down to my height, is grinning too widely. She looks like my babysitter, without the braces, the same long blond braid that starts somewhere inside the top of her head. She shakes Bugs Bunny in my face, making the carrot he's clutching plunge up and down like a knife. I wait for one of the social workers to tell her I'm not allowed to watch Bugs Bunny.

'Look what your momma got you,' I hear.

Momma.

I say it softly like a magic word you use only when severely outnumbered.

'Right here, honey,' the woman with the bunny says. She smiles even wider, looking up at the three surrounding social workers, nodding at them. Their tilted heads grin back. She shakes the rabbit again.

'I'm your momma.' I watch her red, glossy lips, and I can taste the word, metallic and sour in my mouth. And I ache so badly for Her, the real one that rescues me.

I stare out at the blank faces, and from deep inside I scream and scream for Her to come save me.

• • •

When we first get back to the tiny, one-bedroom bungalow, I throw myself on the floor, kicking and screaming for my real momma.

She ignores me and makes dinner.

'Look, SpaghettiOs,' she says. I won't move. I fall asleep on the floor. I wake up in a narrow cot with Bugs Bunny next to me, and I scream.

She shows me the few toys she's gotten me. I have more and better at my real home. I throw hers out the window.

One of the social workers comes by, and I cry so hard I throw up on her navy blue tassel shoes.

'He'll get used to it, Sarah,' I hear her tell my new mom. 'Hang in there, honey,' she tells her, and pats her shoulder.

At lunch she gives me peanut butter and jelly with the crusts on. My real momma cuts the crust off. I fling the plastic Mickey Mouse plate off the table.

She spins around, hand raised into a fist. I scream, she freezes, her fist shaking, a foot away from my chest.

We both stare at each other, breathing hard. And something passes between us, and her face seals up. I don't know what it is exactly.

As my sobs start she grabs her denim jacket and leaves. I'd never been alone before, not even for five minutes, but I know something has changed, something is different, and I don't scream.

I run to my bed, curl up tight, and wait for everything to be different.

The phone's shrill ringing wakes me up. It's dark without the dinosaur night-light I used to have.

'Thank you, Operator, it works,' I hear her say quietly. Then, almost yelling, 'Hello? . . . Hello? . . . Yes, Jeremiah is here . . .'

My heart starts pounding. 'Jeremiah, honey, are you awake?' she calls out, her shadow haunting my partly opened door.

'Momma?' I call out, pushing my sheets away.

'Yes, honey, it's your foster parents.' I run to her and the phone.

'Oh yes, he's here.' I reach up for the phone with every muscle.

'What . . . oh . . .' She frowns. I jump up and down, straining.

'Bad? . . . Well he hasn't been *very* bad . . .' She turns away from me, the black phone cord wrapping around her.

'Momma!' I shout, and pull on the phone cord.

'Yes . . . I see,' she says, nodding, turning away from me farther. 'Oh, is that why? OK, I'll tell him.'

'Gimme . . . Momma!' I yell, and yank hard on the cord.

'So you don't want to speak to him?'

'Daddy!' I yell, and grab hard. The phone receiver flies out of her hands, bounces on the blue, sparkled linoleum, and slides under the table. It spins like a bottle, the mouthpiece facing up. I spring for it, sliding like my daddy taught me when we played whiffleball. Just as my finger touches the dull, black plastic of the phone, it jerks and flies out from under the table and away from me.

'Got it!' I hear her gasp. 'Hello? . . . Yes! Yes! He did that . . . Fuck yeah, I'll tell him.'

I twist around and drag myself from under the table.

'OK, thanks.' She smiles into the phone.

'No!' I reach up with my arms.

'Y'all take care . . .'

'No!' My feet skid under me, leaving me back on my stomach.

'Good-bye.' In slow motion she swirls like a ballerina, a grin wide on her face.

'No!'

Her arm rises into the air, the spiral cord swinging in front of me. I grab for it, her hand sweeps backward, and I catch nothing.

'Momma!' I scream, and I watch the receiver lowered into its cradle on the couch's white plastic end table.

I scramble to the phone and snatch it up. 'Momma, Momma, Daddy!' I shout into it.

'They hung up,' she says. She sits on the opposite end of the couch and lights a cigarette, her bare legs pulled to her chest, tucked under her large white T-shirt.

Even though I hear the dial tone humming, I still call for them. I press the receiver to my ear as tightly as I can, in case they're there, past the digital tone calling to me like voices lost in a snowstorm.

'They're gone,' she says, blowing smoke out. 'You wanna know what they said?'

'Hello? . . . Hello?' I say quieter.

'They didn't want to talk to you.'

'Hello?' I turn away from her and wrap myself in the cord.

'I said they did not want to talk to you.'

'Uh-uh,' I whisper. I twist more, and the receiver slips out of my hands, banging on the linoleum.

'Don't you throw my phone!' She gets up quickly and grabs the receiver at my feet.

'You ain't gonna be throwing things no more,' she says, and unwraps the wire snaked around me, jerking it violently around my Superman pajamas like a whip.

She hangs up the phone and goes back to the couch, crossing her legs. She twists backward to look at me.

'I went through a lot to get you back, and you're going to be grateful, you, you little shit.'

A loud gasp pops out of me, a silent sob. I'm beyond regular crying.

When Momma and Daddy go out without me, leaving me with Cathy the babysitter, I always cry awhile. Sometimes I even scream and lay on the wood floor near the front door, smelling the leftover trail of sweet perfume Momma left. But I always stop crying, remembering my special treats left in the top drawer for being a good, grown-up boy. Cathy and me watch the *Rainbow Brite* video, and she reads three books to me, and when I wake up they're back, Momma and Daddy are always back in their place. 'We always come back,' they tell me.

'Do you want to know what they said about you?' I hear her puff hard on the cigarette. I stare at a huge water bug scurrying under the couch past her foot. I shake my head no, turn around, and go back to my bed.

I grab Bugs Bunny from under the cot where I'd shoved him, wrap my arms around him under my blankets, and between hiccups whisper in his oversize fuzzy ear, 'When you wake up, they'll be back, they'll be back.'

That was the first night I wet. I woke up feeling a cold dampness under my blankets as if an air conditioner had been turned on somewhere beneath me. I'd never wet before, unlike Alex, my best friend from preschool when I lived with my real parents. When he spent the night, my momma had to put the special plastic cover under the galaxy sheets. 'He has accidents,' I repeated to my momma as I helped her stretch the opaque white plastic over the mattress. 'I don't,' I told her.

'No, you use the toilet like a big boy.' She smiled at me, and

I laughed with joy. I had a giraffe ladder I'd climb up on. I'd stand tall as a giant, raise the seat myself, and I'd rain down my powerful stream. I used to float my toy boats in the toilet and pour down on them, sinking them, till my mom explained that's not good to do, so I did it in my bath instead, making my speedboats and tankers suffer under my forceful gale.

When Alex and I lay in bed discussing who had a bigger rocketship that went fastest to the moon, I felt proud every time I heard the aluminum foil-like crinkle of him moving on his sheets against the smooth swishing of mine. 'It's OK,' I'd tell him in the morning, patting his shoulder. 'It's just an accident. You'll use the giraffe one day, too.'

I peel the wet blanket and sheet off me carefully and look down at the wet, my wet. Bugs Bunny grins up at me, his fuzzy cheek fur matted and damp.

I sit up slowly and stare at the bright yellow room around me. I had had dinosaurs painted all over my old walls. Here, tacked up, is a poster of a large clown, frowning, maybe crying, holding a droopy flower.

'Look at the clown, look at the clown, isn't he funny?!' my new momma had said. I nodded but didn't smile. In my old room my momma would complain, 'There's no place to put all these toys.' Two blue milk crates side by side hold all my clothes and toys now, and they're not half-full.

I stand there leaning against the cot, staring at it all: the dark wet patch on my red Superman pajamas, the orange swirly-patterned linoleum lumpy and bubbled like little turtles are living beneath it, the whitish brown cottage-cheese stuff in the ceiling corners, the ABC books I'd outgrown six months ago buried in the crates.

And I know I won't cry. I just know it isn't possible. I undress quickly and repeat to myself all I need to dress myself. I dig in the milk crate: one shirt, two arms, one underwear, two legs, one pants, two legs, two socks, two feet. My old sneakers. I put on the ones I can close and open with sticky stuff by myself, not hers that she got me, ones you have to tie. Two sneakers, two feet.

'You dressed yourself!' she'd say.

'All by myself,' I'd tell her, and I'd get a star on my chart. Twenty stars and I got a matchbox car. I had near a hundred of them.

I go into the living room quietly. She lies on the couch, curled under a fuzzy blanket with a lion on it. Open cans and cigarettes are strewn on the floor and coffee table. The TV is on with no sound, no cartoons, just a man talking.

I tiptoe past her, silently pull a chair over to the front door, climb up, and noiselessly turn the locks. I know how, my daddy taught me in case of a fire or an emergency and I needed to get out.

I climb down, turn the knob, and pull. The light makes me squint, and the coolness of the air makes me shiver, but I know I have to go, it's an emergency. I have to get out.

I walk for a long time, staring at my sneakers, the only familiar thing around me. I concentrate on them, walking quickly on the cracked, weed-filled sidewalk, trying to escape the crooked bungalows, all with sagging, rotting porches, with paint cracking like dried mud. Dogs bark and howl, a few birds chirp now and then, and the slam of car doors makes me jump as people get home or leave for work.

A huge gray factory hovers up ahead, like a metallic castle floating in its thick, yellowish bellows of smoke. I watch my sneakers for directions. They're from home. Like stories about carrier pigeons I loved to hear, I know they'll return me to home. I survive crossing streets by myself for the first time. Even though no cars are visible, I run, my heart thudding, expecting to be crushed suddenly. I walk fast, shaking my hands like rattles to keep me going, like a train's engine forcing me forward, keeping me from stopping, keeping me from curling up in a tight ball and trying to wake up.

Past the heavy-gated factory, chugging and snorting so loud I can't hear the soft padding of my sneakers on the gravel as I run. Run from the gaping, smoking, metal dragon's mouth, trying to swallow me whole. And then I'm going uphill, through a field so thick with brown grass I can't see my sneakers, but I know at the top I'll see my home, my real home. I'll run through the door and into their arms, and everything will be right again.

My foot catches on a half-buried rubber tire, and I fall forward, my chin and hands digging into the reddish brown earth.

I lie there quietly, too surprised to move. I lift my chin and stare at the tilted world around me. The dark clay earth's spread out and glitters from the multicolored shards, as if a pane of stained glass is hiding beneath.

A slow stream of watery red fills the moats my sliding hands made, and the pain, stinging and sharp, stops my breath. I pull my hands back and there are wet dark slits in them. My white T-shirt catches the red tear in my chin.

And I know they're really gonna be sorry now. I get up and run toward the top of the cliff. The tears are coming now and little yelplike screams slowly getting louder as I get closer.

Right over the hill is the house with the big green lawn, and swings and slides, and my castle in the back. My house.

I'll burst through the door and scream till they come running like they did when I fell off my swing and scraped my forehead. But I won't shut up, I won't let them kiss it better. I'll scream till the roof flies off, till all the windows shatter, till they themselves blow apart and explode. I'll make them sorry.

I'm almost at the top of the hill. I can smell the eucalyptus scent of the living room, hear the tick tick of the wood clock that chimes with a colorful cuckoo every hour.

I scream and lunge for the top.

The grass is deep and thick on the flat hilltop. I push my way through the brush. I see the edge ahead where it all drops down, down to the yard fenced in white. I slow down, my breath hitching, my hands balled into soggy fists. I reach out a shaking arm and move aside the last weeds blocking my way home.

I'll let them cover me in kisses. I'll let them hug me long and hard. I'll let them give me hot cocoa and cookies because I'm such a brave boy.

I'll let them, if only their house were down there instead of the tight rows and rows of peeling, rotting bungalows.

At that ledge, overlooking the worn and ruined houses, I understand the world has suddenly become as frightening, violent, and make-believe as the cartoons I wasn't supposed to watch.

When Sarah walks into the brick police station I scream so loud, everything goes silent except her high heels clicking toward me.

I cling to the officer who found me, showed me how to use his radio, bought me a chocolate ice cream, and let me wear his cap after I let a nurse clean my cuts.

'Your mommy's here.' He leans down and tries to push me toward her. They speak above me, and I can smell the strong perfume on her, not like my mom's clean laundry scent.

I hold tighter and bury my face in the soft dark blue weave of his pants.

'I thought you wanted to go home to your mommy,' he says, looking down at me. I shake my head no.

'He's just confused,' she says. She crouches and whispers into my ear, 'If you come with me now, I'll take you back to your momma.' I turn to face her. She smiles, winks at me, and puts out her hand, tan and thin with long red nails.

I slowly let go of the policeman's leg and give her my hand, wrapped in a bandage and stained with chocolate ice cream that looks like blood.

'Good boy.' The officer pats my head. I let my mother lead me through the brightly lit fluorescent station, but my head is turned back to the policeman, watching him wave and smile good-bye, as if I know I will never see the police in that magic, protective light ever again.

She only nods her head while blowing smoke out of the window as we drive from the police station.

'Take me home,' I repeat again and again. She stares straight ahead. She slides her palm up to her forehead in a heavy, slow movement, like ironing.

Soon the road looks familiar, the cracked two-lane tar and the big metal factory, its pipes connecting to itself like silver luggage handles. Panic lurches in my chest, and I turn toward her in my seat.

'You said you'd take me home!' Her lips suck in as she chews them.

I pound on the window. 'Lemme out, lemme out, lemme out!' The car veers suddenly off the road, opposite the gated factory. The ripping sound of the emergency brake reminds me of my daddy pulling up to our house, and I sob. She holds her cigarette up and blows on its red, dusty tip till it glows like a night lamp.

'It's bad to smoke,' I tell her between gasps. 'My momma, my momma says so.'

She looks over at me. 'Is that what they say?' she says, real singsong-like. I nod, spit I can't swallow dribbling from my mouth.

'Well, I'll have to make myself a note to thank them very, very much.' She sucks hard on the cigarette, then pulls out the ashtray, crumbles it into it, and blows a stream of white smoke into my face.

'Does that meet your spec-i-fications?' She smiles, close-mouthed.

The tears are bubbling in my eyes, hazing everything like a cotton film.

'OK, OK. Now before you start wailing, let's you and I have us a little chat.' She turns to me, a leg bent on the bench-type seat between us. I blink at my tears, and the picture clears some, but more are coming too fast.

'Let's get this straight. I'm your mother. I had you. You came right from here.' She pulls up her denim skirt and pats the flat dark under her pantyhose, between her legs. I look away, out the window, toward the blurry factory.

'No, you pay me mind.' She reaches out and turns my face toward her. Before I can scream she says quickly, 'Your momma and daddy want you to hear me. If you want to go home to them, you listen.' I swallow my scream and nod.

'You gonna listen?'

'I go home!'

'You gonna listen?' She reaches under my chin, raising my face to hers. I nod and then shake my head free of her hand. I hiccup hard, and chocolate ice cream runs down my mouth and shirt.

'Jesus . . .' She grabs an end of my shirt and wipes at my face, hard, not the soft dabs my momma does, even as I wriggle my face away from her. I don't try to pull away, though.

As she rubs my face, pressing my lips into my teeth, she says, 'I had you when I was just fourteen years old, can't say I wanted you; can't say I didn't do rabbits' tricks to try and get rid of you.' She spits on my chin and wipes hard, ignoring my Band-Aid.

'If my father'd let me, you'd long been flushed down some toilet. You understand?' I nod, even though I don't. I sob quietly, my lips sucking in.

'They took you from me . . . goddamn social worker cunts.' She lets my face go and looks past me to the factory. 'Now I'm eighteen now . . .' She looks at me, nods. 'I got you back.' She pats my head. 'See, you're mine.'

'Take me home,' I whisper.

'Do you hear what I'm saying to you?' she yells. She reaches down into her denim bag and pulls out another cigarette. I turn toward my window.

'Take me home,' I say louder.

'They don't want you.' She flicks her lighter.

'Take me home!' I yell, and hit the glass.

'You goddamn, spoilt brat . . .' She grabs my hand and twists me toward her. 'Don't make me whoop you!'

I gasp hard, and a little more chocolate ice cream dribbles out. She jerks my arms above my head, puffs on her cigarette, and exhales, her head shaking the smoke out like a released balloon.

'They said they got rid of you 'cause you're bad . . . you understand?'

I try to pull my arms down, my face red and swollen. She leans closer, into my ear. 'Your foster par . . . your momma and daddy . . .' She grabs my cheeks with her other hand and turns my face to her, the cigarette hanging from her lips.

'They . . . shit!' The cigarette drops. 'Shit!' She lets go of me. 'See what you made me do?' She leans down to retrieve the lit cigarette, and I jump over to the door, pushing and pulling at the handle.

'Momma and Daddy never showed you how to unlock a goddamn car door?' She laughs behind me. 'You wanna go home? . . . Fine, I'll take you, I'll take you back.'

The keys jingle in the ignition, and the brake rips again. The car rumbles beneath us. I let go of the door handle.

'Go—go home,' I sputter.

'Yeah, go fucking home!' She rolls down her window and flicks her cigarette out.

She pulls back out onto the tarmac, drives past the factory and the dirty, broken houses, one of which is hers.

I sit back in my seat, heaving, wiping chocolate drool off my mouth.

'I was just trying to help you,' she says quietly.

I look out at the abandoned shacks overrun with grass and vines, like a museum exhibit of another world.

'My guess is they'll just call the police when I bring you back.'

We pass children with sooty faces playing in a turned-sideways refrigerator.

'The reason you're with me, you know, is because they don't want you no more.' I turn in my seat, a little toward her. 'They told me, 'member when they called last night?' She adjusts the rearview mirror. 'They said you're a bad boy, and that's why they gave you away. If they loved you so goddamn much, well then, why'd they get rid of you? Answer me that.'

I sniffle and swallow a snot glob.

'They found out how evil you are, those police . . . they were ready to do you in. If I hadn't've begged them, those cops would've taken out their guns and shot you through.' She adjusts her mirror again, then runs her finger under her eyes, wiping off the black smears.

'I got ice cream,' I whisper.

'Just because I convinced them not to kill you.' She looks over at me. 'If I hadn't taken you from your foster, your momma and daddy, where you think you'd be?'

I choke on a hiccup. She pats my back a little too hard.

'They didn't try to stop the social worker from taking you away, now, did they?' she asks me softly. I look out at the mountains rising and falling into each other, little gray wood shacks lodged between them like food caught between teeth. They hadn't tried to stop the social worker from taking me. They'd even turned away fast from the car once I was in it. As I screamed and banged on the back windshield for them, I saw my daddy hug my momma with both arms, her head on his chest, and they walked back toward the house, they didn't turn around.

'How many times did you go cryin' and throwing tantrums like a spoilt baby if you didn't get your way, huh?'

I look up at the clouds, too gray and weighted to be floating over the mountain peaks. 'Be a good boy and don't cry for Momma,' she had said lots of times. I usually ended up crying, though.

'Why do you think the police got you when you ran away, not your foster, not your momma and daddy, huh?'

I watch a yellow dog chasing what looks like a long-tail fox through the burnt orange bushes near the road.

'I begged the cop not to take long sharp knives and stick them in your eyes so they pop like grapes.' She reaches down to her bag, pulls out and lights another cigarette. 'I had to pay them, too.' She pulls up her bag. 'See my wallet in there . . . go on.' She pats my shoulder, a cigarette ash falling down my shirt. I reach into her bag. 'The wallet with the red heart on it, open it.' I pull the Velcro lips apart; she reaches over and pulls the money out from inside. 'You know what a hundred-dollar bill looks like?'

She glances at me. I nod, my Daddy had shown me, Ben Franklin and kites. She blows a plume of smoke straight up.

'See any one-oh-ohs in there, kid?' she says, the cigarette dangling in her mouth.

I shake my head and swallow a hiccup.

'Ain't in there, right? . . . Huh? . . . Answer me, darlin', I ain't gettin' any younger.'

'No,' I mumble. Her red-nailed hand scrunches them up back into the wallet. 'Well, you said it, kid, no one-oh-ohs, you got your proof. You know who got the one-oh-oh? Huh?' She turns from the road and looks at me while sealing up the pink heart-covered wallet. I breathe in deeply to try to smell the musty, leathery smell of my daddy's wallet. I put my hand on her wallet, but it's not the smooth, worn skin warmed from his back pocket.

'Get offa!' Her hand knocks mine. 'Little thief, trying to get everything. You better not have taken none.'

I blink at her, too disoriented to cry. She drops the wallet into her bag at her feet.

'So you saw for your own self? No goddamn one-oh-oh. So guess who got it?' She jabs me with her elbow. I look out my window.

'The cops, the policeman, he has it, I had to give him all that, one-oh-oh, to not . . .' She pushes me lightly. 'You listenin'? I had to pay them not to strap you down and put you in the electric chair.'

I've seen the electric chair on one of those cartoons I'm not supposed to watch. A cat got tricked into one, strapped down, and the switch pulled. His skeleton glowed, his eyes bulged out, and after, he was just a pile of ashes.

'I've done you a favor taking you . . . so it's up to you . . . we can go to the police and turn you in. If I take you to your fosters, they're only going to call the police and get you arrested.'

My stomach is cramped. Everything looks strangely lit and too shiny under the greenish, mold-colored sky. The clouds aren't even trying to clear the mountains any more, they're too loaded down with dark, smashing into the treeless peaks.

'If I didn't take you when I did, you'd be hung up on a cross. They teach you about Jesus?'

I nod a small yes. When I'd stayed at my babysitter Cathy's house, I saw a picture of Him. He was almost naked, with nails in him, on a cross, and if I moved my head back and forth, his blood flowed, his head tilted more, and his eyes closed, then popped open, looking out in an accusing stare.

'The police will nail you up on the cross, if they don't give you the chair.' She spits on her cigarette, tucks it behind her ear, and reaches out, takes my hand, and opens it in her lap. I watch her press a long red fingernail into my bandaged palm.

'They drive the nail in here.' She presses harder. My hand curls up around her finger, but I don't try to move it.

'Your momma and daddy will hammer another nail in right here . . .' She drops my hand, lifts my T-shirt, and presses her long nail below my ribs. She twists her finger in.

'And they'll stick one here . . .' She slides her nail under my shirt to my chest, under my throat, and digs it in.

My head is shaking, racing all His blood out, draining him, till it crashes like waves and surrounds the big white house with my parents inside and carries them all away forever.

'I want to stay with you,' I whisper.

'Well, we're not that far from the police station . . . they'll be real glad to get their hands on you again.'

I swallow loudly, feeling her hand resting on my throat, pressing.

'I want to stay with you,' I whisper again.

'What did you say?' Her nail flicks against my skin.

When I asked Cathy why He was like that, she told me it was because He loved me and because I was a sinner. Jesus died like that, suffering for me.

'No policeman.'

'You don't want me to take you to your foster parents?'

I shake my head a small no.

'You better learn some manners, kid . . . if I'm not going to turn you in.' Her nail slides up my throat to under my chin, lifting my head toward her.

'Ma'am, you say. Understand? You say ma'am, you say sir, you say thank you, you say please . . . you were rude with your fosters and they got rid of you. You're rude to me and we go right to the police, you hear?'

I avoid her eyes, looking past her to the dark clouds tumbling ahead.

'Ma'am,' I repeat just like the coffee-colored maid would call my momma.

'Yes, ma'am, please let me stay with you, thank you. Is that what you mean to be saying?'

A dry swallow squeezes down my stretched-up neck like a snake digesting a rat.

'Ma'am . . .' My voice cracks. 'Thank you, please, no policeman . . .'

She pulls her nail away, and my head drops some.

'So, if you ever cry about your fosters again, we go straight to the police. You hear?'

I nod, staring vaguely at trees starting to bend and shake in the wind. Her hand flies up quickly and slaps the top of my head, bouncing it back against the seat. 'If I take the time and energy to waste my breath speaking to you, you damn well better afford me the courtesy of replyin'.'

I don't understand her, so I nod again, sucking on my lips to still them from shaking, and I taste the salty ooze running from my nose.

Her fist bangs down on my shoulder, knocking me sideways to the seat.

'You answer when I talk to you,' she says loudly but calmly above me.

I stay down on the seat, my stomach releasing a horrible trembling that spreads throughout me. A loud sob fills the car.

'Don't you dare cry!' Her hand searches in my hair. 'I've had about enough of you crying to last me a lifetime.' She yanks my head up by my hair and then pulls my face back to look up into hers. Her eyes gleam like glazed blue enamel, her mouth turned into a red semi-smile.

'If you cry any more, not only will I give you something to be really cryin' for . . .' She shakes my head. 'I will drive you straight to your foster parents and watch while they and the cops nail you up, set you on fire, and chop you up, while everyone cheers and laughs and spits at you. Understand?'

A car horn blares at us; she lets go of my hair and swerves back to her side of the road. The other car is still honking as we pass.

'Jesus!' She grabs the cigarette behind her ear.

The click of her lighter sounds bizarre in the sudden silence inside the car.

There are many times I've cried when I didn't have to, when I'd only bumped myself lightly or something, but I'd wail anyway, nice and loud to let them know I'd been injured and to punish them for letting me get hurt in the first place.

They're not here to come running, and if they were, they wouldn't just walk in the opposite direction while they sent me away again. This time they'd laugh and spit and do to me what I did to Jesus. They'd tell me I was a bad boy, and I'd watch them rip down, off my chart, all my stars.

I feel my tears cut off, stopped up somewhere below my throat. I swallow hard and flush them away.

'So should I turn around, kid?' She puffs a few times. I start to nod but stop myself.

'Yes, please, ma'am. Thank you,' I say clearly.

'Very good!' She pats my head hard. 'We'll turn you into a good boy yet . . . now all we gotta do is make sure the cops or nobody don't get you before that time.'

She rolls up her window as the first few heavy drops of rain splat inside her door. The car fills with her smoke, and she pats my leg softly.

'You know, we only have each other from now on, you see. I fought for you. You'll have to fight for me. I'm all you got.' She smiles.

And I watch the big yard with the white house with the room with dinosaur-covered walls and a racing car bed, and shelves of toys and charts with stars and a smiling momma and daddy, I watch it fold up neat like a gas station map, and I bury and hide it like a treasure map.

The car slows some, the tires screeching as she turns around on the black road top.

I watch the storm sky, a bruised blue black, following right behind us.

We have to leave, have to pack up right away and go. The digital clock on the Formica counter says 3:47 A.M. I stand in front of her, rubbing my eyes. She hangs up the phone; it was them again, my fosters. They've called almost every night for the last week since I first got here. I don't cry and reach for the phone any more. Last night I didn't even jump out of bed when the phone rang, I only got out of bed because she called me to the phone. I stood and waited, my thumb anchored in my mouth, Bugs Bunny pressed to my chest, while she nodded and shook her head as she listened to and repeated all the bad things I'd done and how they wanted me to go to jail. I didn't ask to speak to them. I waited until she hung up, waited to see what she would decide.

'They really want me to turn you in.' She pats the phone. I press my face into the stuffed rabbit's fake fur; he smells like saliva and pee.

'But we're a team, right?' She sips from the open beer next to the phone. I shift my weight from leg to leg.

'While I was at work you did all I asked you to, didn't you?' She pulls the black web net off her pulled-up hair and unpins the Sarah nametag that has a smiley face off her short pink dress.

I nod. I had made myself a peanut-butter-and-jelly sandwich, and I washed the dishes standing over the sink on a chair, the way she showed me. I hadn't let anybody in, and I put myself to bed at eight P.M., as she said.

'All the lights was on,' she said, lighting a cigarette. 'I have to pay for the electricity around here. You see any sugar daddy pickin' up the tab?' She gazes around the room, then sits on the couch, crossing her feet on the coffee table. 'You think I like dealing with coked-up truckers all night? Letting them feel my ass for their goddamned quarter tip?' She kicks an empty can off the table toward me, drags deeply, and blows smoke out through her nose. 'So you can be burning my money up?'

I shake my head and stare at her sneakers, dirty white with silver laces. 'No social workers dropped by, right?'

'No,' I mumble.

'Mind!' She leans forward.

'No, *ma'am*.'

'You didn't answer the phone, right?'

I shake my head no, then quickly add, 'No, ma'am.'

'When they come again, what do you say?' Her foot taps.

'When you're at work I got a babysitter.' I think of Cathy, and falling asleep listening to her talking and laughing on our telephone.

''Cause they're just testing you. You answer wrong and you go straight to the jailhouse. You hear me?' She knocks off another empty can with her foot.

'Yes'm,' I whisper.

'You are so spoilt, and you don't know it. Well, it's all over with now. I'm all over your shit, kid.' She reaches in her dress pocket and pulls out some crumpled dollars. 'Fifteen fuckin' dollars, OK? Fifteen! How the fuck am I gonna feed you with this shit?!' She kicks the money off the table. 'Goddamn spoilt brat.' She leans over her lap, folding her arms around her head. I stand there watching the quivers traveling down her spine like a breeze rippling water, listening to the little gasps escaping her. She raises her head, her eyes dripping black ink. 'Get the fuck into bed!' she screams.

'We gotta go, we gotta get the fuck outta here.' There are garbage bags partially filled on the kitchen floor. She unplugs the clock and drops it in.

'Get dressed . . . go, hurry!' She waves her arm at me. I go into my room, flick on the light, and dig out my clothes from the milk crates. They're all clothes I've worn already. I don't have my own hamper here. When I told her all my clothes were dirty and showed her the pile, she said if she wears her clothes until they're ready to walk, so can I. I feel comforted by the dusty smell of my clothes as I put them on.

'Goddamned social workers telling me what to do,' I hear her mutter. 'Stuck-up cunts, fuck them, fuck them . . . let's move it in there, kid!'

She comes into my room with a big black garbage bag.

'Pack.' She opens it and throws my clothes in, then hands it to me to do. She starts pulling my blankets off my bed. 'Goddamn it, you pissed it again!' She pulls them off and shoves them into the bag. 'I told you, you'll lie in it till you learn it ain't the god-damn fucking toilet! Jesus!' She finishes stuffing it in and leaves my room. I hear her swearing and tossing things into bags while I put the rest of my clothes in on top of my blankets.

'We'll have fun!' she shouts. 'I'll take you to Disney World. I'll get me a job as a character, I'd make a good princess or some-body. You can be there all the time, you like Mickey Mouse, don'tcha?! . . . It'll be better there, you'll see . . . I'll get you so many fuckin' toys your fosters'll seem like poor damned slobs.'

I hear her tossing things across the room. 'I take care of my kid . . . fuck them!' Something slams into the wall and breaks. 'Fuck them.'

Everything is loaded into the car. Plastic bags are in the trunk, in the backseat, and under my feet. 'Isn't this fun?' she asks me while snapping open a beer.

'Yes'm,' I whisper, and yawn, looking out at the sky, a thick, pasty black. She backs out of the cracked, concrete driveway and onto the gritty tar road. Insects and dust zoom by in the head-lights like crashing meteors.

'You're mine. Fuck them, telling me what all to do.' Yellow porch lights blink by. 'Pay a goddamn babysitter four dollars an hour, and I don't near make that in tips when it's slow. Fuck 'em.' She hits the dashboard with a fist, and I jump.

'We got two hundred dollars waiting in a wire for us when it gets day.' She grins to the windshield, then turns to me with a sly look on her face. 'Know who sent us that money?' I don't answer. 'You won't believe who sent us that two hundred.' She laughs. 'The only thing your grandfather hates more than an unrepentant sinner like myself . . .'—she slaps her chest—'is the god-damned government telling people all what to do with their own life, money, and childrens.' She laughs louder. 'And Lord does he hate them social workers.' The sky seems to be getting blacker, not lighter, or maybe it's just the mountains rising up around us.

'One tried to come into his house, somebody made some complaint saying they'd seen Noah, my brother, whipped . . . well, after he got done speaking with all those folks he's donated the church's money to . . . well . . .' She shakes her hand like it's too hot. 'Not only was she fired, but no uninvited government folks ever set foot on his land again.' She laughs so hard, she has to rest her head on the steering wheel for a few seconds.

A thin, pale blue ooze of light streaks the sky ahead of us. My grandparents, my foster grandparents, live up north, and at Christmas they bring me so much candy that my momma, my foster momma, takes it away and hides it.

'How do you think I got you back, darlin'?' She reaches her hand out to ruffle my hair, and I jump. 'Social worker's callin' him up, askin' him to sign the papers, like you're some pound dog, just sign you away so some stuck-up sinners can adopt you, steal you forever.' She fishes in her jeans jacket breast pocket for a cigarette.

'He'd be damned if he'd let the government steal his blood . . .' The cigarette flaps in her mouth. 'Got me a lawyer, paid for my clothes, laid out more for you now than when I squirted you out, he wouldn't pay for a diaper then, cheap son of a bitch.' She combs her hair back with her fingers. 'He said if he has to call out the goddamned Mountaineer Militia, he would. 'Course he didn't cuss, be a damned sight if he did, tight-assed fucker.' She tucks the cigarette behind her ear.

'I feel good, damn.' She leans over and pats my head again, a little too hard. 'We're a good team . . . you an' me . . . nobody takes what's mine.' I yawn suddenly. She reaches into another pocket. 'You tired? Don't be tired, I need your company . . . here.' She hands me a ball of tinfoil. 'Open that all up . . . be careful.' I pick the tight ball open to reveal little blue pills. 'Take one . . . no, no, OK, take one and bite it in half.'

'Is it medicine?' I push the pills around the silver. They're just like the ones in the cabinets, locked above the refrigerator at my old house, not the big chewable ones I get.

'Yeah, it's medicine . . . so do what Momma tells you—bite half.' I hold one up to my mouth and bite it. The whole pill crumbles into my mouth, tasting bitter and chalky. My tongue rolls out.

'No! Swallow it! . . . Swallow!' Her hand cups my mouth. I taste her palm, salty and dry. Her voice rises. 'Swallow now, god-damn it!' I pull my tongue in, forcing the pill slivers to the back of my throat, and swallow. She presses her hand hard against my lips. 'You swallow?' I nod. 'Don't drop those pills!' I hold them carefully in the foil in my hand. 'I'll take another one myself, I reckon.' She releases my mouth and takes the pills from me, popping one into her mouth before she balls them up and shoves them into her pocket.

'See, now you'll feel good, too.' She grins and pats my head again.

'See, I take care of you, tellin' me I don't, when I was fourteen maybe I didn't take care of you right, but then the voices you were throwin' was enough to drive a bean field Mexican insane.' She shoves the cigarette from behind her ear into her lips.

'You was possessed . . .' She rubs my shoulder and smiles strangely. Pinks are leaking into the pale blues like eye shadow.

'What was I supposed to do, anyways? You spoke in dev-ils' tongues, middle of the night, you'd start up, then Satan's voice . . . Jesus, went to healings for you, not his church, mind you; see, he ain't want nothin' to do with you then. You weren't his grandson then, huh?'

I yawn again and feel my eyes getting heavy. I wish my Bugs Bunny wasn't in the trunk.

'Naw, you ain't took the pill?' I nod.

'You took it?'

'Yes'm.' I yawn again.

'OK, all right. We got a drive ahead of us, and I'm doin' this for you, for you, so you ain't leavin' me . . .' She leans over toward me and shakes me hard. 'Hold on, hold on, it'll be soon!' she shouts in my ear.

I can see the outline of trees along the mountain against the glazed dark blue sky. My eyes start to blink closed.

'Stop that!' She pulls my thumb out of my mouth. I had quit sucking my thumb a year ago and gotten a big star on my chart. But I'd seen her when I woke in the morning; she'd been curled up on the couch, her blankets tangled at her feet, her thumb deep in her mouth. It had made me laugh, although I said nothing.

'That was quick . . .' I jolt awake, the sky a deep violet, and the blood pounding too loudly in my ears.

'Not tired any more, huh?' I gaze around, unsure of where I am. I feel panic surging, the same as when they left me, sent me away.

'You look like a bug-eyed rabbit. Told ya to only take half. You'll learn to mind me . . .' Her words come too fast and quiet past the hollow ringing in my ears. 'Soon we'll be gettin' big money . . . don't you worry, your grandfather won't ever let your fosters get you back. Fuck them socials, tryin' to tell me . . .' Her voice turns high in imitation, 'Maybe he's better off with them. Fuck 'em. They try and get you back, your grandfather will squash them again!'

'They want me back?' I say loudly, my body shaking.

'What? Hell no, hell no . . .' She hits the steering wheel. ''Member the call, that phone call, just a few hours ago?' I nod and can't stop. 'Well, that was the call, they all died. Your fosters, they're dead as doornails.' She pats my head hard again. 'Cops killed 'em . . . 'cause of you . . . that's why we hadda go. So you better not talk to cops or social workers, nobody . . . or we'll get killed, cut up . . .' She makes chopping motions with her hand.

I wrap my arms around me. My skin is peeling off, and soon I'll step out of it. I claw at my body to help the sloughing skin come off.

'What're you doin'?'

I shout past the loud buzzing in my head, 'I'm digging myself out!' and watch clean, cold shafts of sun shadows rip into my flesh.

A small thread of lightning spools through the black sky. I sit up on piled-up blankets and keep my eyes on the bar's big screen door. Pickup trucks and beat-up old long cars pull in and out next to ours. It's not raining, but short distant claps of thunder break the crickets and jukebox noise.

I used to run to their bed and she'd hold up the blanket like a tent, and I'd climb over her body, warm and soft like dough, to the empty center between them, and the thunder would attack around us. My fosters, fucking fosters, like Sarah calls them.

The screen door kicks open and a wobbly man in a cowboy hat leaning way too heavily on a small, yellowish woman, walks onto the muddy dirt. 'Where's goddamned car gone at?' he yells, pushes her away, and stumbles behind the club.

I watch the door again. Sarah went in to use the bathroom some time ago when it was still light; now it's been dark awhile.

'Don't move,' she told me, and I haven't. I watch the door for her and the road for cops.

'While I'm in there going to the bathroom, you see any of 'em you hide down.'

Cops almost got me once already. We were pulled over on the side of the road, I was asleep in the back, she was in the front with the seat leaned down.

'Ma'am, ma'am, you OK, ma'am?' I heard her jump up. The flashlight waving above the blanket pulled over my head made me feel like I was hiding in a deep lake, breathing air from the sun's penetrating rays. 'Fine, I'm fine, just dandy, sir.'

'Don't mean to startle you, but you can't camp here, ma'am. You in need of assistance, ma'am?' His voice was soft like the boys that came around to cut the lawn had been at my fosters, fucking fosters.

'No, no . . . just on my way to Florida, see some of the family, got a little tired . . .' Her keys rattle and turn in the ignition.

'Sorry, ma'am, there's a cheap motel up a ways . . .'

'Oh, I will check it out.' The car rolls forward slightly. 'Well, thank you, sir.'

'Yes, ma'am, have a safe trip.'

The car pulls onto the road. 'Righty-right, see ya . . .' Her hand taps a good-bye. 'Motherfucker,' she mutters.

'You up?' Her hand gropes behind the seat. 'I'm up, you're up,' she says, and the blanket is pulled off me.

I raise my head cautiously. 'You were wise to stay down or they woulda taken you. And that woulda been that.'

The car door opening and loud laughter wakes me.

'Can't you all but wait till we get on to your place?'

'Pretty flower like you, ah won't let you be wiltin' on me.'

I stay quiet against the backseat.

When they settle into the seats, I raise my head slightly. A big cowboy hat with a man under it is where she should be, driving. They smell like smoke and the beers she drinks.

'I ran them boys away from you with but a fly swatter and shotgun, sugar. Claim you for my own some.'

'They did all clear away like jackrabbits when you brought me that Jack and ginger.'

'Damn straight they would.' He snorts. The dark of the road floods the car.

'Lemme see in there, girlie.'

'That's all you get for now.'

Outside their laughter I fall back asleep.

The door buzzer on the small gray house glows orange, like a lit Halloween pumpkin's eye. A tinny, high-pitched buzz comes out of it.

'Goddamned,' a man says from behind the door. Crickets silenced briefly by my footsteps to the house from the car have dismissed me as a danger and are singing even louder. I step closer to the door and buzz again.

'Who!' the man's voice shouts from inside.

'Me,' I whisper, not sure what to say. She told me to never say my name.

'Selma?'

'Me.' The crickets have quieted down some, to listen in or because there's something else out there bigger than me.

'Who is it, goddamn it?!'

I reach my hand out and scratch at the wooden door, like my dog did when he wanted back in.

The door opens with a jerk and I look up at the man, naked

except for his cowboy hat that's not on his head but held in front of his lower self. The light inside is dim and flickers.

'Come on, Luther . . . carry yourself back home.'

'There's a little kid here,' he says over his shoulder. 'You a boy or a girl?' He taps my head. I stare at a hole in the top of the cowboy hat and say nothing.

'A kid? Oh, shit!' I hear her say, then the sound of blankets being kicked off.

'What?' he says, but steps aside.

She fills the doorway, wrapped in a sheet like a ghost. My heart contracts.

'Momma,' I start to say, but stop. 'Sarah' she had told me to call her: 'I ain't old and haggard enough to be Momma except in front of social workers—then I'm Momma. Got it?'

But since we've been on the run from the law that are after me, I can't be me and she can't be she, and I don't remember who we are.

'Jesus, I fuckin' forgot!'

'What the f . . .' He stares at her.

'Don't go frownin', Luther, or your face'll stay like that.' She walks past him, takes my arm, and pulls me inside. A bed fills the room, sheets tangled and rolled off the mattress so the blue prison-type stripes of it show.

'This is my brother . . . I'm sitting him.'

'What? He been in the car the whole time?' The room smells sour, like sweat and farts.

'No, no, somebody dropped him off . . .'

'Who?' He swings the door closed with a slam. The candle flickers from the draft of it. He switches on the light.

'Goddamn, you are something, baby.' He moves his hat from his front to his head and walks naked toward the bathroom.

I stare at my feet, lost under the lime green shag rug. The bathroom door slams.

'He won't be no bother,' she shouts over her shoulder.

The sound of pissing and then a flushed toilet answer her.

She walks toward the bathroom and goes in, shutting the door behind her.

'I coulda gone home with any cowboy there, and I picked you. Now you wantin' to drive me back. I'll tell everyone a four-year-old scares you from the best pussy you'll ever have a chance to be takin'!'

I stare at the poster on the bathroom door of a girl on her knees, her mouth on a man's thing, no cowboy hat in front of it.

They're arguing. There are other posters on the walls, all the girls have yellow hair like Sarah, and they're all naked.

She comes out still wearing the sheet; he follows wrapped in a towel. They say nothing. He goes into the little kitchen, where I hear him open the refrigerator. She grabs some pillows and a blanket off the bed and goes into the bathroom.

I watch him, through a small window cut in through the kitchen wall, unwrap some chicken.

'You hungry?' he calls out, opening the microwave. My mouth's suddenly wet.

'Naw. The chili dog you got me is still settin' in me.'

'OK.' He shuts the microwave door and punches buttons that beep.

I say nothing.

I learned about being greedy. I wouldn't eat the sandwich she had made, Spam on day-old white bread. We pulled over on the side of the road to eat. I kept my lips compressed as she pushed the sandwich against my mouth.

When it was dinnertime she got a drive-through burger and fries.

'You got your sandwich now, don'tcha.' I watched her eat, and I didn't touch the sandwich sitting on plastic wrap on my lap. When she was asleep I opened the chocolate-chip cookies hidden under her jacket in the backseat. I ate them all.

She woke up and saw the crumbs and the empty package at my feet. She opened the car door and held her finger down my throat until the cookies came back.

'Those were mine, greedy pig. Steal from me again, pig, and see what happens.'

'Johnny, come in here!' she yells from the bathroom.

She's not talking to me, so I don't move.

'Get in here!'

The smell of fried chicken fills the room. She comes out of the bathroom.

'Hey.' She motions me over. 'You deaf? . . . Come in here.' I follow her into the bathroom. She closes the door.

'You're Johnny, remember? I'm Monique. Got it?' I nod. There are more posters on the wall. One girl has brown hair.

'You'll sleep in here.' She points in the tub. A few pillows cover the bottom, and a blanket's on top.

'Get on in . . .' I climb into the tub, its sides low enough for me to get over easily. I stand on the pillows, staring up at her.

The sheet is still wrapped around her like a dress. I know she has all the same stuff the girls on the posters do. I've seen her changing in the car.

'Take off your shoes. You gotta go?' I shake my head and sit on the pillows and pull off my sneakers. I do have to piss but can't with all the girls on the wall watching, staring out with vague smiles in poses like snakes.

'Johnny, OK, remember, Monique. Johnny.' She points at herself, then at me.

She flicks the light off.

'Good night.'

She closes the door. I look around. I feel my eyes to make sure they're open. A thin line around the door glows yellow, and I hear hushed laughing and talking. Soon the light around the door disappears and their voices melt into grunts and moans.

I pull the blanket up around me to block out the sound. I know what he's doing to her, I knew all along what he would do and I said nothing. I didn't warn her.

I lay in the tub, squeezing my eyes tight against all the blue eyes blankly gazing out from the walls into the black.

I hear her cry out. I should go and do something. I hold the blanket over my ears.

When I wake she'll be gone and there will be a new poster on his wall.

She yells out again, and I know it will be her up on the wall like the others, frozen and trapped forever staring out and hating me for forgetting her.

'Only way your *brother* is gonna learn not to piss himself is a whipping he remembers.'

The pillows I slept on lie stained and wet on the floor next to the bed. She found I'd had another accident when she went to put the pillows back.

He's pulled out a brown leather belt from the small closet near the kitchen, and he's clutching it doubled.

'Luther, I didn't know you had it in you to be so fatherly.' She's in a T-shirt; it's too big and stained yellow under the armpits, it looks like his.

When she first came in the bathroom earlier this morning and sat on the toilet, all I could do was sit up in the tub and stare at her.

'Who are you to be sittin' in judgment of me, huh?'

'You're not one of the posters!' I said.

She wadded up some toilet paper and ran it under the sink tap. 'How rude are you? Well, that's how you got here, got news for you!'

She threw the wet toilet paper, it splattered and stuck in the center of my chest.

'Get over here.' He motions me to the bed.

'He's never been spanked before, Luther, my parents spoilt him bad.' She puts her arm around his bare waist and smiles at him. He adjusts his boxers.

'Gonna be a lot more than spanking goin' on here.' He hits the bed with the belt. I jump. 'Let's go!'

'See, you would so make a real good daddy . . .' She pats his chest. The flattened morning light streams past the venetian blinds, making thick bars on the floor between me and the bed.

He reaches out, grabs my arm, and jerks me toward the mattress. He pushes me over it, my face bounces on the crumpled sheets. My teeth start chattering. I try to push myself up, but he shoves me back down.

'Get his things down,' he orders.

Sarah leans over and yanks on my jeans and pulls them down.

'They're wet again! I told him too many times already, next time he wets that's it . . .' Her hands slide into my underwear waistband.

'Your parents oughtn't to be spoilin' him . . . he wouldn't be messin' my good goose feathers pillows.' The belt slaps at the mattress again. 'Damn, he smells like a alleyway in the city.'

She slides my underwear down to my ankles with my jeans. 'He pisses it, he wears it. Won't wash it till he learns.' She moves away from me.

'Now, son, I'm gonna whip you a beatin' you can be proud of, and you won't be wetting like a little baby no more. Ya hear?'

I nod my head small. I want my clothes to smell like Sarah's do. When she sent me into a gas station to buy us chips while she put in gas, a girl behind me on line tapped me on the shoulder. As I turned she said, 'You stink.' A man with her shushed her, but she stuck her tongue out at me and held her nose when they walked back to their car.

'Where your cigarettes at, honey?'

'Table . . . you sure you wantin' to stay for this?'

I hear her sitting at the table, and the crackle of the cigarette pack.

'Oh, I've got and seen my father give so many hellfire beatings I could sleep through it.' She flicks the lighter.

'Thought they didn't give no whippings?'

'Huh?' She coughs some. 'No, no, just him, spoilt just him.' She waves away her smoke.

''Coz once I start, I ain't stoppin' till I'm done, you hear?'

'I'm so proud of you, I know I picked right last night.'

He steps back. I hear the belt whistle down and then a loud crack against my body, but before I'm aware of the pain it happens again and I feel it, a sudden deep slashing into my flesh. I scream.

'Goddamn spoilt brat . . .' He leans over, pulls my head back, and covers my mouth with his hand. 'I can't have him hollering, Monique.'

'Put the sheet in his mouth,' she says, exhaling.

'You're only makin' it worse off for yourself, now be a man.' He moves his fingers off my mouth. I gasp and scream. His hand smashes back against my mouth, his other hand grabs some sheet and balls it. He frees my mouth, and as I open to scream the sheet is stuffed into my mouth. It's wet and sticky. I try to pull it out.

'Goddamn it!' He jerks my arms backward and holds my wrists behind me. 'You didn't wanna make me madder!'

The belt hurls down across my ass, and I scream against the sheet. The thick, salty wetness on it coats my mouth, and I retch, while the belt keeps coming harder and harder and harder.

The Heart Is Deceitful
Above All Things

The heart is deceitful above all things,
and desperately wicked: who can know it?

JEREMIAH 17:9

The ones that buy me candy don't last long. The ones that slap her last longer, but not as long as the ones that beat her with their fists and me with their belt.

We live in the car, driving until she meets the next one. Sometimes she tells him about me, her brother. Sometimes I'm her sister. 'Men like girls, not boys,' she says. 'You wanna come inside, don't ya?'

Sometimes I stay hidden in the car until he's gone to work. I lie in the cradle at the foot space of the backseat and disappear.

Sometimes she gives me the halves of the pills I ask for. They're white, but they make it all dark, not the dream where my limbs are blown across the open brittle road until red-winged crows descend from the white sun, carrying my limbs farther and farther away until I wake up screaming, struggling to reattach.

Sometimes we go into stores and I borrow what she tells me. Under my coat inside my pants, the bologna packages go. The cold beer bottles slide down my sleeves, the ends held closed with thick rubber bands so by the time I'm back in the car my hands are numb and bright white. When I borrow right we drive away fast, laughing while stuffing our mouths with strings of bologna and drinking the sour dull fizz from the bottles. When I borrow wrong—a bottle falls out when I loosen a rubber band or I get stopped on my way out the sliding doors—then the world moves like in those old hand-cranked movies I'd looked at in arcades. Everyone surrounds and moves away from me at the same time. She yanks my pants, and her hand comes down fast across my bare ass again and again. It's a trick, she had told me. They usually stop her, tell her it's OK. They calm her down, give her coffee or something. She tells them I'm a behavior problem, and she cries. They stare at me, shake their heads, and suck their tongues. Sometimes we have to really trick them if they're really mad by spanking me again. Sometimes not in the back private room, but with everyone seeing. It works 'cause they never call the police on me. But when we get back to the car she doesn't drive away fast and laugh. She stays mad, sometimes for a day or two, not speaking to me at all, not giving me any of what she had to buy, making me be in the back and out of her sight. I know it's not real, though, I remind myself she's just tricking them in case they have 'eyes in the back of their heads' like her father, and maybe their eyes went in our car.

Sometimes when she stops at a bar, she comes out and goes in his truck. 'Man don't drive a truck, can't drive home a fuck,' I whisper her rhyme while they drive away. But I know how to go with the flashlight from under the seat when everyone is gone and it's quiet, just like we do together; going around back, dig-

ging into the bags and finding food 'hardly bit, not wet with spit.'
When I do it alone I pretend she's next to me being lookout.
I even whisper to her about what I find.

'Bag of pretzels.'

'That'll do us fine. What else ya got there, kid?' I make her say.

Then there's the one she married. I stay in his apartment
while they drive up to Atlantic City for their honeymoon. They're
supposed to be gone for two nights. The door is locked with a key
on the inside as well as out, which makes me feel safer. But as the
nights keep going by and my Kraft singles go down, even the end
pieces of Wonder are gone, I watch out the back window as the
garbagemen load up the bags I can't get into.

I keep all the lights on at night and sleep in the day after my
favorite Bugs Bunny cartoon show. After four nights I know they
aren't coming back, so I stand on a chair and draw pictures of her
on the white walls with a black marker. I do it all night until the
first violet blur of morning creeping in lets me feel my hand is
cramped and see the walls are covered.

After six nights he comes home without her. 'She married me
and run off when I runned out of money,' he says, his head in
his hands. He says nothing about the walls, even though I have
already prepared and stand holding a belt, doubled over. He only
cries looking at the potato figures of her stuck flat on his walls.
While he cries I pull the cellophane film off the last cheese slice,
eat it, and go to sleep even though the moon is still a yellowish
scar in all the black.

I wake up screaming; the crows' red wings flash over my eyes
as he pulls my legs apart, his hot breath against my neck, claws
push my face down into the pillow. And for the first time they
peck at me, and it's worse than I ever imagined. It's a drill blade
twisting and hollowing me out between my legs, and he cries her
name again and again in my ear until it bleeds.

I stop trying to crawl away. I float up with my marker and draw her on the ceiling whenever the crows attack again.

The towel under me is turning crimson and soggy like tomato bread soup.

'Les' go,' he says when it's night again, and dresses me, putting a new towel on me instead of my underwear, inside my pants. He carries me to the car, where I fall against the wall waiting for him to unlock the door. He drives me in our car she'd left, not his truck.

We drive a long time and turn onto a dirt road. Suddenly the car stops. 'Sorry,' he says, takes the flashlight from under the seat, and leaves. I pull myself up and watch the torch he carries swing over the crowd of skinny trees like a flame scanning a match-book. I stare until the glow of light is gone, only the funneled moon through too many trees.

A flash in my eyes blinds me, but I can hear them. 'Nurse, hold him still now!' Another flash. I struggle, but I'm held firm. 'Turn him round.' I am moved to my stomach, my legs held apart. Another flash behind me. I squint past the floating spots and see two policemen across from me, standing, frowning, and drinking from steaming paper cups. I scream and kick. 'Help us out here, Officer, if you don't mind.' One moves forward, putting down his cup, and presses down on my back. Another flash. 'To the side, turn him.' My body is turned and held sideways on the white paper spread beneath me.

'What's your name?' the cop says, his stale breath coating my face. I kick out hard as I can. 'Goddamn it! He hit the camera! Hold him still!' The hands clamp down on me, pushing my head and chest down hard onto the mushy vinyl tabletop, the paper ripped and soaked from my drool. 'What's your name?!' the cop says again. 'They found ID in the car?' Another flash above me.

I see my clothes crumpled in a corner, and the red-stained towel pokes out from a trash basket. I'm naked.

'He needs stitches, you about done?' Another flash. The cop blocking the door, still drinking, rests his other hand on his gun. I scream again. 'Nurse, restraints!'

'One more photograph! Turn him sideways . . . spread his legs . . . wider . . . perfect, OK, great! Thanks, guys. Hope you get the bastard that did this, see ya.'

'Let's get these restraints goin'.'

I'm pushed onto my stomach, my arms are pulled out, as are my legs, and soft cuffs freeze them to the board. Something is sliding under me, lifting my hips, and straps are pulled across my legs, back, and head. Voices rumble around me. 'Tell me your name!' the cop standing above me orders. 'You want us to catch this guy?!'

'OK, you're gonna feel a sharp stick,' the doctor says.

And off in the distance I hear the beating,

'OK, one more stick.'

of their wings . . .

'And one last stick.'

and the room bleeds with their jagged red feathers

'OK, here we go . . .'

and razor beaks filled with

'Gonna fix you right up.'

parts of me.

Toyboxed

The woman holds two dolls. Her hair is in a tight yellow bun that pulls the ends of her eyes back into slants. She smiles quick little flashes at me, then frowns down at the dolls. The big man doll's pants go down, she takes them down. His thing sticks out, dark yarn surrounding it like a dirty mop head.

'The little boy doll is blond like you,' she says.

The room we're in is pink, with pictures of smiling children hanging on the walls. There's a dollhouse in the corner with a rubber family inside. I'm sitting on a rug that has games woven into it, like hopscotch and a marble circle. I'm sitting on the alphabet Indian style, the way she is. The boy doll has a round hole for a mouth and 'freckles like you have,' she says, and pats my nose.

The man doll fits his thing into the boy's mouth like a puzzle piece. She makes him do it. Her shoes end in sharp little points, and some of her foot skin hangs over the edges.

'Pay attention,' she says, and clears her throat. 'This is bad.' She shakes her finger at the dolls. 'Bad, bad man.' Her fingernails are red, like Sarah's. She makes the man pull the little boy's pants down with his mittenlike hands. I dig my fingers into the Day-Glo fuzz of the alphabet rug and make them disappear.

'Are you watching? Watch the dolls now, pay attention.' She shakes the dolls. The man's thing bounces up and down. The little boy's thing wobbles. There's no yarn around it. 'Owie owie,' she says while she puts the man doll's pink thing into a round hole in the boy doll's bottom. She shakes them in the air, their feet dangling like they've just been hung. 'Owie owie,' she says as she brings them together and apart, together and apart. They sound like two pillows hitting each other.

'How does the little boy feel?' she asks me, not stopping them. There's a large box behind her. It's painted like a toy drum, blue with white Xs. A large braid with a red bow hangs out over the edge.

'Watch now, come on, pay attention.' She shakes them harder. 'How does he . . .' She taps the little boy. 'Feel? Hmm? You can tell me, it's OK. *You are safe now.*' She smiles vaguely and extends her arms so the dolls are closer to me. There's a little brown stain on her peach blouse. I'm careful not to stain my clothes so Sarah doesn't get pissed, because people will think we're trash.

'Stained clothes is how you can tell trash,' she says while reaching into her bag for the small bottle of Clorox bleach. 'My father is rich and educated, a preacher.' She pours the bleach onto some McDonald's napkins, then rubs it on the ketchup stain on my T-shirt. 'Not trash,' she says, then wipes my face and hers with more bleach until it stings. 'You gotta look and smell clean.'

Sometimes we go into the ladies' room. I go into the stall with her. We pull down our pants and our underwear. I hold two clumps of toilet paper. She pours the bleach onto them, soaking them. I hand one to her. 'Folks can smell sin on ya,' she whispers. Our hands holding the bleach-soaked tissue disappear between our legs. She covers her mouth with her free hand and cries into it.

'Are you paying attention?' The woman holds the dolls on her lap. 'This isn't the little boy's fault . . . see?' She picks them up again, the thing going in and out of the hole in the little boy's behind. 'Ow ow ow,' she says in a high-pitched voice. 'Bad man, bad man,' she says in a low, growly voice. 'Repeat after me,' she says, and scoots closer. The dolls slam together faster. 'It's not . . . c'mon, say it, you want cartoon privileges back?'

I said nothing last time I visited with her and the dolls, so I hadn't been allowed to watch TV or go to the game room in two days. I stayed in my room and reread the same books. I didn't mind not seeing the other kids. Some are bald and bloated, their lips peeling like fingernail paint. Some are in wheelchairs or on crutches, with tubes that wheel around with them. One boy has to be hit on the back all the time. He coughs all night when he isn't crying. I especially don't mind not seeing their parents. They come with shopping bags filled with goodies. They don't like to unpack them in front of me in the day room. 'Let's go to your room, honey,' they say, glancing at me. They usually have to talk loud, because as soon as I see them coming I raise the sound on the TV until a nurse comes running in and takes the remote away from me.

'It's not . . .' I whisper.

'What? Yes, good, you spoke. See, it's easy . . .' She bounces the dolls on the rug. 'It's not the little boy's fault,' she repeats. I stare at them jumping up and down across the alphabet, held together by the man doll's thing. 'The little boy's fault,' I mumble.

'Great. See, that was easy . . . now you can watch cartoons after dinner. You're getting better.' She leans over and pats my head. 'Time to go.' She gets up, wiping rug fuzz from her beige pants. She carries the dolls to the drum bin and drops them in. 'Let's go.' She holds open the door that has a cartoon poster of laughing children on the outside. I walk past the box of dolls; it looks like a massacre grave pit, some naked, some dressed, and on top lie the boy and man. The man stares up at me with his arms around the boy. I can tell by the blond boy's face that the man is still inside him. I reach down to pull them apart. 'No, no,' she shouts, 'leave the toys.' She walks toward me. 'We've got to get you back upstairs for dinner. You can play more tomorrow.' She pushes the lid down, and it seals with a slam.

Some children disappear. They're kept in their rooms, wrapped in tentaclelike tubes, and suddenly their rooms are empty, just the fluorescent light beaming down on the military-made bed, all cards stripped from the walls, all balloons that were tied to the bed gone. Some kids leave with their parents. They take their balloons and stuffed animals in big shopping bags, and the nurses hug them good-bye. But I tricked them all; they never discovered what I'd done to my fuckin' fosters. I kept my mouth shut the way Sarah taught me so nothing could escape and I wouldn't get arrested and sent to hell.

I left without any hugs or waves or shopping bags of goodies, but I did have a stuffed bear a nurse gave me when I first came and only stared at the walls. 'He's yours,' she told me. He looked almost like the one I'd had way before, the same yellowish fur. I didn't say thank you. I left him on the floor of the day room. She put him in my bed. 'He has no place else to go,' she told me. Later that night when I woke up suddenly, my heart bursting inside me, my sheets wet with sweat and pee, I grabbed the bear and buried my face in his neck fur. That spot was wet for days.

I leave with a woman the nurse says is my grandmother. 'They have custody of you,' she says. I nod, not understanding but excited to be leaving with someone. The woman signs papers while I stand quietly behind her, arms stiff at my sides. 'You haven't visited before,' the nurse says.

'It's a long trip,' my grandmother says, her voice a soft, musical lilt, her hair a tight crisscross of blond braids on top of her head. Her face is a stern, drawn version of Sarah's. I follow her to the elevator and look around, and cough loudly, hoping that everyone will see me leaving with somebody.

'In God is my salvation and my glory,' she says, staring straight ahead as the car winds through the cracked mountain roads laced with frost. 'The rock of my strength and my refuge is in God. Trust in him at all times; God is a refuge for us.' I hear her swallow. 'Psalm 62:7–8.' She says nothing else until we get to the house.

The trees open out onto a wide clearing. Horses run inside fences as our car drives past. A steeple is visible over a distant ridge. The road smoothes out to soft black tar. An older blond boy on horseback gallops next to us. He stares at me, then whips the horse twice and races away over the low green slopes.

We drive past gray weathered wooden barns that look propped up by haystacks. Another five minutes and we turn into a wide pebbled driveway. Four white columns hold up a sloping overhang. Two oak and stained-glass doors sit in the center. It looks like a museum. 'This is a house of the Lord,' she says, and stops the car in front of the doors. We get out and she opens the unlocked door and light streams into the dark hall. I squint hard to see.

'He shall redeem their soul from deceit and violence: and precious shall their blood be in his sight.' She pats my shoulders. 'Psalm 72:14.' She walks away from me into the gloom of the hall. I stand still, waiting.

Foolishness Is Bound in the Heart of a Child

I hear the footsteps long before I see anyone. The click click sounds like an eggshell being torn apart rhythmically and with anger. 'The way of the wicked is an abomination unto the Lord: but he loveth him that followeth after righteousness.' The voice echoes down the hallway, staccato and sharp.

'Jeremiah, do you know where that is from?'

My grandfather is suddenly standing in front of me. He says my name the way Sarah does; she's only said it a few times, but when she does I feel reassured and remembered. 'Jere-my.' My, like you're mine.

'The only reason you're here is the bastard wouldn't let me give you a wire hanger for a head,' she said between swallows of the Wild Turkey that she called 'chicken' when we went to the liquor shop. I got used to the bitter taste of 'chicken' in my Coke and how easily I fell asleep after I drank it. 'Trip on the train' is for Midnight Express. It's the same sour burning as 'chicken,' but I liked hearing Sarah ask for train more.

'Once you got here,' she said, wiping her mouth with the back of her hand, 'he wouldn't give a dime to feed or keep ya.'

But he had wanted me. He had protected me. He had saved me. I had made him look like my fucking fosters' grandpa, but better, with a white Santa's beard and rosy cheeks and chocolate coins in his pocket. I'd show him I wasn't bad. It was her, Sarah. I smile up at him, we're on the same side, you saved me, I'm Jere-my, I'm yours.

'You know where that's from, Jeremiah?' The damp air from his words smells like peppermint.

My, mine, yes.

'For the Lord knoweth the way of the righteous: but the way of the ungodly shall perish.' His mouth is turned down. I tilt my head to the side, and now it looks like a smile. He doesn't have a beard; his face is thin and tightly stretched across his wide cheek and jaw, which he's working back and forth as if he were chewing leather. His eyes are the same distant clear blue as Sarah's; they give his delicate features an ominous look, like ragged ice glaciers overhanging a smooth cave entrance. Even though he's not really smiling, his eyes are squinted as if he were. I smile wider. He nods once and steps back. I nod in return and wink the way Sarah does. He lifts up the thick black book that he has been holding behind him.

'You will not mock the Lord, Jeremiah. You will learn not to mock me. Jeremiah, you will find these tracts.' Each time he speaks my name I force a wave of warmth through me. All he says after my name sounds garbled, as if it were floating through water. 'Jeremiah, you will know them. If you cannot read, you will learn quickly.' He lowers the book and hands it to me. 'Jeremiah, is that clear?' I watch his other hand to see when the hidden chocolate will appear.

'This is your pillow, Jeremiah. You sleep on it. You keep it
with you always. Jeremiah, is that clear?'

I open the book, but the tissue paper page is only words.
I turn some more pages but can't find the pictures yet. 'Thank
you,' I mumble. I was going to call him Grandpa, but something
chokes off the word.

'We will begin tomorrow at seven A.M., Jeremiah.' He places
his hand on my shoulder. I tilt my head toward it. 'Do not lean
in my presence, Jeremiah.' He pulls me forward with a short jerk.
'Or in the presence of the Lord.' He releases his hand and turns
and walks back down the hall, still talking: 'He *maketh* a way to
his anger: He spared not their soul from death, but gave their life
over to the pestilence.'

I look down at the book, flip through some more pages. I still
can't find the cartoons.

A boy a little taller than me comes down the hall. He's whitish
blond, like me, hair combed back. He's in white pants and a blue
blazer, and he has a tie on. I've never seen a kid in a tie. I feel
jealous.

'How old are you?' he asks me, and pushes himself up on his
tiptoes.

'Seven . . . in ten days.' I stand straighter and stretch my
neck up.

'Tell him you want a big birthday party.' He smiles, his teeth biting into his bottom lip, his opalescent eyes guarded yet prowling.

'You'd like that, wouldn't you, huh?'

'How old are you?' I ask.

He points at my book. 'I know the Psalms One through Fifty.
How many do you know?'

'I know a lot of songs.'

'What?! Damn,' he whispers, 'you're an idiot.'

'I'm not. I can read.' I stare right back at him. He smiles wider, crinkling his small upturned nose, finely sprinkled with freckles like nutmeg.

'Tell him you know songs . . . from there,' he says, pointing at the book and laughing. I laugh because he is. 'What songs do you know? Sing some.'

I roll my eyes up to think. Sarah's next to last boyfriend had a mohawk. He'd given me one, but I didn't like it; people pointed and kids laughed. 'That's the idea of being a punk, you gotta shock 'em,' he told me. I wet it down, making it look like a raised yellow highway divider line across my otherwise bald head. In disgust he shaved it off. He dyed his pink until the sheriff threatened to arrest him for disturbing the peace. Then he shaved his off, too. He taught me to sing along with the Sex Pistols. I didn't understand the words, but it made Sarah laugh when we sang them, sneering and spitting. Sometimes she joined in.

'I am a annie-christ. I am a annie-kiss, dunno what I want, know how to get it, wanna this toy, the buzzer by.' He stares at me wide-eyed, mouth hanging open. 'I wanna be annie-key.'

'Jesus Christ,' he gasps.

'Go piss this toy,' I finish singing, and spit. It lands in a little bubbly pile on the wooden floor by his black, shined leather shoes. 'Sex Pistols,' I say, smiling at him.

'You're possessed,' he says, not smiling any more. 'You gotta sing that for him.' He nods and smiles slowly. 'You gotta.'

'I know more, too.'

'Uh-huh, he'll love it.' He laughs.

'I know Dead Kennedys.'

'How's that go?'

'Too drunk to fuck,' I sing, 'I'm too drunk to fuck.'

He slaps his leg. 'Yeah, yeah, sing,' he says, covering his mouth, but I can still hear him laughing. 'Sing that one, too.

Promise you will?' I nod. 'But don't say I told you to. It'll be a secret. I'm just helping you out.'

'What's your name?' I ask.

'Aaron,' he says, wiping the tears from his eyes.

'Do you know Sarah?'

'Sarah, yeah, she's one of my older sisters, yeah, she's a sinner.' He adjusts his tie.

'She's my momma.'

'Yeah, I know, that's why you gotta sing for him . . . got any more?'

He takes my hand and leads me to our room.

At five A.M. Aaron wakes me up. I reach around for my Bugs Bunny and then remember what Micah, a different blond boy with rosebud lips and sleepy eyes, told me before bed.

'It's worshiping idolatry, you'll burn in hell.'

He took it from my bag, and I never saw it again. I slept with my thumb in my mouth, and I wake up to a girl that looks like a smaller version of Sarah yanking it out. 'No, no, you can't do that.' She says nothing else and leaves the room.

Aaron is dressed in jeans and a sweatshirt. He's standing next to a carved wood-framed bed, same as mine, with the same thin mattress, except that he has a pillow. His bed is tightly made, with no blankets hanging over the edges.

'Make yours and get dressed. We got chores to do before prayer.' He points to a wooden dresser. 'Clothes in there, they should fit ya. Fit me when I was your age.'

I get dressed, staring at the stark, blank walls.

'Let's go!' Aaron half shouts. 'We got chores to do.'

We sit on a worn grayish wood stool in a dirty brown brick room next to the kitchen, peeling potatoes. A huge sack of potatoes sits beside us.

'So, you'll tell him about your songs.' He points at me with the peeler. I nod and yawn. He smiles down at the potatoes.

At six-thirty A.M. Aaron and I stand upstairs in another long, wood-floored hallway. The walls are bare, reflective white. Four other blond boys stand behind us. They're wearing the same long, scratchy robes that Aaron and I are wearing. They keep leaning over and staring at me. Someone hits the back of my head. When I turn around, Aaron smiles. 'It wasn't me! And I'll swear on Christ's nails!' They muffle their laughs. A wooden door opens next to me, and the escaping steam makes my lungs hurt. A tall, sinewy, but fleshy blond boy motions me in.

'Get in.' He points at the huge porcelain tub, steam rolling off it like fog. I stare up at him. His catlike face scrunches up. He sighs, rolls his eyes up, and says like he's bored, 'If any man's seed of copulation go out from him, then he shall wash all his flesh in water and be unclean until the even.' He licks at the beads of sweat above his lip. 'Leviticus.' He shakes his head. 'Come on.' He reaches out his hand. All he has on is white boxers. His chest is bare and covered with a light film of sweat. I take his hand, and he leads me to the tub. Its edges are covered with small black cracks that look like bloodshot eyes. His hand is warm and moist. 'Let's go,' he says softly. He leans over and slides off my robe and underwear, his hand brushing against me as he does. He smells like salt and chlorine. 'Here, I'll help you in.'

He clasps his arms around my waist. I feel his breath against my neck, and it tickles and I laugh. 'You're a light one.' He lifts me up and holds me over the tub. I lean my head back against his chest. 'OK, here we go . . .' He lowers me down fast. It takes me a few seconds to feel the heat of the water. I yell and grab for the edges. 'No, you don't!' He grabs my hands with one of his and covers my mouth with the other. 'I ain't gettin' whipped 'cause of you. Now, come on, shut up,' he says in a low voice into my ear.

My vision is blurred with tears. I scream into the hand across my mouth. 'You'll get used to it,' he says. He reaches past me to a thick bristled scrub brush resting on an edge of the tub. 'But ye are washed . . .' He reaches into the water and rests the brush against the skin of my lower stomach. 'But ye are sanctified . . .' He presses the brush into my flesh. I smash my lips against his palm, trying to escape it. 'But ye are justified in the name . . .' He begins to move the scrub brush slowly across my stomach. 'Of the Lord Jesus . . .' His eyes close. The brush moves down lower. 'And by the spirit . . .' His eyes open and roll around in their sockets. He moves the brush in deliberate strokes between my legs. My teeth press against his palm. 'Of our God . . .' I bang my head in small stiff bounces against his chest. He leans his mouth against my neck. 'Amen,' he whispers.

He lets go of the brush, wraps his arm around my hips, and, while still covering my mouth, lifts me out of the tub. He stands me next to him. 'If you scream or cry, you'll go back in.' I nod. 'So be quiet.' I nod again. He removes his hand, and I gasp. He stands over me. 'That wasn't so bad, was it?' My body feels numb. I look down at myself, a bright pinkish red with blood pinpricks and scratches marking my skin where he scrubbed. I feel the burn between my legs. A towel is dropped around my shoulder. He begins patting me dry.

At seven A.M. I stand in a hall downstairs, outside my grand-father's thick oak door. Aaron lines up behind me, other boys behind him. They all look unnervingly familiar, like seeing a mir-ror cut up of parts of my face stuck on different people. They're all dressed like I'm dressed, like Aaron, in a blazer, tie, and soft black pants. Aaron whispers in my ear, reminding me, again, to sing my songs and to complain about the tub being too hot. My skin still aches, and I've left off my underwear because of it. 'Tell him you're not wearing them, tell him!' Aaron said when he saw me getting dressed. His skin was red, too. He didn't seem to care.

The door opens and an older blond boy dressed like I am walks out slowly, wobbly. His face is turned down. He doesn't look at me. I watch him walking carefully down the hall like he's on a tightrope. He puts his fingers out against the wall to balance himself now and again. 'Jeremiah,' my grandfather calls from inside his study. I jump and then press myself against the wall and quiet my breath. 'I will not call you again, Jeremiah.' His voice is flat, commanding. My body involuntarily moves to the doorway.

The morning light streams from the window onto his desk. 'Step in. Close the door, Jeremiah.' I walk in, closing the heavy door behind me. I watch my hands move the brass knob that sticks out like a dog's tail until it clicks in its lock. 'Jeremiah . . .' I turn around slowly. Long rows of books, not library books, but leather bound, in blacks, burgundies, and browns, line the wooden shelves up to the ceiling. They're the kind of shelves where if you remove the right book, a secret passage opens and a slide takes you to a secret dungeon. 'Jeremiah . . .' He taps his foot in rapid succession. I turn back to face him. As my eyes adjust to the light, I can see him better. He's frowning. His hands are pressed flat on the black inlay on top of the wide desk. I want him to smile, to be better than my fucking fosters' grandpa, and to know I'm me: who he saved. 'I know songs, sir,' I whisper, and immediately I feel as if I've tossed a water balloon off a roof and I'm watching it, powerless to stop it, as it hurtles toward a crowded street.

'You've learned Psalms, Jeremiah,' he says, half like a question.

'Aaron told me to sing them to you,' I take a breath, 'sir.'

'Aaron told you to sing them to me, Jeremiah,' he repeats. He folds his hands one on top of the other. His hands are bright white with delicate blue veins, raised like worm tunnels. His little pinkie taps slowly.

'I am a Annie-christ,' I sing without melody, 'I am a annie-kiss—'

'Jeremiah,' he interrupts, 'what psalm is that?' He cocks his head to the side like a dog listening to a silent whistle.

'Sex Pistols,' I say, excited he's interested.

'And where did you learn the Sex Pistols psalm, Jeremiah?' Now his ring finger is tapping along with his pinkie.

'Um . . . from Stinky.' I examine the bookcase again. There's only one white book on the fifth shelf; that must be the one you pull.

'Jeremiah . . .' I turn back. He tilts his head to the other side. 'And who is Stinky?'

I laugh and cover my mouth. He smiles back without humor. 'Stinky has a pink mohawk, but he cut it.'

'Yes . . .' His whole hand is tapping now. It's making me jumpy.

'He lived with us, he's a punk rocker, and I get to be one, too, he said. He's learned me guitar so I can be one, too, but we ran away because he was boring, Sarah said . . . we didn't even say bye-bye. We sole his guitar at the pone shop. We didn't say bye.'

My grandfather just nods.

'Oh, Aaron 'minded me to tell you the Dead Kennedys, I know them, 'Too Drunk to Fuck.' I know that one, too. I know more. Wanna hear?'

'No, Jeremiah, I—'

'Oh!' I interrupt him. He looks down at me with surprise, his eyebrows raised. 'Aaron 'minded me to tell you my bath was too hot, it hurted. And Job scrubbed me hard. And I taked the bath at the hospital before, anyways. They don't scrub ya.'

'What other things did Aaron remind you to tell me, Jeremiah?' His teeth lightly bite into his bottom lip.

'That I ain't got no pillow, and the blankets ain't warm enough, and we haded too many potatoes to peel. But you know what? He can make 'em look like naked peoples.'

'What else did he say or show you, Jeremiah?'

'Well . . . he said he gets candy from your drawer, and if I do his bed for a week, I can get me some.' He says nothing, only nods like he wants me to tell him more. I rub my head. 'Oh . . . he says my mom is a sinner and a slut.' His hand starts tapping again, louder. 'Um . . .' I can't think of anything else. I think about making stuff up because I'm enjoying the attention, but I decide not to. 'That's about it.' I sigh. 'Sir,' I remember and add on. I half smile up at him.

'That's all, Jeremiah,' he says with his white lips thin as a woman's eyebrows pulled together.

'Oh yeah, I'm not wearin' any underwears.'

'OK, Jeremiah.' I smile wider, but he frowns back. He stands up and moves rigidly to the door. He opens it, steps into the hall, and says Aaron's name. As they enter, Aaron stares at me from the corner of his eye. My grandfather sits behind his expansive desk and folds his hands one on top of the other. He's only looking at Aaron. Aaron's head is turned down. I watch the dust swirl from my grandfather's breath as he repeats to Aaron all that I told him. Aaron never raises his head. Never moves. My grandfather stands and leans forward on his knuckles.

'Is this what you said, Aaron?' Aaron's body twitches, but he says nothing. His gaze stays fixated on the floor. My grandfather walks around his desk in front of Aaron and repeats the question.

I didn't realize that I'd been staring at the floor also, until the loud slap makes me look up. Aaron's face is askew and bright red. Fingerprints are across his cheeks. I look up at my grandfather standing tall and dignified above us, his hands calmly at his sides.

'I didn't say it, sir,' Aaron mumbles to the floor.

'What didn't you say, Aaron?'

'None of it, sir,' he whispers.

'So Jeremiah is a liar?'

'Yes, sir.'

'Am not!' I spit out.

My grandfather looks at me in so direct a way that my outrage is quickly evaporated. I gaze down at the almost black wood slat floor.

'Aaron, I'll ask you one last time.' I can hear Aaron's breath almost a pant. 'Is Jeremiah a liar?'

I grind my teeth together and tighten my hands into fists.

'Yes, sir.'

'Liar!' I glare at Aaron, who's still staring down. My grandfather taps his foot, once, almost softly, but it's enough to quiet me. I don't feel afraid, and I don't even feel all that mad at Aaron. I like the feeling that my grandfather and I are a team. I think he believes me, because he saved me, he's protecting me now, like he did from Sarah, and I love it.

'Aaron. How did Jeremiah know I keep hard candy in my desk?'

Aaron says nothing. A loud crack of another slap across Aaron's face breaks the silence. I don't look up. I bite my teeth into my lip so I don't smile.

'Who is the liar, Aaron?' My grandfather's foot taps like a metronome. Another slap echoes in the room, and the words start out of Aaron.

'I am . . . sir,' he says, sniffling, 'I am the liar.'

I bite harder into my lip.

'Aaron, show me how you steal from my drawer.'

Aaron slowly raises his head. His cheek is red, with blues and purples spreading like watercolors on a paper towel. Tears line his eyes. 'Please, sir . . .'

'Go ahead, Aaron, pretend I'm not here. That's when you thieve, isn't it, Aaron?' My grandfather steps away from the desk. 'Show me, Aaron.'

Aaron closes his eyes longer than a blink, then walks slowly to behind the desk. He stops in front of the drawer and looks up at my grandfather.

'Yes, Aaron. Show me.' Aaron closes his eyes and slides open the drawer. He reaches inside quickly, pulls his hand out, and then closes it like he'd been burned. He stands waiting, eyes closed, his long blond eyelashes fluttering.

'Aaron, show me,' my grandfather says almost sweetly.

Aaron opens his eyes but stares down at some floating invisible spot. He walks from around the desk, his leather shoes clicking against the wood. He holds out his right arm, turns over his fist, and opens his fingers like in a game of guess which hand. Two candy cane peppermints stand in the center of his shaking hand. I let myself smile.

'So, Aaron, you told Jeremiah to sing those songs to me?' Aaron nods, his hand still extended. 'And you told Jeremiah to complain about the bath?' Aaron nods. He nods a quick head jerk for each of the things my grandfather repeats to him. Then my grandfather asks Aaron to repeat it all, saying each thing he did, including lying about it all and his intention to get me in trouble. By the time Aaron's done, his outstretched hand is shaking so much, the candy's jumping in his palm like popping corn. I quietly step to the side to stand a little behind my grandfather, in his shadow.

'So, Aaron, what should be done? I've taught you otherwise, have I not?'

Aaron nods to the floor, his whole arm trembling in the air and his body jerking in little spasms.

'Yes, sir.'

'What should be done, Aaron?'

Aaron lets a little moan escape, and my grandfather slaps him again, his whole arm swinging back. A little pool of blood forms at the corner of Aaron's mouth.

'Foolishness is bound in the heart of a child . . .' As Aaron speaks, the blood trickles down his chin. 'But the rod of correction shall drive it far from him.'

Sarah doesn't like to hit my face. She hardly ever does, only if she really has to. I plan to tell Aaron how she's never slapped my face.

'Where, Aaron?'

'Proverbs, Chapter 22:15,' he whispers, the blood moving and painting his lips like gooey lipstick.

My grandfather walks to behind the bookshelf and returns carrying a thick leather belt. He reaches into Aaron's hand and removes the candies. 'What else does Proverbs say, Aaron?'

Aaron swallows loudly. 'Withhold not correction from the child'—his voice is soft but clear—'for if thou beatest him with the rod, he shall not die. 23:13.'

My grandfather reaches out for Aaron's stretched-out hand like he's going to shake it, but he flattens it instead. Aaron's hand stays extended. The strap folded over crashes down across it. Aaron closes his eyes and pushes his hand farther away from his body. I blink involuntarily with each hit. Sarah's never done this to me. I hope it hurts.

After I hear my grandfather count 'ten' he stops. Aaron's outstretched hand is shaking and lined in swollen dark colors. Bright red seeps along tiny cracks in his palm like bloody canals. My grandfather's face is as composed and as calm as before, if not more so. Aaron slowly lowers his hand. Tears roll down his face, and he blinks at them as if he were only cutting onions. It makes me mad.

'Thank you, sir,' Aaron says loudly. I squeeze my hands into fists.

'You've been punished for stealing. What should be done about your other sins, Aaron?' my grandfather asks him, the belt still at his side.

'I need to be punished, sir,' he whispers. I nod my head yes. '23:14 Thou shalt beat him with the rod and'—Aaron's voice breaks—'shalt deliver his soul from hell.'

'Remove your clothing, Aaron.' His foot taps quietly.

Aaron unbuttons his shirt with his left hand. He avoids moving his right hand. He takes off his pants and underwear. He covers himself with his left hand, not touching, just in front. My grandfather nods at Aaron, and Aaron walks to his desk and leans against it on his elbows. I feel jealous that Aaron knows what to do and my grandfather doesn't have to tell him. My grandfather steps around and behind Aaron. He takes his left hand and rests it on Aaron's head. My grandfather's never touched me like that. He hasn't touched me at all.

The belt swings up and snaps down across Aaron's back, then across his ass. I know what that feels like. I hear Aaron whimper after each stroke. My grandfather has let go of Aaron's head, and I'm glad. The belt cracks hard against his ass. She holds me sometimes, her hand on my thing, and it's so nice. It slaps again on his ass. Sarah holds me while her boyfriend, any boyfriend, brings the belt down. Little flecks of saliva spray from Aaron's mouth. But her hand is beneath me, stroking me. The strap hits against Aaron's back again. Her hand is so soft and comforting that I don't mind the belt, I don't care.

Aaron's body raises up in response to each stroke. His skin is looking like his palm. What always ruins it, though, is my thing, growing, and then evil sinfulness takes over, then her nails . . . Aaron is crying now, he's crying hard. Her nails dig in and rip at me, at my sinfulness. That's when I start to feel the belt. 'You sinful, dirty fucker,' she had said, and it hurt so bad, but she still holds me. The belt blurs down in front of my eyes. And it's hard, my thing, it's hard. She holds me. He'll hold Aaron after. She holds me and it's hurting, but she holds me. And it feels like heaven. The beating has ended, and now I hope it's my turn, before he holds Aaron and forgets about me and my turn.

Lizards

We pass other boys and a few girls. They look briefly at us and turn away quickly. I walk slowly with Aaron, staring at the floor in front of us, like he does, like the other kids do. We walk down red-carpeted stairs. He sucks in breaths with each step down. His grip is so tight that my fingertips are red by the time we reach the landing. We go behind the stairs to a white-painted wood slat door. Aaron releases my hand, turns the lock, and opens it, and we stare down into blackness. He reaches in and flicks on a light. The cool smell of must and mildew wafts over us as if a fan were blowing it up. He takes my arm again and we descend gray concrete stairs. At the bottom a small wood-paneled hall faces four different doors. Aaron lifts his hand, holding mine to his face, and wipes his eyes and nose with our hands. We walk over to the door on the far right. He releases my hand and unbolts and opens the door. He flicks on the light; it flickers above us like a strobe for a few seconds. We stand staring at a raw wood box maybe four feet high and not very wide. There's a wooden stool in front of it and a black book on top of the stool. It looks like a dog cage without the wire. The prayer box.

A small door is latched on the front; he reaches out carefully and opens it. Inside it smells like bleach. He pulls me over to the stool. 'Take the Bible,' he whispers. 'Deuteronomy,' he says. '32:22.'

'What?' Our voices sound spooky in the dead silence around us.

'Here.' He takes the book, thumbs some pages. The book shakes in his hand. He points at some words and hands it back to me. 'You can read, right?' I nod. He points at a paragraph. 'We start here,' he whispers. He wipes his face against his shoulder and turns his back on me. A wet spot marks where he pointed. He lowers his pants and then steps out of them; the skin of his upper thighs is red and swollen like a blister. 'I'll say it till time, OK, you make sure it's right, OK?' He sucks up snot. 'You can tell him how many times I mess up. I don't care, OK?'

'OK,' I say to the cracks in the cement floor.

He takes my hand and pulls me close to the box opening. He climbs inside, still clasping my hand. He lets out a few gasps, and I feel sick. His hand is wet, and I'm afraid he'll take me into the dark, chlorine-smelling box. He's kneeling in the box. That's all there's room for. 'Close the door and lock it,' he says. I start to close it, and it hits against his hand stretched out behind his back, still clutching my hand. He turns and looks at me, his face like a surprised, big-eyed animal in the shadows. He had looked so old to me, but now he looks like a kid younger than me. He presses his lips together, eyes wide and blinking at me. He starts to slide his hand out of mine, but I hold on to it tightly. Suddenly I don't want to let go. He looks at me with sad, determined eyes, and his hand slips from my grasp. 'Close the door, lock it,' he whispers. I do.

'For a fire is kindled in mine anger,' Aaron says from inside the box, his voice muffled but clear '. . . and shall burn unto the lowest hell.' I wipe my hand dry on my pants and sit on the stool. '. . . shall consume the earth with her increase . . .' I notice little airholes on the side of the box at the bottom. '. . . and set on fire the foundations of the mountains . . .' There's a framed picture of Christ on the wood-paneled wall. '. . . I will heap mischiefs upon them . . .' Jesus is not on the cross. He looks like he's in a good mood, friendly, almost smiling. '. . . they shall be burnt with hunger, and devoured with burning heat . . .' There's a black bug crawling slowly toward my foot. '. . . and with bitter destruction . . .' I wait till it's close enough, and I raise the Bible over it. '. . . I will also send the teeth of beasts upon them . . .' It suddenly curls up tight into a little ball. '. . . with the poison . . .' I stand up and slam the balled-up bug as hard as I can with the book. Aaron pauses slightly, then continues. '. . . of serpents of the dust. For a fire is kindled . . .' I sit on the stool and try to find the place Aaron showed me. '. . . in mine anger . . .' I kick the squished bug under the box.

Some time before my grandmother opens the door of the room we're in, Aaron stops reciting. I only hear him whispering to himself and moaning. He doesn't answer me when I try to talk to him. I think about opening the door, but I'm afraid he's been taken down to a fiery furnace, and a wild hell dog is in his place, waiting for me. I start reciting because I know the chapter by heart now. He says nothing, only whines like a dog.

When I hear footsteps coming down the stairs, I grab the Bible I had put up against the box door to try to seal the evil inside of it, like in vampire movies.

'Someone's coming,' I whisper to warn whatever's in there. My grandmother steps into the room, and I feel relieved but still frightened. I clutch my book up to my face like I'm reading it.

'It's been one hour,' she says, her lips set in a disappointed line. She knocks on the wood roof of the box. 'Up to a bath,' she announces.

'How many mistakes did he make, Jeremiah?' She doesn't

look at me. She leans over and unlocks the door to the box. I hear Aaron moving inside. The door pushes open with a long creak. I hold my breath. 'Jeremiah!' she snaps.

'None, he made none,' I whisper, and stare at the black hole in the box.

'Your mother never taught you your Bible, did she.' She shakes her head as a foot, then a leg sheened with sweat, appears. 'Come on, Aaron.' She knocks on the box. Aaron's other leg pushes out and then the rest of him. He sits hunched over in front of the box. 'Aaron, I have chores to get done,' she says impatiently. He reaches up to my stool, I give him my hand, he grabs it tight and pulls himself up. He stands shaking. His knees and the fronts of his calves are pocked with little deep round red craters. 'Upstairs.' She turns and walks out of the room. Aaron takes wobbly baby steps behind her, wincing at the light. Little brownish green round things fall away from him. She switches off the light, and they walk into the next room. I stare at the open mouthlike hole in the box. I drop down and reach into the floor of the box and grab. 'Jeremiah,' my grandmother calls. I run out and catch up with them on the steps. Aaron's walking like a cripple. My grandmother rushes him with clicks from her tongue. I lean behind Aaron's shadow and open my hand in the fluorescent light of the staircase. I roll around in my palm little round peas, hard little round peas.

Aaron taught me Bible and the rules, and I learned. I learned well enough to go on a long drive to the city and have my own street corner. I carry my pamphlets in one hand and pass them out with the other. All day I preach hellfire and damnation. Plain and simple. Kids ride by on bikes and skateboards and spit at me. Grown-ups either bless me or squeeze my cheeks and pat my crew-cut hair. But I know I'm going to heaven. I know the evil's left me. When police pass by, I don't hold my breath any more. I can feel him working through me, working his miracles, healing and curing. And when I fall, when I displease him, I pay, like Aaron, leaning over the desk, breathing in the rich lemony wood polish, and waiting for him to rest his hand on my head for a minute. I cry, and I'm cleansed. I'm with him, my grandfather, just me and him and the rod of correction, restoring me.

And the truth is sometimes I mess up my lessons on purpose and make myself not say ma'am or thank you, I let myself get caught reading a book from his study, I start to crave the strap that hangs on the silver hook behind the bookcase in his office. I need to be put into myself, to feel his hot, minty breath against my back and hear him pant quietly as he brings the strap down, to watch him dab his brow with the white embroidered cloth napkin that he carefully unfolds from his pocket. I always thank him after, like the others do, but I mean it. I don't cuss him later, telling everyone that it didn't really hurt. My heart feels full after, until it slowly seeps away. Sometimes I need more than the nod I get when I've memorized more Bible than anyone, when I've helped Job scrub me so hard that my skin is raw and cracked, when I've turned in Aaron again for not using toilet paper as he holds his thing to pee. I feel his love vaporizing out of me. I let Aaron turn me in. I let him feel closer to Jesus, I give him the gift of letting him feel powerful with my grandfather as he reports me. But all he gets is a nod from my grandfather like I get when I turn Aaron in. He gets the same closed-face nod and dismissal, but I get to stay inside and I get to feel his love.

Then one day she comes. I hear her voice from downstairs, loud and slurring. She's preaching. I race out of my bed to the banister and look down. '. . . but he is powerful,' she shouts, '. . . and never lets the guilty go unpunished . . .' She says unpunished slowly like it's many words and a swear word, too.

'. . . Nahum 1:3 fucker!' I hear a face slapped. I run down the stairs. 'Guilty, guilty, guilty,' she says.

'Get out of this house immediately,' I hear him say, but without his commanding sermon voice.

'Jere-my-yah!' she yells out singsong. 'My kid, right?' she says. 'Or is he yours? I'm the whore, I can't remember, maybe you can.' Slap again. She laughs, then screams my name. 'What will you do, calls the cops?'

'Leave immediately,' he says, but there is something strange in his voice. I stand at the bottom of the stairs, panting. Neither of them turns to me.

'We're going,' my mother says to him. My grandmother stands off to the side, wrapped in a robe she pulls tight. Her face looks defeated, but her eyes watch with a fierce gaze. 'Jeremiah . . .' Sarah reaches out her hand. Her skin glows like warm honey, and her fingers wiggle like little twigs off branches. She doesn't look at me, but I walk slowly toward her like I'm in a trance. I extend my hand out and up, but when I'm near her I don't have to reach up like I used to. I slip my hand in hers, and it's warm and it closes tight. My grandfather says nothing. My grandmother says nothing. 'See ya,' she says, and starts walking to the door, taking me with her. I turn my head toward my grandfather. His jaw's working back and forth, but he says nothing. 'God bless you, and thanks for turning my kid into a Jesus freak,' she says, and opens the door. 'Fucking hypocrites, fucker!' she shouts, slamming the door behind us.

The concrete is freezing against my bare feet, but I love the silky freedom of standing on it. 'Jesus . . .' She sighs and turns and spits on the door. I can't help but laugh. 'Like that, kid?' She looks at me for the first time. 'Damn, you're huge. He must be feeding you more than he ever fed me.' Her hair's cut short and spiked with a green streak in it. She's got a ring through her nostril. 'He won't fuck with me,' she slurs. She pulls me down the stairs with her. 'I got it over him.' There's a semi idling in the shadows. She motions wildly, and it backs up. 'Told you, we're partners,' she says, patting my hand. When we step on the grass, I wiggle my toes in the damp fuzz and laugh again. She lets go of my hand and reaches for the truck door. 'This is your new daddy,' she says.

My smile folds as the man in the turned-backward baseball cap nods at me. I look back to the sealed front door. 'Let's go,' she says, and clicks her tongue like my grandmother. I climb up and stand behind her seat mechanically. She hops in the front. 'So fuckin' easy . . . told ya he wouldn't fuck with me.' She drums on the wide dash. 'Not with what I got over him.' I keep wanting to ask what, but I can only turn and watch the front door get smaller and smaller.

'This is Kenny's. Owns his own rig,' she says, and passes the bottle in a brown paper bag back to him.

'So, little man. Ain't seen your momma in a while, huh?' He's got a blunt, stubby, but friendly, handsome face.

'Two years,' she says, and reaches back for the bottle, 'two years.'

'If we hadn't been driving by, it mighta been another two.' He laughs. 'This ain't like a stop for cigarettes.'

'What's mine is mine,' she says.

'Gotta mighty fine momma,' he says, and grabs a handful of her short hair in his thick, hairy hands and pulls her in for a kiss. 'Now, I know you learned some religious instruction, but we-all can't be havin' none of that here.' He points to a silver crucifix hanging on his rearview mirror. 'I got my own thing with the Lord, but if'n you start up any preaching, I'll tell ya . . . there's the door, don't let it hit ya in the eye, understand?' He winks at me. 'Now there's a little bed on back there.' He points to a satin silver curtain behind him. 'Go on back to bed'—he motions with his head—'go on.' I walk through the curtain to a little room in the back of the truck cab. I climb under sweaty-smelling blankets on the mattress, and I fall asleep listening to the low rumble of the truck competing against their laughter.

'You be listenin' out for me, Kenny.' Through the gap of the curtain I can see Sarah flip her head down into a platinum wig and come up tossing long curls, her shoulders bare in a tube top.

'Always do.' He thumps the wheel.

'Always don't, and I won't be gettin' my arm broke while you're doin' some goddamn lizard.'

'Gonna be right here listenin' out for you and fixin' up my comic book.' He flips pages in his logbook. 'Last weigh station set us back some. Gotta toy with it some.' He shakes his head over the pages. 'Plus pickin' your kid up . . .'

'Fuck that, I'll bring in more than your whole run.' She bends her leg and places it between his. He runs his hand along her thigh.

'Why you think we're stoppin', sugar?' He puts his hand behind her head and starts to pull her head down.

'No, don't even be messin' my lips up, 'less you wanna pay for it.'

He laughs and lets her go. 'Do good tonight. I'll be listenin' for ya.' He pats her ass, and as she slides her leg off the seat, she whispers something in his ear that makes him laugh.

'Later,' she says, and I hear her open the door.

'You know it,' he says, and stares down at his book turned spine out on his thigh. The door slams, he sighs and tosses the book off his leg. He switches on a country tape and jumps around, making the cabin shake like on a Ferris wheel ride. I cover my mouth not to laugh out loud as he shakes his ass wildly and sprays deodorant under his arms, inside his jeans, and on his hair, which he brushes and pushes till it rises like an overpass across his head. He squeezes a big blue glob of Crest into his mouth. I wait for him to spit, but he doesn't. He licks his lips and slips on cowboy boots that look like they have cheetah skin on them. He opens the door and I hear the metal tap of his boots on the truck steps, but he comes back, grabs the crucifix off the mirror, and slides it around his neck. Then he leaves, switching off the light and slamming the door behind him. I hear his heels clicking away, and I pull myself out of bed to the door window. I watch him disappear down a long line of trucks like his, lined up like sleeping dragons.

It's dark in the cab, and I don't know how to turn the light on. There's a little toilet in the back behind the curtain, and I need to go, but it's too dark back there. I stare at the silver curtain and wait to see the red eyes of Satan staring back out at me. My heart throbs in my chest, and I put my hand on the door handle next to my mother's empty seat. My bladder is almost bursting. A harsh light glares through the windshield, and I tell myself it's another truck, but then I see the red eyes floating inside the light, disembodied, glowing like fireflies, and I pull on the handle and push out as hard as I can. The door swings out, and I do, too. My feet dangle over the tar black of the lot like I'm bait on a fishline. I let go and fall to the ground, stumbling slightly as an eighteen-wheeler barrels past. I quickly regain my balance and reach for the truck door and slam it with all my might before Satan can escape. I stand there panting, staring at the sealed door, expecting Satan to start barking and clawing at the window. I wait until my feet start freezing, which isn't very long because I realize, looking down, I'm barefoot in my pajamas. 'Shoot!' I say out loud, and my voice sounds small and flat in the cold, windless air. The pressure on my bladder stabs into me. I look around. There's nobody, so I lean against the tire and piss, my eye on the cab door. I hear the click of a door opening. Satan's coming out. I step back, my piss forming a lazy arch shooting up and out of me. 'You have a good night, baby,' I hear from behind me. I jump and turn suddenly, the pee still flowing out of me, refusing to shut off. The cab door of the truck next to ours slams and a girl climbs down the truck steps, her eyes on me.

'You gonna hose me down now, or what?' The pee tapers off to a drizzle. She smiles. 'I think you're about done,' she says, standing across from me. 'Why don't you put that little baby bean away before you frighten everyone.' I blink at her and then down at my thing in my hand. She laughs, and dimples form in her rouged cheeks. I shove my thing back in my pajama bottoms and turn back to our truck, forgetting Satan and wanting only to get away from her. I climb the steps and yank on the door, but it's locked. I try again.

'Here . . .' She steps up next to me. 'Let me help.' She pulls the handle, but it doesn't budge. 'Wake 'em up.' She knocks loud on the door and smiles at me. She's got a lot of makeup on, and it sparkles like glitter. She doesn't look old, though there's something worn about her. Her black outlined eyes roll up. 'They in there?' She bangs again. I shake my head. 'Where are they?' she says, and steps down. Her skirt is so short that when she steps down I see her red panties. I shrug my shoulders and try the handle once more. 'You're locked out,' she says, sucking on her thin lips. 'You'll have more luck banging your head against a wall.' A plum-colored outline extends past the boundaries of her mouth, giving her a tough appearance. 'Come on.' She motions to me and starts to walk away. 'Come on, you can't stay out here, you'll freeze . . . come on . . .' She motions hard. The cold metal of the steps is starting to burn. 'Come on!' I jump down and follow her.

'Milkshake,' she says without stopping or turning. She reaches back her hand. Her nails are painted gold.

'No thanks, ma'am,' I mumble. She stops and turns to face me.

'I ain't offerin' you one. I'm Milkshake.' She rolls her eyes and puts her hand out again for me to shake. I give her my hand, and she pumps it once hard. 'And you?' She lets go without waiting for an answer and starts walking. She walks in her high heels like they're sandals, her feet lost inside them, making flip-flop noises. I catch up with her.

'I'm Jeremiah,' I tell her.

'Cool,' she says. 'Glad to meet ya, wouldn't want to be ya.' She laughs. 'Just kidding.' She flips her hair back again. 'See, there . . .' She points to an old station wagon sandwiched between two trucks. She starts to run a little, her shoes dragging like scuffs. She wraps her arms around herself. She's only wearing a tank top, red like her underthings. 'Come on,' she shouts, and I run to catch up. She digs in a little leather purse hanging across her shoulders. I can see money crumpled up inside it. She takes out keys and opens the back. 'Get in.' She gets in the front and turns the keys in the ignition. I panic. I've heard stories about kids being kidnapped, sacrificed, and eaten. I grab for the door handle. She turns back at me. 'Relax!' She grabs my arm. 'We ain't goin' nowheres. Just turning it on to get the heater goin'.' She points to a dirty beige metal thing near my feet. 'The heater . . . see?' She climbs over the seat next to me. 'What the fuck would I do with you, anyways?' She pulls off her heels and rubs her feet. 'Damn,' she says. There are runs up and down her stockings. They're black. 'So, that your daddy's truck?' she says, pulling on her toes.

'He ain't my real daddy,' I say. I rarely say ain't at my grand-parents. I almost taste the soap in my mouth. Sarah says ain't. She says it a lot.

'But that his truck?' She spits on her feet and rubs harder.

'He owns it, Sarah, my momma, said.'

'He thinks he's a bad-ass. That's a chicken car,' she says. 'Spends most of his money on the chrome.' I shrug. 'It got a toilet?'

'Uh-huh, TV and fridge, too, and a bed.'

'It's a condo, damn. What's he haulin'?' I shrug. 'He an ass-hole?' I shrug again. 'You know those lights all along the outside? Chicken lights. Any trucker with them's an asshole . . . I know truckers.' She sucks her lips. 'I like Kenworths men myself.' She sniffs her feet. 'Damn, they stink.' She puts one up to me. 'Wanna whiff?' I jerk my head back, laughing. She shoves her foot in my face. 'Won't charge ya none. C'mon, take a whiff,' she says, laughing. I try to push away her foot. I slide down the seat, laughing so hard my eyes tear. She climbs on top of the seat and puts her foot above my face. I'm pushing up as hard as I can, but laughing makes me weaker. 'Beg for mercy,' she says.

'No.' I push harder, but her foot lowers.

'Mercy,' she laughs, 'beg . . .'

'No!' I shout.

'Then suffer,' she yells, and forces her foot down on my face.

I thrash and yell between laughs, 'Mercy, mercy!' She rubs her foot around my squished cheek and then pulls it off and col-lapses back in her seat, wiping black mascara tears off her face. We sit in silence, catching our breath. After a few minutes she asks me if I'm hungry.

'I got Dunkin' Donuts somewhere,' she says, and reaches into the back.

'This your car?' I ask.

'What?!' she says, bringing out the pink-and-white box. 'How old do you think I am?' I shrug. 'This is my momma's.' She flips open the box. 'Help yourself.' I grab a chocolate sprinkle one. She takes a cream-coated one. 'How old do you think I am? Guess.' She's taller than me, not much, even in the heels, but she's wearing makeup and dressed old. I shake my head and wipe crumbs off my mouth. 'I'm twelve, almost thirteen. I can't drive yet, stupid.' She talks with her mouth full.

'I'm ten,' I lie.

'You look younger.' She takes a big bite, and cream gets on her nose. I don't tell her.

'Where's your momma?' I ask.

She snorts. 'My momma's a toss-up, you know, hubba.'

'What?'

'Crack. Crackwhore. She goes on runs. She won't be back for days.' I nod, though I'm not sure I understand. But I'm glad her momma won't be back. She licks her fingers. 'I take care of myself, plus all the lizards look out for me.'

'Lizards? My momma was worried about Kenny doin' lizards.'

'Well, she should be at this truck stop.' She swallows. 'They don't stop for nobody, most ignore the signs, not me. They don't want me, I ain't a-knockin'.' She takes another bite. 'Your daddy didn't have no signs on his truck.' She laughs, showing me her doughy mush.

'What signs?'

'Lizard signs, stupid.'

'What are lizard signs?'

'You don't know what a lizard is?' she asks, her mouth open and pieces of doughnut falling down her tank top. I shake my head. 'OK'—she swallows—'a lizard is a prostitute. Sex for money.' I nod. 'If you're workin' a truck stop, then you'—she points to herself—'are a lot lizard. Got it?'

'Uh-huh.' I reach into the box between us and take a cream doughnut like the one she has.

'Now a sign is . . . OK . . . hole up.' She gets up and digs in the back. She turns around with a flashlight. 'C'mere.' She shines the light out of the window and onto the door of the darkened truck next to us. I lean in close to her. She smells like perfume, but it's too heavy and I feel a little sick. The light dances over stickers on the truck door. 'Lookit.' She shines it on one of a cartoon lizard garishly dressed, with a red slash through it. 'See?' She turns to me. 'That means he don't want any.' She switches it off. I slide back to my seat.

'Kenny doesn't got one of those stickers.' I say got, not have, like Milkshake does, like Sarah says sometimes, like Aaron and the others would never say in front of my grandfather.

'I tole ya,' she says, and nods.

'Your mom's a lizard?'

She nods. 'So am I,' she says, and turns away to look out the window. 'Frosting up,' she says, tapping on the window. 'You're lucky I found you.'

We fall asleep in the backseat. I wake up before her. Her head is cradled between my feet, and her bent legs are on the seat. I don't move, even though I feel stiff.

When she wakes up, she pulls herself quickly off my legs and sits up. I pretend to wake up slowly. 'Gotta piss,' she says as I sit up. 'No condo in here.' She digs in the back and turns around with toilet paper, boots, and a jacket. She puts the boots and coat on. 'Be right back.' She goes behind the car. The sky is lightening with blue slashes, and the mountains in the distance look like purple humps. 'Your turn.' She jumps back in and hands me the toilet paper. 'Wanna get breakfast?' she says, opening a small mirror. 'Yuck, what a mess.' She spits on a finger and rubs at the black under her eyes.

'I haven't got . . . I ain't got no money,' I tell her.

'No kidding. Didn't think you hid it up your butthole, now, did I?' I feel my face redden, and I look away. 'My treat, but we gotta put you in some clothes.' She climbs in the back and unzips bags. 'Here . . .' She tosses a pair of jeans over, and a sweatshirt. 'Put 'em over your PJs and they'll fit, OK?' She tosses more stuff around. 'Here . . .' She hands me a pair of sneakers and two pairs of socks. 'Put 'em both on and try 'em.' They're a little big but will stay on. I hold up my foot and show her. 'Now you're set cowboy.'

We leave and head to the restaurant, the only one open twenty-four hours. A sign at the entrance says 'Truckers,' and an arrow beneath it points one way, then 'Everyone Else' points the other way. We head opposite 'Truckers.'

We eat eggs, and steak, and French fries, and coffee and hot chocolate, and she points out men walking by. She tells me who have no teeth and who cry like a baby when they come. She explains it all to me, coming, white goo, and how much it's all worth. 'I make a lot,' she says. 'A lot of 'em like little girls. And if I tell 'em I'm a cherry bomb . . . a virgin . . .'

'Like Mary,' I say.

'Yeah'—she laughs—'like that. They'll pay big bucks.'

'Then why don't you get a house or a truck?'

'More coffee, baby?' The fat waitress smiles over us and fills Milkshake's cup.

'Thanks, Cilla.' She opens and pours in ten half-and-half containers. 'My momma smokes it all,' she says, looking into her white coffee. 'It's my fault. I always believe her, then the money's gone.' She blows on the coffee. We watch it ripple. 'But if I leave her, she'll die . . .'

'I know,' I tell her.

We both look out the window and watch truckers pull out and disappear.

We stop at Kenny's truck after breakfast, but nobody answers my knock. So we go back to Milkshake's car.

She pulls out a tiny battery-run TV, and we watch her stories and game shows. I want to watch cartoons, but I'm embarrassed to ask. I really haven't seen any since before being at my grandparents'. We didn't watch TV there. Once when I was preaching near a TV shop, I gave in to temptation. I went in and watched *Rainbow Brite* and *The Smurfs*. I sat on the floor in the corner until it was done. I was afraid I was going to hell, and two days later I confessed to my grandfather. I didn't sit for a week, but I was relieved of my sin.

We eat more doughnuts, then go see if my mom's back yet. I'm afraid to go, scared that there'll just be an empty space instead of a truck. 'My mom's probably very worried,' I tell Milkshake.

I hear yelling inside the cab. Milkshake stands off to the side. I hold my breath and knock. The yelling inside continues. I knock louder. Sarah opens the door, dressed the same as she was last night, similar to Milkshake.

'What?!' she says.

'I'm back,' I say.

'Not now,' she says, and turns back inside, slamming the door. The shouting continues.

I don't want to look at Milkshake. I stand staring at the closed truck door. I feel her hand in mine. 'C'mon,' she says, '*All My Children*'s on.' I let her lead me back to the car.

I go back several times and check on the truck. There's always shouting inside, so I don't knock. When I go back after the sun goes down, the cab is dark and there is no answer when I knock.

'Watch this,' Milkshake says, and climbs into the front seat. She's changed into a different short skirt, a metallic gold, and her face is painted in glitter again. 'This is a CB,' she says, pointing to the radio box in the dash.

'I know, Kenny's got one . . .'

'Bet Kenny don't do this . . .' She switches the CB on. Static and men talking fill the car. She looks at me and winks. She holds the mike and presses down on it. 'Break 1–9,' she says.

'Go ahead, breaker,' a man's voice responds.

'Milkshake here for R 'n' R, over.'

'Calf Roper here, darlin', where ya wanna take it?' he says.

'Twenty-eight for my 10–20,' she says.

'Is the pussy free tonight?' a different man says.

'Milkshake goin' to twenty-eight. Visit and ya'll find out.' She reaches out and changes her channel. 'Break 2–8,' Milkshake says.

'Hold a minute, Breaker,' a woman's voice says.

'. . . suck the life outta ya, sugar,' a throaty-voiced woman cracks over the CB.

'I'm a-waitin' over the chicken coop,' a man responds.

'Be right there, Smokestacks,' she says.

'Go ahead, Breaker,' the first woman says.

'Milkshake here, for R 'n' R.'

'Calf Roper pullin' you in, baby,' the man from before says.

'Can't get enough of me, can ya?'

'No, ma'am, I can't.'

'I'll be on over.'

'Milkshake, you need help with that cradle robber?' a woman asks.

'Naw, Sweet Lips, I'm gonna rob him all myself. That's a 10–7.' She reaches over and switches off the CB. 'I just made us dinner and video game money.' She leans back and laughs.

'But you gotta do stuff with him?' I ask, staring at the CB.

'No big deal. I sit on his face, jerk him off, and I got me twenty-five dollars.' She puts her high heels on.

'He said he wanted all that just now?'

'No, I know him, he's a repeat, did him last night.' She looks at herself in her little pink compact mirror. I shake my head. 'Beats knockin' on doors like your momma does.' She snaps her mirror shut.

'What?'

She opens the car door. 'You don't know . . . your momma's a lot lizard, too.' She shuts the door. She waves and walks off.

I say nothing to Milkshake when she comes back and fires up the CB again. I pretend to be asleep. She turns the CB louder. I want to cover my ears. I'm afraid I might hear Sarah. Milkshake leaves on another date, but she leaves the CB on. I raise the volume on the TV as high as it goes, but I can still hear the moans from the CB.

In the morning we eat ice-cream sundaes at the restaurant. 'I wanna do one,' I tell her.

'Do one what?' she says, scooping out hot butterscotch fudge.

'One date, like you do.' I tap my spoon on the table.

'You can't, you're too young, and you're a boy.'

'Am not!'

'Am not what?' She stares at me, her makeup colored splotches on her face. 'Not a boy?'

'Sometimes I'm not,' I tell her, looking down. She reaches under the table and gropes between my legs. I jump away, my spoon clattering to the floor. 'Damn!' I shout, and then bite my lip hard for having sworn.

'You are a boy, though I've had my doubts.' She laughs. I remind myself that my grandfather isn't here, and I let myself breathe again. 'Damn!' I say once more, and smile.

We take free showers at the truck stop, wearing her sneakers because the showers are too slimy to do without them.

When Milkshake goes to her car to sleep, I walk back to the truck. I try the door, and it's open. I enter quietly. 'Kenny?' Sarah calls out from behind the silver curtain.

'No—no, ma'am,' I stutter. 'It's me.'

'C'mon back here.'

I walk cautiously to the silver drape and pull it aside slowly.

Sarah is in the bed and covers her eyes from the shafts of light. 'C'mere,' she says, and motions to me.

I move to her heavily, like I'm walking through peanut butter. She'll want to know where I got the clothes and where I've been. She pats the bed for me to sit next to her. I do carefully. 'Lie down,' she says. I blink at her. Her makeup's smeared like Milkshake's. 'Lie down,' she repeats. I can't read her tone. It's not angry, not even annoyed. I lie down stiffly next to her, my head half on her pillow. 'You're all I got,' she says. She throws an arm around my waist. I stare wide-eyed around the cab, at the white toilet glowing like a fluorescent moon and the tiny humming fridge filled with iced coffees and Cokes. 'No one can take you away from me,' she says. I stare at a used syringe on the floor and the cotton ball next to it, lying there like a fallen cloud. 'You better not leave me,' she says, and her hands move sloppily to my crotch and rest there lazily. I notice a thin trickle of blood running from her arm like a sink leak. She breathes in heavy, a partial snore. I reach my hand to her arm and wipe up the blood with my fingers. She snorts, then moans. I put my fingers in my mouth and clean the blood off them like I've seen a cat licking her newborns do.

'I'm yours,' I whisper, and lean into her dead weight and try to sleep.

I wake up feeling the truck rumbling beneath me. Sarah doesn't stir as I pull myself out from under her arm and go up front. 'Where ya been?' Kenny says, sitting in the driver's seat and starting to pull out of the truck stop.

'We going now, sir?' I ask, looking back at the lot, searching for Milkshake's station wagon.

'Goin' now? Shoulda gone yesterday.' He reaches in his pocket for a Marlboro.

'Please, can we not go yet, sir?' I grab on to the back of his seat as we pick up speed, following the interstate signs.

'Not go yet?! Hell, no! Boy, I just tole ya, we shoulda done been gone!' He lights up. 'What were ya doin' back there that ya don't wanna go? Where d'ya get them clothes at?'

'I met a family and they took care of me, lent me clothes and these shoes. And I really should give 'em back and say thank you or something, sir.'

'Well . . .'—he laughs—'you just got yourself some new clothes, you needed some anyways. We ain't goin' back.' He waves at me. 'Lean over here and I'll let you pull my new train horn.' My mouth feels dry as I move to his side. 'This here is a brass lever.' He takes my hand and puts it on a golden chain hanging from the cab roof. 'When I tell you pull down on it . . . you pull down on it.' The truck enters the interstate ramp and heads into the stream of traffic. 'Now, pull it now.' My arm jerks down, and Kenny smiles. 'Isn't that the most beautiful sound?' he says as the wah-wah cry of the train horn echoes around us. 'Seventeen hundred dollars that cost me!' We speed past the truck stop, and I yank the horn's lever once more and put my good-bye into it like a smoke signal floating in the air.

I hear Kenny's train whistle for the last time while eating alone in a truck stop diner outside Orlando, Florida. I look up and around me, but it all continues, the haggard waitresses in dirty white sneakers, glittering gold hairnets, and short pink skirts, tending to the big men and their bigger wives packed into the orange plastic booths with their dull-eyed children.

Nobody notices the train horn. A train horn on a truck, and no one looks up to wonder who was in the way and if they moved fast enough.

I bury my spoon under the milk in my Cheerios mix. Sarah showed me how to make Cheerios. 'Just Cheerios, no milk . . . Milk's on the table, don't need to pay for what they're givin' away.' She dumps the silver container into her cereal and points to me to grab the container off the empty table behind us and do the same. 'Jelly's free . . .' She spoons half the jar of sugary strawberry jam in, then does the same on my Cheerios. 'Butter's free, too.' She opens five little plastic packages and pushes out the bright yellow blobs into the bowl and motions for me to do the same. 'The classier places leave out the maple syrup . . .' She pours half the slow amber liquid into her bowl, then mine, pouring it on the table while traveling between her bowl and mine. 'Now this rounds it out . . .' She reaches for the red plastic ketchup bottle and squirts a big mound of red squiggly lines in our bowls, and again she doesn't stop squeezing the bottle in the space between our bowls. 'Now, if ya got a extra fifty cents, you order yourself a cottage cheese ball.' She grabs a fork and begins to stir the mixture. 'Then you're really stylin'. More cream,' she tells the waitress when the waitress asks her too loudly if that'll be all. 'White trash, cunt,' Sarah mutters as the waitress walks away. 'Here . . .' She reaches out, gripping the glass sugar container like a machine gun, and dumps half of it into our bowls and on the table.

The truck's train horn sounds again, farther away, three quick fuck-you-I'm-out-of-here blasts. 'Gotta let the hearts know when to start a-breakin',' Kenny would say every time he would pull the horn chain when we left a truck stop. 'More like their wallets to start a-achin',' Sarah would say, laughing.

The train horn echoes through the diner, but nobody even looks toward the big mirrored plate-glass window. If you stare for a while, you can make out the huge black box outline of trucks in the night, like some hidden underworld nobody wants to remember exists. I hear Kenny's horn long after it must have stopped, long after he must be on the interstate and finally getting to play his country tapes, the ones Sarah didn't toss out the window.

A teenage girl with frizzy red hair she keeps combing and holding down with her hand as if it were a hood in a windstorm has watched me prepare my Cheerios from a table across from mine. She picks at her fries, then frowns at me when I pour something free into my bowl. When I pick up the ketchup her face goes sour. I pretend to only be examining the container, and I put it back down. I wait till she turns to her mother, and I squirt my ketchup in fast. We do this dance for a while, her even faking me out, not really going for her fries, making me panic and squirt a red slash line across my chest. I expect her to laugh. She only looks more lemonish. I feel disappointed and ashamed. I don't start to eat until she and her mother leave.

The horn sound is still ringing inside my head. It's not a surprise; I thought it would happen sooner, I thought I'd feel relieved, relieved that I wouldn't keep waiting to hear the hollow bellow of it every time I left the truck.

'I hate punk rock,' Kenny had said, and pulled her tape out of the cassette player.

'Only faggots call it punk rock, Kenny. How many times I have to tell you, you ignorant, country-listening, white trash, cocksucking, hillbilly, motherfucking . . .'

He grabs a handful of her tapes and tosses them out the window. She screams and attacks him, whaling at him with her fists so violently, he almost hits another truck. He pulls over and runs along the interstate like a jackrabbit, returns an hour later, holding up three tapes, his face cut from her fingernails. He cradles one tape, its guts roped and glittering around his fingers. 'Maybe we can rewind it, baby,' he says, looking down as he enters the cab.

She grabs the broken tape. 'The Subhumans, you fucker!'

They don't speak until they get to the truck stop. She dresses in her wig and shiny dress. He says he'll listen out. She leaves, telling him he'd damn well better. He doesn't get dressed up like usual. He asks me if I want another comic book. He gives me $5 and tells me not to spend it all in one place. 'Go on now, before the gift shop closes up.'

I don't go to the gift shop. I go to the diner. I don't buy a burger like I could, I don't even get a cottage cheese scoop.

And I feel the bill in my jeans pocket, the jeans Milkshake gave me and I keep up with Kenny's belt, doubled around me. I run my palm along the smooth leather of the belt and reach my hand in my pocket past the five-dollar bill, like I do at night sleeping on the foam bed in the front of the cab when I snake my belt out from my jeans loops and guide it gently under the fuzzy polyester blanket. It's Kenny, holding me from behind, breathing out in my ear, pressing into me, draping the belt over me, like I wish he would but never does, my grandfather preaching, his minty breath stinging and his face set like a stone carving so solid, so absolute, you know there's something between you and the bottomless pit. Every package of candy and comic book I've stolen from truck stop gift shops is laid out, and I whisper, 'Please punish me, please,' and I rub, so hard it'll hurt when I piss the next day. I rub with the belt, wrapping it and squeezing. I dig my nails deep into the tender skin of my thing until I cry, until I feel that point of breaking, but there's no one to fall into. I hold the belt close until I finally sleep.

'Daydreaming at night's bad for your health,' the blue-haired waitress says above me. My eyes jerk open, and I pull my hand out of my pocket. 'Waitin' for your momma?' I shake my head. Children are always eating alone at all times of night at truck stop diners. Some kids get dropped off before their parents go honky-tonkin'. There'd usually be a few kids sleeping in a booth in the back. Some truck drivers ride with their whole family. I'd seen seven or eight kids tumble out of one cab. Some waitresses smile at you for being alone and bring you free milkshakes and burgers. Some tell you they ain't no goddamn babysitter, and tell you kid or not, she'd better get a goddamn tip. Most just treat me like a non-truck-driving customer, relaxed and with indifferent friendliness. I eat another spoonful of Cheerios and imagine Kenny laughing and pulling on the chain, the brass chain he polished every day. I can't be sure Sarah isn't with him; to think about that makes it impossible to swallow. Her hand on his, pulling the brass lever together. I pay for my Cheerios and run to where the truck was parked.

It's empty, like I knew it would be. There's a black garbage bag sitting on the black tar between oil spots. Our stuff is inside, mostly Sarah's. I find my comic books next to her red spiked heels. I dig around and find the markers I'd stolen from a truck stop goods shop in Georgia.

I tear out a piece of paper from a small notebook I stole. I write on it with a red marker and fold it up. In my notebook I have written five words on each page. As we drove, I wrote stories but only put one word of it down here and there, so when Sarah grabs it to see what's so damned interesting she won't know the code, won't know the story, and can't take it from me. But I see the words fit snugly between the printed ones and could read the story the same way fifty times. I sit on the plastic bag and wait for her return.

I hear her heels clicking, echoing down the rows of sleeping trucks. I peel my cheek, glued with drool, away from the garbage bag. She says nothing, only moves her eyes over the empty space like it must be a reverse mirage, seeing nothing when something is really there. Her makeup is smeared, and her wig is crooked. I reach up and hand her the folded notebook paper. She holds it close, reads it, laughs, and drops it. 'That orange truck . . . there . . .' She points down the line. 'I'll be in there.' Her voice slides around the edges of her words, not quite pronouncing them, but I understand her. 'Come by tomorrow and you're my sister.' I nod. She steps on the note, the words melting into the oil. 'Somebody stabbed you,' she says, and points to the ketchup stains across my chest. She turns and wobbly walks toward the orange truck. 'Bring the bag,' she says over her shoulder. As she walks she reaches up and yanks down on an invisible chain three times.

I stare at the note, almost drowned in oil. 'I love you' is covered, the red 'Goodbye' slowly slips into black.

In the morning I find the Schneider National truck, not shiny and covered in lights like Kenny's, but ugly and bright orange, like construction site cones, which is why truckers call the cones Schneider eggs. 'What's your name, darlin'?' He makes a tight-lipped smile, but because of his droopy eyes it looks more like a frown.

'Chrissy, that's Chrissy,' Sarah says, taking the garbage bag from me and pulling out her red heels. I nod hello and watch him dance his fingertips along his leather belt and then through his crew cut.

'Pretty sister you got, Stacy,' he says to Sarah.

'Uh-huh,' Sarah says, stuffing balled-up tissues into her bra.

'Sure is pretty.'

I smile back and blink my eyes like the bleach blond wait-resses do on the trucker side.

I don't like the smell of Schneider Truck. His moldy flan-nel mixed with women's flowery deodorant nauseates me. His hands are pale, and his fingers are long and floppy like daisy stems, not cracked and heavy like Kenny's, not the kind that can crush you quickly if they wanted to, and for some reason that makes me feel cold and hot at the same time, they just don't. Schneider Truck pinches my ass when I move past him. He rubs my cheek with fingers that feel slippery and wet like spaghetti. He tells me I'm a pretty girl like my sister. I like that, and I smile while looking away from his filmy gray eyes. Sarah hates him. He doesn't understand her medicine. He won't help her tie her arm for it, so I do while he paces in front of the cab and whines for her to hurry up. She gives him the finger behind his back; sometimes he turns, catching her, and she pretends to be picking her nose. He doesn't like punk, either. He only listens to boring radio talk shows. He shakes his head when they talk about the perverts teaching in our schools. 'They should be castigated,' he says.

He gets a room for us, paid for one month while he's away.

Sarah wants it far from the truck stop but still in Orlando, on Orange Blossom Trail. He likes her away from the stop, but, 'Orange Blossom Trail ain't no place for my future wife . . .'

'It's cheap, ain't it,' she yells as we drive down the wide dark street, passing gated deserted warehouse lots and neon 'GIRLS, GIRLS, GIRLS' signs every two blocks. She heard from someone that it's the place to stay. Schneider Truck doesn't like it being situated right behind the sleaziest striphouse he ever saw. 'It's cheap, ain't it?' Sarah says again, and they go to check in.

I sleep in the cab that night. They sleep in the efficiency motel room. She insists they get the room with the gas stove so she can cook for me. The next day Sarah gets a job stripping at the club in front of the motel. 'Fuckin' Mickey Mouse tips again.' She pulls the fake Disney dollars mixed with real dollars out of her bra. 'They think they're so original . . .'

Schneider Truck calls every day for a month. Since there's no phone in the room, he rings on the pay phone at the end of the line of chipped-wood motel doors. Sarah either isn't around or won't answer when someone bangs on our door for the phone. I go instead.

'How's your sister, sweetie?' His voice has a raspy, lung-cancerous tone to it.

'Fine, sir.' I run my dirty nails over the silver metal armadillo back phone cord.

'What's she up to . . . no good, honey?' He coughs and laughs nervously.

I look at the flashing blue neon outline of a naked girl on the club about a stone's throw away. 'It's all fine, sir,' I say.

'You can tell, baby . . . I'm gonna be almost like your daddy, buy you lots of pretty little dresses . . .'

I dig my nail in the black rubber under a chink in the phone cord's armor. The idea of going shopping for dresses makes me happy. 'I've seen a real nice Sunday dress at T. J. Maxx,' I tell him.

'What color is it, sweetie?' he asks.

I wrap the cord around me and pull the phone in tighter. I turn away from the club. 'Kinda pink,' I say quietly.

'You got'—he coughs—'got panties to match, sweetie? Little pretty pink panties to match?' His voice is high, like he's talking to a puppy.

'No'—I dig my nail in deeper to the sticky rubber—'sir.'

'I'll get ya some, for you, sweet-pie.'

'OK . . .' I push dirt with my sneaker over a busy anthole.

'Tell your sister I love her . . .'

'OK . . .'

'I love you, too, sweetie . . .' I nod. 'Now say you love your daddy.'

The ants are scurrying, searching for the entrance to their home. 'Say you love your daddy,' he repeats louder, but he sounds like he's cupping the phone.

Some of the ants have found another way in, a back door five inches away from the main one.

'Don'tcha love your daddy?' He coughs.

I'm mad at myself for not covering them both.

'Sweetie? Chrissy baby?'

I lean over and kick dirt over their back hole.

'You still there?'

Now they're panicking again. I smile.

'Chrissy!' he shouts.

'Yes, sir . . .'

'I got to go . . . kiss your sister for me.'

'I saw a pretty yellow dress, too,' I say.

'Anything you want. I love you, sweet-pie.'

I nod and press my nail in so hard into the crack in the phone cord that I can feel the wires.

'Bye'—he coughs—'love to your sister . . . my two pretty girls.'

I nod. I wonder if I can get electrocuted if I go too deep in.

'You there? . . . I'm hangin' up now . . . Hello? Good-bye . . . bye-bye . . .'

The phone clicks. I push my nail in as far as it can go. Nothing happens. I hang up the phone and stomp on ants.

One morning from our room I hear Sarah screaming into the pay phone. Schneider Truck must have caught her on the way home from the club. 'Fuck off, pervert fucker!' she screams. 'No, you ain't comin' back, unless you want your shriveled-up balls as a butt plug.'

I turn the Bugs Bunny cartoon louder, but I can still hear the phone slam down again and again. The dresses weren't really that nice anyway.

I don't leave our room much. We go to a diner for Cheerios, and there's a Hostess outlet nearby, where I walk every two days to buy us Ding-Dongs.

The police are after me again because the evil is in me again. Sarah said a cop came to the strip club and flashed a picture of me. I didn't believe her at first, but a week later sirens and blue lights surrounded the club.

I hide under the bed. The police bang on the doors, straight down the line of rooms. I hear keys jingle outside the door, then in the lock. I flatten myself to the dusty, moldy rug. 'See, prostitutes no here, amigo,' the Cuban manager says. Flashlights sweep across the floor. I can see their thick black shoes walking toward me. 'No here! No here!' he says. The shoes walk to the bed, I hold my breath. They pause and then move past into the bathroom. I see the flashlight shine into it. 'No here, see?'

Sarah doesn't come back for three days. 'I was fuckin' arrested!' she yells. She pulls off her heels and throws them at me. I don't step out of the way this time. 'Thank fucking God the club got us out . . . or I'd've turned you in!' Her face is yellowish, and her hands shake.

I had pretty much stayed under the bed while she was gone. I came out to grab the Ding-Dongs and to sneak into the bathroom, but sometimes I was too scared to make it. I prayed to Jesus to heal me, to save me, to restore me. I recited every psalm, every proverb, every chapter and verse I knew, hundreds of times, till it filled my dreams when I slept.

'I'm sorry, I'm sorry,' I whisper to Sarah. 'I've . . . I've tried to cast Satan from my soul . . .'

'Well . . . you're gonna have to fuckin' try harder!' Her eyes are rimmed raw like chopped meat. She sits on the bed, her head between her legs. Her body raises up with a sob.

'I prayed for Jesus to bring you back. I prayed and prayed . . .'

'Shut the fuck up.'

'The . . . the . . . police might not want me any more, though, He might have cured me. He brought you home . . . "In God is my salvation and my glory: the rock of my strength." '

She reaches fast over to the night table and grabs a heavy motel glass. It hits me on the collarbone with a thud. I hear the crack. 'You're lucky . . . I was aimin' for your ugly-ass fuckin' face!' Pain races like an ice shear through me, but I don't move. I blink the tears away. 'Don't stare at me like that, you evil fuckin' piece of shit. What? You think you're better'n me? If it weren't for me, you'd be burnin' in hell right now!' She reaches for the glass where it bounced off me and rolled near her feet.

'I p-prayed very hard,' I whisper.

'You forgot how to shut the fuck up!' I watch in slow motion as she winds her arm back and hurls the glass again. My eyes close against the coming impact across my face. It hits me in my stomach. I lean over from the force of it and gasp. 'You've gotta learn when to shut the fuck up!' I lean down and try to catch my breath.

She didn't hit my face. I smile up at her. She didn't even aim for it. I wrap my arms around my stomach and rock myself gently, feeling soothed and comforted.

'Get the fuck out,' she says, her voice throaty and raw. 'You're a fuckin' demon.' The smile stays frozen on my face, and I hold on to my stomach and keep rocking. She staggers over to me. She grabs a handful of my hair and pulls me backward. Without thinking I put my hand up and over her hand so I won't be carried only by my hair. My collarbone throbs as I lift my arm. 'You possessed piece of shit.' I try to walk my legs backward, but I can't stand. The room is blurry. I hear her opening the door. 'I never should have come for you.' The skin on her hand is soft like polished leather.

'Let go of me, let go, you evil fuck!' She's shaking her hand in my hair. I feel a thud on my side, then another. It's her foot. I let go of her hand and fall backward, half out of the door. 'Go to hell,' she says in a low, hushed voice, and kicks again so I'm out the door. 'If the police find ya, they're gonna burn you up. First they'll chop you up.' She spits down at me. It hits my mouth. 'Then you burn . . . in hell. So if I was you . . . I'd stay away from cops!' She looks nervously both ways down the row of room doors. 'If I so much as see you, I'll call them myself.' Then she closes the door softly, as if she were shutting it on a friendly salesman.

I sit there staring at the footprints and dents on the bottom half of the door. Someone once kicked hard to try to get back in.

I lick the spit off my lips with my tongue and listen to the flux of pain like rotating arcade lights, the throb moving from my scalp to my collarbone to wherever. I get on my hands and knees and pull myself up. I blink away the blurriness. The lights are off at the club. There's only the hum of moths batting against the caged-in lightbulb in the middle of the row, crickets, and the low rumble of an isolated truck driving down Orange Blossom Trail.

I walk around the motel to the clump of bushes and trees. I've often seen men fast asleep back here, smelling of alcohol and urine, their cars the only ones left in the lot at the club. I crawl into a flattened patch and curl up. She didn't aim for my face, I repeat to myself, and I taste her saliva in my mouth.

The next day I stay hidden behind the motel. I drink from a leaky spigot. I cover myself with fallen palm leaves and sleep. When I hear a police siren race by, I wet myself.

At night I listen to the different women chatting, going off to the club or coming back. Finally I hear her. 'I better get my pay, that's all,' Sarah says.

'They might raid again,' another woman says.

'That's what happens when cops get stiffed on their fuckin' bribes,' she says.

'Just keep your shit away from the club, is all I heard, or your ass gets fired on the spot . . .'

'I better get my pay, that's all,' she says again, and I hear the loud click of her red heels along the concrete walk. I walk around the back to the manager's office. He's a small, brawny Cuban with a single thin eyebrow across his forehead. He recently put new bedspreads in the rooms, bright Day-Glo with hallucinogenic geometric shapes on them. Whenever he sees any of the women with lit cigarettes, he screams. If he sees Sarah walking from the club back to the room, a cigarette dangling from her red, shimmering lips, he runs out of his stale, fart-smelling office where he sits all day blasting soccer games in Spanish, ringing the service bell on his counter when his team scores.

Usually she grins and tosses the cigarette, crushing it under her high heels, her leg stepped forward and twisted from her fluid hips. Her eyes hold his gaze, causing the dark stain under his armpits to spread. Other times when she's had too many Mickey Mouse money tips and not enough medicine, she flicks the cigarette at his feet, making it spray like an electric spark while he yells at her.

I knock on the screen door that he always keeps locked on the inside. '*Qué?*' He doesn't look up from the soccer game.

'I'm locked out,' I mumble.

'*Qué? Qué?*'

I look past the tiny mesh stitches of the screen door and glimpse chubby little legs sticking out from behind a wall. Their kid, that Sarah told me about. 'He's retarded or something, and they treat him like a dog, feed him from dog bowls,' she said. 'Heard they tie him up sometimes, too. See, you don't even got it so bad.'

The manager hits wildly at the bell. '*Goal, goal!*' he yells. When I look back the fat baby legs are gone.

I start to knock again, but he moves from around the counter.

'I hear you once, you think I don't hear you, I hear you.' He opens the door and walks past me, jingling the keys. The sound gives me a chill. He stops at our door and opens it.

'*Gracias,*' I whisper.

'You look not so good,' he says, and turns and walks away. I close the door, turn on the light. I pull the chair over to the cabinet above the sink. I climb up stiffly and take down the bottle of Wild Turkey. 'Chicken,' I whisper. I grab the glass still on the floor and fill it halfway. I run the tap, wait till the rust clears as

much as it will, and hold the bottle under it, then my glass. I put
the bottle back.

I swallow down the drink as fast as I can while walking into the
bathroom. I slowly take off my clothes. The ache in my shoulder
is starting to fade fast. I climb into the tub and turn the water on
as hot as I can stand. I wish I had a scrub brush.

Baby Doll

When Jesus died the angels cried and their tears turned to stones.

My mom's new boyfriend is born again, so we scour the dirt like gold panners for the fingernail-size rocks with crosses naturally formed on them. Angel tears. We try to escape from the busload of Baptists giving praises and hallelujahs, which echo loudly all through the forest of Fairy Stone Park, Virginia.

I always find the best ones, with clearly defined crosses rising out of the brown stones, not the broken crumbly ones my mom finds.

'You find 'em like an old horse finds glue, don't ya?' Her eyes squeeze up jealously, her nostrils widening.

'Lord smiling on you today, son.' I look up into his big face, long and black bearded exactly like Paul Bunyan, smiling down at me, with the emerald treetops shifting the light above his head in glints and glimmers.

He reaches down and takes the cross stone from my outstretched palm. 'Have to show this one at services.' He nods. 'Let the Lord guide you to more, son.' He pats my ass as I turn away. I catch my mom's jagged glare and my smile folds. We continue to hunt, bent over the dark peaty moist earth in silence.

'Look at this one, Jackson!' My mom rushes over to him. She

holds out her hand like I did, her other hand pushing her yellow hair back against her skull repeatedly. He leans over her palm, she shifts back and forth, he turns it over and shakes his head.

'Not as good as his, baby doll.' He nods toward me. I look away, grinning. I hear her throw it into the bushes.

'I found another one!' I yell, and raise up my arm, holding another perfectly formed tear of an angel.

'You're my baby.'

I raise my head silently from my pillow; there's only a thin divider that doesn't reach up to the trailer roof.

'My sweet little girl,' he half whispers, and I hear blankets moving and sticky skin noises.

'Yes, I am.' Her voice sounds too high and babyish.

'What are you, darlin'?'

'Daddy's little girl,' she answers right away.

'Daddy needs his little girl.' I hear the patting of flesh, and I lay my head back down. She makes purring noises.

'Tell me you're Daddy's good girl,' he growls. She says it. I reach under my blanket.

'Ya want Daddy to fuck ya?'

She says yes, says 'Daddy' twice. I reach between my legs.

'C'mon, baby girl, c'mon, give it to your daddy.' His voice rises. 'C'mon. Good girl, good girl.'

I take my thing and push it backward between my legs, and I feel the trailer swaying. I rub the smooth skin where my thing was, in time to the rocking.

'Good girl, good girl, Daddy loves you.' I close my eyes.

I watch her from the side in the morning, leaning into the tiny mirror over the kitchen sink, smoothing tan foundation over her face with a small triangular white sponge. She dabs it on heavily over her nose and cheeks, covering the spray of freckles that she hates. The same ones on my face that I hate.

'Make mine disappear?' I ask her suddenly. She turns to me in surprise that I'm even there. I step back. She smiles.

'Pull over a chair.' I drag over one of the red metal folding chairs.

'Climb up.' I stand on top and see our faces in the mirror.

'Let's get rid of those.' I nod my head and watch her dab the sponge into some beige liquid foundation that's open with the rest of her makeup above the sink ledge.

'Here.' She rubs it over my nose and cheeks, not gently like she did to herself; but my freckles are darker. I enjoy her touching me.

'There! Look.' I stand on my tiptoes and lean into the mirror. They're gone. I smile up at her.

'We gotta do something about your nose,' she says. I look at hers, delicate, upturned, and thin.

'Somebody fucked their nigger slave, and you got the nose to prove it.' I look at mine, short, turned up like hers, but with thick nostrils, wider and almost flattened.

'Nigger—nigger nose!' She laughs.

'Fix it? Please?' I don't want to cry.

'Sure, nigger nose!' She laughs again, and I smile, my lip shaking.

'Camouflage it . . . see, I learned that in beauty school.' I watch her take a small brush and dip it in brownish eye shadow.

'One day I'll go back, I'll get a shop for the models in Hollywood . . .' She sucks the wooden end of the brush. 'Or I'll be a model.'

'Take me?'

'Hold still.' She runs the brush along the sides of my nose like she's dusting.

'Well, we'll see if we can fix this nigger nose.'

I try to look in the mirror, but her hand's in the way.

'OK, now I lighten it with concealer.' She dabs some creamy stuff onto my nose.

'Blend, OK, now . . . look at me.' I look up at her, feeling excited and nervous.

'Can I go with you?'

'Take a look.' She pushes my face toward the mirror. My nose has brown beige strips on its sides like war paint.

'Definitely camouflaged!' I nod hard.

'OK, now your eyes . . . you have my eyes, so you're lucky. OK, close your eyes.' I do, and I feel brushes gliding across my lids, her coffee breath warm and moist against my cheek.

'Look up, look left . . . right, blink . . . again.'

It feels like she's writing on my eyes. I don't want it to stop.

'Look at me!' And when I do it is freeze-framed in my mind forever, her licking her finger and running it gently under my eyes. It reminds me of those nature films of a mother bird regurgitating food into its baby's mouth. I feel so happy, I almost hug her.

'Can I look?' My hands flap at my sides.

'No, you ain't half-done. Let's see if we can give you lips . . . you ain't too lucky—you got the nose, I got the lips. Even a chicken's got more lips than you.' I trace my finger across my thin lips with little crowned points. Hers are big, shiny, and red.

'Look here.' She holds a rust red pencil. I pucker my lips.

'Nooo . . . relax 'em,' she says, a little irritated.

'You ever see me pucker when I do my lips?' I shake my head. 'Close, just natural like.'

The pencil moves around my mouth.

'OK . . . now . . .' I hear her opening lipsticks. 'Open.'

I look up at the white corkboardlike ceiling. She dabs lipstick on my lips.

'Hmmm . . .' And then a brush with mushy wet goop sweeps across my lips. I look up at her, so close to me, staring at my mouth; she catches me, I look away fast.

'Here . . .' She holds a toilet paper sheet to my mouth. I open and close on it like I've done a million times copying her, but now I leave red kiss marks. I laugh and try to turn toward the mirror.

'Not yet!' She grabs my head. 'Blush?' she asks.

'Yeah, yeah,' I practically yell. 'Please.' My eyes flutter as she lightly sweeps a big fuzzy brush across my cheeks and over my face.

'I won't do your nose, don't wanna bring no attention to that, do we, niggey nose?'

'Uh-uh.'

'OK, now, to set. Close your eyes.' She dusts me with translucent powder, her hand over my eyes to protect them, and again I feel overwhelmed with joy.

'Can I look?'

She regards me. 'Go ahead.'

She turns my head toward the mirror. I blink at myself and try to recognize what I see. They're her eyes, a mottled mix of pale blue gray green, painted and outlined, only smaller. My lips are full, almost like hers, and satiny red. I don't even notice my nose.

'Well?' She sounds impatient.

'I, I look pretty,' I say quietly.

'See, I told you you were meant to be a girl.'

'I know,' I mumble, and bite my lip.

'Stop that!' She hits my head, not hard. 'Don't mess my lips!'

'Sorry.'

'Now, ain't you glad I didn't cut your hair short?' She reaches for the curling iron. I nod yes and I realize I've gotten used to it and I like it when we go to the shops and the store owners say I'm a pretty girl like my older sister. Sometimes I get free candy. Only once did I correct someone.

'She's my mom and I ain't a girl!'

The tall, pimply man behind the meat counter leans forward. 'Pardon?'

Her hand reaches out, grabs the back of my hair, and gives a quick, sharp yank. She laughs.

'Playin' games . . . she always is . . . now say thank you . . .'

Later she unloads the groceries silently into the trunk. I climb into the back where I sit when she has a boyfriend, if he's with us or not.

'Sit up front,' she says. I watch her start the car and push in the lighter.

'I want a haircut!' I feel strong in my anger. She says nothing, just starts to drive.

'Everyone says I'm a girl. I'm not! Even Kevin!' The lighter pops out and she pushes it back in and starts humming.

'I'm not a girl and I want a haircut, OK?' I'm yelling, my body turned toward her. She pulls onto a dirt road.

'I want a haircut, I want a haircut!' My fist pounds the vinyl seat. 'Grandfather would never let my hair be long!' I say spitefully. The car jerks to a stop.

'Wait here,' she says really friendly, smiling.

'Huh?'

'Wait here.' She puts on lipstick.

'Where you goin'?' I feel my anger draining. I try to hold on to it. 'We gettin' my haircut?'

She points wordlessly to the back of the sheriff's tiny brown wooden building. She turns to me with a wide smile, all her teeth showing.

'I'm turning you in. You are too evil and bad.'

I swallow hard. She starts to pull open her door.

'No! . . . Wait!' The world starts to tilt and melt.

'I've hid you, changed your name, my name, how many times now?'

'Please . . .' My air is choking off.

''Member when those workers came 'round last time? I moved and changed everything so they wouldn't get you.'

I start to see colors swirling around the windshield, making it hard to see clearly.

'They warned me Satan was entrenched in your soul, that you should be put to the chair and sent to hell to burn forever.' She caps her lipstick.

'I'll be back with the sheriff in a jiffy. They'll cut your hair for you, they'll shave your head for the chair, unless they stone you, or . . .' Her eyes turn from corner to corner, then stare straight back down at me. 'I won't be surprised if they don't just lynch you when word gets out who you really are.' She adjusts the car mirror to see herself and rubs lipstick off her teeth.

'Don't go . . .' I'm crying.

She doesn't turn. 'They usually take a knife and cut your evil tongue out first and then your eyes—scoop 'em right out, and they laugh and celebrate. They'll be extra pissed 'cause you've tricked 'em all.'

'Please . . . please.' Spit rolls down my chin.

The lighter pops out. She shoves it back in and gets out of the car.

'I tried to make you good. I see I've failed. Wait here.' The door slams and I squint to see past the fireball of reds, blues, and yellows cycloning around me. She crosses the street and enters the sheriff's station.

All the voices inside scream at me, and I can't see outside any more, I can only hear the taunting. I see the huge wooden electric chair, wired, waiting, and empty, and the silver gray switch. I see all the faces laughing and jeering, and the Horned One clutching his blood-soaked pitchfork. And I'm alone, and I deserve it all, and there is no one to take it away.

I lean forward and bang my head on the dashboard. My mom told me that when I was a baby I used to bang my head all day and all night long. She kept me in the top dresser drawer. It drove her nuts, she said. It was Satan fighting for my soul. It would get so loud, she'd have to close the drawer.

'Stop it, stop it!' I feel a hand holding me down, pushing me back into my seat, keeping me still. The sheriff's large, hairy hand is reaching through the open window, resting on my shoulder. My mother is standing next to him.

'See why I can't send her to school?' I hear my mother's voice. 'She should be in fourth grade. Can't attend without causing problems.'

'How long you been in town?' he asks, gravelly voiced.

'Month.'

'Well, we'll see about some special classes. You livin' with Kevin Rays?'

'Yes, sir,' she says sweetly.

'So you wanna get home schoolin', huh? Well, I'll see what I can do.'

'Much obliged, sir.'

His hand releases me. 'Y'all take care.' He walks away. She gets back in the car and pushes in the popped-out lighter.

'I convinced him not to take you. I'm gonna try to fight Satan for your soul and make you good, do you understand me?'

I nod stiffly. We're both staring straight ahead at the deserted, tree-lined dirt road.

'You'll have to be punished.' I nod again, the colors settling, my vision clearing.

'Or if you don't want that, you can go cross the street and turn yourself right in.' I shake my head.

'Very well, then . . . take your thing out.' Her voice is calm. My stomach is tight and I hiccup up a little vomit; it burns as I swallow it back down.

'Take your thing out!' The lighter pops out, and she knocks it back in. My hands tremble as I pull down my zipper and pull out my thing, small and pink.

'Hands under.' I swallow too loudly.

'Do you want to go in there?' She points at the sheriff's. I shake my head and slide my hands under my legs, like I've done other times. Her hand wraps around my thing; I stare straight ahead at a stray dog sniffing for something to eat in the dirt. Her long red nails flash.

She leans over me and whispers in my ear, 'Do you think Kevin would let you stay if he knew about this evil thing?' Her hand starts to move slowly, gently. 'Mmm, do ya?' She smells like baby powder. I shake my head.

'Do you think tellin' people I'm your mother and you are a bastard is gonna help any?' I shake my head a small no.

It looks like the skeletal dog found some food. My thing moves through her fingers. I try to imagine the electric chair and hellfire. I sob.

'Do you really think the butcher will give us free cuts if he knew you weren't no sweet little girl, but had this evil thing?'

Fire burns me alive, stones pound into my flesh, everyone laughs. Her fingers give soft little yanks.

'Let's see how evil and bad you truly are.' Her fingers stop their caressing. 'You failed the test,' she says gravely.

I look down and see it sticking straight ahead, leading me into hell.

'Do you want to turn yourself in?' I shake my head no. Tears roll down my cheeks.

'Feeling sorry for yourself is further proof of your unrepented evil.'

The lighter pops out. Her fingers, red tipped, pluck it out.

'Well?' She looks at me.

'I want to be good,' I whisper. I feel everything close up inside me. I see the coils, red and glowing, disappear down to where her fingers hold my thing. I dig my hands, sweaty and cold, under my thighs. I watch the tip of my thing disappear into the lighter. I don't move, I don't scream, I don't cry. I've learned the hard way that lessons are repeated until learned properly, and silently, and Satan is, even temporarily, exorcised. I stare straight ahead and watch the dog eating its own foot.

I listen to the sizzle of the hot iron wrapped tightly around a lock of my shoulder-length hair.

'My hair used to be white like yours,' she says. The iron pulls on my scalp. 'Yours'll get darker, too.'

She releases it, and a tumble of white blond curls roll back. She slides her fingers through another section of hair. I'm aware of every touch as her hands move against my scalp.

'You better appreciate this.' I nod as she wraps my hair in the iron jaws and rolls it up tight.

'You look so beautiful.' She beams, and leans down next to me while holding the iron up, her face next to mine in the mirror.

'We're beautiful girls, ain't we?!' The iron is too close to the back of my ear and it's burning it, but I don't dare say a thing. I smile at us, two beautiful girls in the mirror, and ignore the scent of burning flesh.

Usually when I'm alone and not allowed out, I walk around the narrow trailer and turn on the TV and all the radios as loud as I can take. I sit somewhere between the sounds and let the voices and music compete for my attention. I enjoy deciding which appliance will win me over. I'm proud of my ability to concentrate totally on whatever I choose to hear and tune out what I don't.

If Jackson or my mom gets home early and catches me, they get pissed.

'How can you hear anything?' Jackson asks, not really wanting an answer. 'Only put one thing on at a time,' he orders. 'Otherwise it's too much, you'll go crazy.'

Today, though, I don't need my noise. I stand on the chair, staring at the pretty face that isn't mine any more, but my mom's. At first all I do is stare, and hardly blink, as if a wrong breath could shatter her face. But slowly I get bolder and start winking like she does to guys that whistle at her. I practice for at least an hour, that fast wink, quick like a gunfighter that draws and shoots before the other's even touched his gun. Then I work on the kiss blowing—head tilted slightly, lips barely puckered, and the uplift to launch it properly. Then the combo kiss and wink: wink–wink, kiss, kiss–wink. It takes me all morning.

Later I go past the divider into their side of the bedroom and open her drawer. I carefully move aside the strawberry car air fresheners and dress her in a lacy baby-doll nightie Jackson just ordered her from Victoria's Secret. It hangs down to my ankles, though, so I have to pin it up to show her legs. I even dig out a pair of the panties he got her, white, lacy, with ruffles on the backside.

I accidentally put both legs in one opening. I fix it and pin it to the front and run to the full-length mirror on the bathroom door.

'You are so beautiful, baby doll!' I giggle and swirl my nightie around.

'Thank you, honey.' I shake my ass in the mirror, wink, and blow a perfect Fire Red Temptation gloss kiss. 'Daddy's sexy little girl . . . uh, oh.' I lift the frilly front of my nightie. 'Shit! Why do you gotta ruin everything?' I reach in her panties and push it back between my legs. 'Go away!' I scream down at it. I keep my baby doll raised and run my palm over the smooth, flat crotch.

'How's my baby doll's honey pot?' I wink at the mirror. 'Needin' all your lovin', Jackson.' I walk sexily toward the mirror, and my thing pops out.

'Shit, goddamn it!' I punch it hard with my fists. 'Owww!' It starts aching. 'Go away!'

I close my eyes tightly so the tears won't ruin her makeup. And then it comes to me. I run over to the sink and dig beneath it, past the Windex, Turtle Wax, and Comet, until I find it.

'Why didn't ya think of this before, baby girl?' I hold up the Krazy Glue and laugh until it hurts.

All the lights are off, leaving just the strobe-light glow of the TV. Jackson sits in his brown velour easy chair, watching the satellite services live from Sermon Mount and sipping steadily on his fourth beer.

She walks toward him, slow and slinky, like a spider doing the creepy crawl up to its catch.

'C'mere to Daddy.' He waves her over, not looking up. She stands a few feet in front of him, spinning in circles, making the white frilly baby doll he special-ordered from Victoria's Secret glow a ghostly blue gray in the twilight TV light of the trailer.

Her blond curls twirl out like cast fishing lines. She twists around and around, weaving her magic love spell that no man can resist.

'What the hell you doin', in Lord's name and creation?'

The spinning stops. She blinks at him, winks, blows a kiss.

'Jesus Lord above, what happened to you?' He's not watching Sermon Mount any more, he's watching his baby doll: me.

She moves closer, one foot in front of the other as if on a tightrope, in the shiny black leather open-toed, sling-back heels, being careful not to trip. She blows a kiss, fingers held out, displaying Red Lust nail paint.

'What the hell . . . ?' He motions with his beer and spills a dark patch on his Day-Glo orange forklift operator's jumpsuit leg.

'Your mother put you up to this?' He wipes the spill with his hand, staring at her, his face narrow and pointy, a perfect triangle from his nose down. It's hard to see both his eyes at once.

'I'm your baby girl.' Her voice is shy and sweet, the way he likes it. He laughs, muting out the sounds from the sermon.

'She home early?' He takes a long sip of the beer, smiles, and looks her up and down.

'Sarah!' he leans past her and shouts.

She giggles. 'It's me, Daddy,' she whispers.

'Jesus.' He finishes off his beer, and the empty clank of it dropping on the linoleum floor echoes through the trailer. He reaches around for a full one, never turning from her.

'Jesus, you look like your mother . . .' He pops open his beer. 'Few years on back, I reckon.' He grunts. She puffs out her lips, pouty and hungry, and slowly slides her thumb into her mouth and begins to suck, the way he likes her to do.

'Take that thumb out, you know you ain't to do that.' She pulls it out, then slowly slides it back in and out, in and out.

'There is something wrong with you, son.' He slowly wipes

the foam from his lips. 'Or whatever the hell you are. Jesus.' He smoothes out his pants lap.

'Lord . . .' He chuckles. 'You do look . . .' She turns around, raises up the back of the baby doll, and shakes her ass, making the panty ruffles flutter like wings, the way he likes to see. He gulps more beer.

'Your momma's gonna whip the daylights out of ya.'

She wiggles her bottom a few more times, then turns to face him, thumb still buried in her mouth.

He always tells her, 'Baby doll, I love ya best when you're sucking on that thumb, makes me think you're an angel.' When she asks him for money, or anything, she puts her thumb right into her mouth; she'll sit on his lap and lean on his chest, and he'll stroke her hair. 'Tell Daddy what ya need, baby doll.' If she takes out her thumb to speak, he pushes it back in. He doesn't tell her she's too big for acting like a baby, doesn't rub hot peppers on her thumb so she'll quit, doesn't laugh and tease her for it. With her thumb in her mouth she gets what she wants. Always.

She faces him silently, mouth sealed with her thumb, blue eyes wide and ringed in black, standing in lightning flashes of color splashing from the TV, waiting for recognition. And he stares, his eyes circling like a plane waiting to land. And then he burps, deep and resonant. His gaze turns downward like an ashamed child's. 'Pardon,' he mumbles. And with his shame she knows she is recognized. She jumps on his lap, into his arms still lying on the armrests, his nails combing the velour to expose its shiny, silver brown underbelly.

'Lord help me, what's got into you?' His eyes squint and his chin doubles as he thrusts his head back like a chicken. His mouth is frozen in a half grin.

'Ain't your baby doll pretty?' she asks with her thumb half pulled out, against his chest. It vibrates, bouncing her delicate, sculpted head with his stiff laugh.

'Ain't your little girl pretty?' she whispers past her thumb, deep into the padding of the wiry curled hair of his breast. Her other arm is wrapped around his waist tightly, the way he likes her to do.

He says nothing, stares past her to the TV sermon, turns his gaze back to her, then to the TV, back and forth, his eyes shifting like dull metal weights on a balance beam weighing. A slight frown makes little gullies on the ends of his mouth. She pumps her legs, dangling from the edge of his lap, like on a swing, forcing it higher. One of her oversize shoes flies off and lands with a crash somewhere in the dark silence of the trailer. It makes him jump. She giggles, causing her front teeth to bite down on her red-ringed thumb. He looks down at her legs, wiggling, thin, and shiny, white like sheets of pasta. He clears his throat and lifts his beer.

'Uh, want some?' His voice quivers, while the other hand drums the armrest. She slides her thumb out slowly as if savoring the last bit of a Popsicle, sucking it, the way he likes her to. She takes the beer and sips it while blinking up at him.

'She, uh, cocktailin' till late . . . uh, not home early, is she now?' His eyes shift from one armrest to the other. She hands the beer back to him.

'I am your sweet little girl, Daddy.' She leans up against his chest in the comfort of a heartbeat outside her own, both arms wrapped around his Day-Glo orange torso. He sits there in the quiet of the trailer's electric hum, not moving, staring intently at the soundless sermon. The beer is empty. He crushes it in one hand and drops it. His breath gets louder. She leans in closer and rubs her fluffy curls against the end of his beard. He shifts his legs. She wiggles on his lap. He clears his throat again. Her hands slide along his sides, thick and solid.

He always tells her, 'You're safe in these arm, baby doll. Nobody's ever gonna hurt you again.' She reaches her hand out and runs it down his arm like a child sliding down a banister until she hits his fist clutching the remote.

'Play with me,' she whispers to him, the way he likes her to say. His fist slowly uncurls.

'Please . . . Daddy?' With a violent pop and flash the light of the TV is sucked back and it's all dark except for the orange and blue dots of appliances glowing like one-eyed cats.

Whenever she wakes up to the black of the trailer, screaming and flailing, he holds her until it's passed. 'Just a nightmare, my sweet little girl, just a bad dream.' He doesn't yell at her for waking everyone up, doesn't spank her for wetting, doesn't laugh at her for crying like a baby. 'Let Daddy make you safe,' he tells her.

'Hold me . . . Daddy,' she whispers the way he likes her to.

He doesn't give her only quick little pats like a dog, doesn't avoid touching her like she's contagious, doesn't not take her on his lap even for a spanking. The ache is severe, pounding, and relentless.

All that's left are the words only she is entitled to say.

Because she's beautiful.

Because she's his baby girl.

'I need your love, Daddy.'

She lifts his hand to her waist. The remote clatters at his feet. He stares at the dead TV. His hand, like a paperweight, rests above her jutting hipbone.

'Make me safe,' she whispers into his heart.

'My sweet little baby girl,' he answers, and his hand starts to move.

'Ungrateful little bitch!'

The water separates into pretty pink pools like Easter egg dye inside the sink.

Something—clock radio?—flies across the trailer, its plug streaming like a comet's tail. It crashes and escapes through the window next to me.

The white silk folds in the middle of the pastel water look like egg drop soup.

'Let fuckin' go of me, you faggot! I'm gonna kill him, let go!'

Things are falling and smashing apart.

Sitting in the center of the white, no matter how hard I scrub it, is a red, bleeding, unblinking eye.

'Let me go, you fucker! Let me go!'

I swirl the white silk around and around, the water spreading pink from its leaking, wounded heart.

'You motherfucker!'

A shoe bounces off the red metal chair I'm standing on.

'Let go of me, you fuckin' traitor!'

She screams with such a guttural force that the trailer vibrates like a tin can and a few loose glass shards from the newly broken window tumble down and shatter.

I lay both my hands onto the cool water, stilling it.

She screams again, but this time it's muted, as if through a hand.

The bloody clump stares up at me, accusing me, claiming me.

And the silk is undulating like it's breathing, in the dying waves in the sink.

'Offa my mouth!' she yells, muffled. They're panting heavy and fast as if they're behind the divider, on their bed. I twist my head toward them.

What I can see of her face not covered by his hand is bright red; her hair looks brown from sweat and is stuck all over her face and is twisted up in his curly black beard. Her eyebrows jump up and down as if she's lost control of them. She twists and turns in his grip. His other arm's stretched around her. When she sees me looking she struggles harder, her hands balled into fists.

He just looks sad and confused, like he's holding a vicious animal that he doesn't know what to do with.

'You better get out of here,' he tells me, but looking at her.

'I didn't get the stain out yet,' I sort of whisper.

'You better get out of here,' he says again wearily, still holding my mother tightly, his fingers pressing white dents into her arms and cheeks.

I jump down off my chair and reach under the sink for the sacred white jug.

'It'll be OK,' I tell them.

I climb back up and carefully pour half a gallon of the magic liquid into the water. Its bitter smell reassures me. Bleach is the true holy water, and I know salvation is near.

'This will help to save you.' She holds me by my right wrist. In her other hand there's a large mason jar filled with a fluid so clear it's like liquid glass.

'You forgot how we taught you?' She nods her head yes, I shake a no. 'Your mother should've taught you, at the very least,' she scolds, dropping my wrist and resting the jar on a wooden shelf next to the huge porcelain tub with large lion paws for feet.

'I'm sorry, ma'am,' I whisper, and watch a glob of snot, and tears, fall from my chin. I don't move my right hand to wipe it, I can't trust it, even now.

'I'm sure you are now, Jeremiah.' She leans over the tub, her baby-corn-colored hair, the same as my mom's, pulled up tight into a bun. Her full-moon face collects little steam drops as she leans over the tub, adjusting the chipped silver cross knob.

'I'm very sorry, ma'am.' I sniffle and concentrate hard on holding my right arm still, next to my side. I block out the stinging pain and blink my tears away.

'I can see why she's left you. Not that she's much better; devil's claimed you both, sad to tell,' she says into the rising steam, occasionally dipping her hand into the water.

'You mustn't give in to dirty temptation,' she says, leaning over the swirling tub water.

'Yes'm.' I sniffle up some snot. Each time she turns to me my heart contracts, I see my mother's face in hers, but heavily creased and thicker.

'I hope you are not feelin' one bit sorry for yourself.' She shakes her finger at me. I shake my head no and stare down at my bare feet. I'd only been at my grandparents' an hour since the social worker had left me there. I'd been taken out of the last foster home when the social workers found out I had grandparents. I liked it there, though; they had a pet pig that came right up to me as soon as I got there and with his snout flipped my hand onto his head to scratch him. But the foster father found out I was evil; he yelled at me to pull up my pants and to be behaving. I tried to tell him it was OK, and to sit on his lap, but he pushed me away so hard that I fell. I knew that if he put his thing in me, he'd let me stay, not throw me out. I was just trying to get it over with. He yelled at his wife to call the social worker. And then I was standing naked next to my grandmother, my right hand held away from my body and all possibility of evil doings.

'This will burn, Jeremiah.' Her lips, full like my mother's, turn down in a frown. 'But not one-billionth of what hell's fire will be if you are not saved.'

I hold my right hand farther out from me as if it's a contaminated fish.

She lifts the large mason jar and silently unscrews the lid. The strong chlorine scent fills the bathroom. I breathe in deeply the smell of summer and swimming pools and let the warmth envelop me.

'Jeremiah!' I open my eyes. She grabs my right hand away from my thing and jerks me toward the tub. 'Does he need to whip you again?!'

I stare wide-eyed at her, shaking.

'Do you feel the evil creep back into you? Do you even try to fight it?' I just stare at her.

'I want my momma,' I moan, and the tears come so fast I can barely breathe. She sighs and pours the contents of the mason jar into the tub and swirls the water around with her hand.

'She left you; too much for her to take, I believe.' She wipes her sweaty brow with her arm. 'If you stop giving in to the devil, well, she'll want you again, I believe.'

'Like last time?' I ask, wiping my face on my bare shoulder.

'She came and got you, didn't she?'

I swallow some snot. 'But I messed up again.'

'Well, you just have to be hard on yourself, Jeremiah, and not give in to the devil so easy.' I nod eagerly.

'You can even be an example to her. She needs help, too, I believe.'

'I want to, ma'am.'

She wipes her brow again. 'Good, that's good Jeremiah. You

have to want Jesus' goodness and love to fill you, and he will, he will . . . now let's get you in here.'

She places me closer to the tub and pats the wooden stepping stool next to it, for me to climb on. I do and look down into the tub, seeing the water, like a mirror with steam rising off it. I inhale the chlorine too deeply, expecting comfort, but it only stings my nose, throat, and eyes.

I turn and look up at her. Her hand pats gently on my shoulder, reassuring me.

'Hold my arm.' She reaches it out to me like a steel bar on the seat of a roller coaster.

I lean over, smelling her kitchen grandmother scent of nutmeg, lemons, and allspice under the heavy bleach fumes.

'I can't, ma'am, it's too far,' I whisper, hoping she'll lift me in her arms and put me into the tub like she did when I was last here a year ago.

'Yes, you can, Jeremiah.' She steps away and holds her arm out to me. 'You're big now.'

'Please?'

'Do I need to call him up here?'

I grab her arm and stretch my left leg up and over the porcelain lip of the tub and pull myself up until I sit on the edge, my foot curled up tightly above the water like I'm dangling over the edge of the world.

'Go ahead.' She nudges me. I dip my foot in and pull it out immediately.

'It's too hot.' Some snot falls from my nose and splashes into the tub.

'Jeremiah, I'm going to call him up here if you're not in this tub by the count of three . . .'

'OK, OK!'

'One.' I put my foot in, steam crawling up my leg. The water has a heavy silky feel to it.

'Two.' It lands on the tub bottom. I swing my other leg over and stand in the water up to my thighs.

'It's too hot!' My tears are back, and I jump up and down, trying to escape the water.

'Not as hot as hellfire! You want to go there? You want to feel hellfire for eternity?'

'Please!' I reach my arms out to her.

'Reverend!' she hollers out.

'Please . . . ma'am . . . please!' I cry so hard I can hardly speak.

'Reverend!' She puts her hands on my head and presses down, keeping me from jumping out. Still, I keep moving as much as I can.

We hear his heavy footsteps marching up the carpeted stairs. As he comes closer she releases my head, and I slow my bouncing.

He opens the door and a blast of cool air hits us. I don't move. She says nothing to him or me, just turns and leaves, closing the door behind her.

His eyes are as clear and burning as the bleach water I'm standing in.

'Sit,' he says loudly, the 't' spitting out, echoing off the white porcelain tiles of the bathroom.

I quickly lower myself down until I'm submerged up to my neck in the water.

He leans over me.

'Hands,' he says sternly.

I reach my arms up to him and he ties a cord hanging over a brass towel rack on the wall behind me to one of my wrists, then the other.

He pulls the cord tight so my arms are stretched up and can commit no sin.

'I am right down the hall. I so much as hear a sound from you, Jeremiah, you will regret the day you were born.' He turns around and walks out, closing the door halfway.

I've turned it all off. The welts and sores on my back, ass, and thighs burn like a fire someplace behind me. The hot water turns my skin bright red, but I've already left.

I'm with my momma in Vegas, winning lots of money. She's so happy, she's hugging me and she keeps telling me how good we are, how clean.

I press my hands into the bleached water and rub lightly on the bloodstain. And like invisible ink, it starts to fade.

'Kill you!' my mother screams, still muffled.

'Son, I can't hold her much longer, you best git now.' I wish the sink were big enough for me to climb inside of.

'You hear me?' he shouts.

I lift the underwear, the white ones with a ruffled back that he bought especially for her from Victoria's Secret, spin around, and display the panties.

'Look, it's OK! It's out! It's OK!'

Water flows from the sopping wet underwear onto my feet and down to the chair, ending in a big puddle.

We all just stand there staring, the water making ticking noises as it splats onto the floor.

I hold the underwear out to them, up toward the fluorescent light, and there, clearly, is the faded outline of rust-tinged blood. My blood.

My mother screams again, kicks backward in her bare feet at Jackson's shins, and struggles free.

I stand frozen, her panties spread out between my outstretched hands like an old lady's knitting, as she barrels toward me.

'You're always trying to steal what's mine!' she screams, and grabs a small lamp off the table and hurls it at me.

I watch it flying toward my face in slow motion, and somehow I jump off the chair so the lamp sails straight into the mirror above the sink. Glass shatters and water sprays everywhere.

I crouch on the floor where I landed, like a frog. I look up into my mother's face, covered in red splotches. Jackson's hands cover her mouth again, and her blue eyes roll wildly like spinning marbles.

'Bleach don't always work,' I say quietly.

'Go on,' he says, holding my mother, who's rocking back and forth and moaning.

I rise quickly and go past the divider to their bed.

I pull off the white baby doll that he'd bought for her.

I lay it as neatly as I can on the bed, the sleeves crossed in front like a burial gown for a child that has disintegrated away.

I go to my side of the room and pull on jeans, a T-shirt, sneakers, but no socks and grab my jacket from the hook that's my height that Jackson had put up especially for me.

I walk past them. She's turned toward him now; he's still holding her arms, but her head is against his chest, bobbing up and down with her sobs and moans. They don't say a word.

Jackson motions to the door with his head.

I step over a chunk of mirror and I see a face, red and splotched, with black raccoon eyes, lipstick smeared across it like a clown, just like hers.

But it's me. It is me. And I have to go.

'Bye,' I whisper, and leave.

It's not too cold out, but it feels it. It's still dark. The only light is from our trailer; we're very far away from other trailers. I can see the black dinosaur shapes of the woods of the Blue Ridge Mountains rising around me and hear the night sounds of crickets and rustling animals. I turn back to our trailer and catch glimpses of movement behind the closed shades. I check to make sure the trailer's still on cinder blocks, not wheels. It is.

In my head I turn daylight on to drive away any wolves or vampires. It's so sunny I have to squint to see, but I know where I'm going. I walk quickly, cautiously, keeping my sneakers from crunching too much on the loosely packed dirt, so nothing knows I'm here.

Some empty lots down there's an old doghouse that some-one had built and left. It's wooden, with a red, peeling roof and 'DOG' glued on in tarnished gold letters.

I go there a lot. To keep the raccoons out I've put wood from a crate in front of the entrance, like a boarded-up, abandoned building. Inside I keep a pillow, blanket, an overdue library book, and a small flashlight that I stole from a trip with Jackson to Malcom's Auto Supply shop. I slid the thin silver light up my jacket sleeve and prayed to Jesus that no had seen me. No one had.

Once inside the doghouse I wrap the blanket around my shoulders, with the pillow on the wooden floor, under me. I turn the piece of crate sideways so it still blocks the door but I can see out some. I turn my flashlight on, but I'm careful not to shine it around too much, just enough to see that all the walls are still there and didn't open to another dimension like a wardrobe in a book I read did.

I'm relieved, and disappointed, that it didn't. I don't inspect the pointy roof because I know what's up there and I don't need to see their shiny webs and dusty strings. I like to think of them as taking me in as one of their own, ready to swing down, like Tarzan, and attack whatever tries to hurt me. We, the flesh-eating predators of the house of DOG, protect our own.

I breathe in the mustiness of my blankets, mixed with old dog smell and the faint smell of urine I cleaned up as best as I could from the last time I had an accident. It's so comforting, I decide never to leave; I will wait until a wall finally dissolves away and I escape into another dimension.

I lie on my pillow and shine my flashlight on the faded picture on the wood of the crate. I stare at the smiling, freckled, red-haired boy in a large sombrero climbing a ladder leaning against a tree dripping with plump peaches. He's waving with one hand and reaching for a peach with the other. If I jiggle the flashlight, his hand moves, waving to me to join him. I lie on my stomach as I always do, resting on the pillow, with my flashlight under my chest pointing like a spotlight.

I start to rock up and down.

'Come have a peach with me,' he always tells me. 'We'll go into my treehouse and eat peaches, just you and me, and we'll never come back.'

My hands under me start to reach for my thing.

'You can wear my sombrero,' he promises, and stretches his arm out to me.

I open my fly and grope around because it's not there sticking up like a miniscrewdriver handle against my lower stomach. I feel panicky and excited all at once. God finally cured me, the bleach worked! I pat my hands on the flat skin of my crotch, terrified to go any lower.

I feel something there, between my legs, but I'm not sure what it is. I sit up fast, the blanket wrapped around me, and lean against a wall. Holding my breath, I lift my hips and slide my jeans to my knees and shine my flashlight down. I think I know what I'll see, just more hard, smooth, white skin, like on a Barbie doll.

I open my eyes and my flashlight shines on my thing, yellowish pink, Krazy-Glued backward between my legs. And suddenly I feel pressure on my bladder and I need to piss. I move my shaking hand and pull on my thing; it stretches out slightly like gum stuck on a sidewalk but snaps right back.

I yank again, hard, but it only makes my eyes tear. And then I find a string stuck on the side of my thing and I follow it back with my fingers. It disappears inside of me. I tug hard and it feels like my bowels are being pressed. I moan from the ache of it.

'Oh, Lord's mercy,' I say again and again, the words sounding too big and empty inside the wooden box to have any effect.

I lie on my back on the pillow and close my eyes.

I turn off the flashlight and reach under my legs to the string. It's definitely attached to something in my asshole and I can't remember how it got there. I pull again, and it's like trying to rip off a thick scab. I tug again, but it barely moves, and the tears roll down the sides of my face. I reach again for my thing, but it's stuck backward.

'It's stuck,' I cry into the spider-filled roof.

My mouth jerks open in a convulsion of sadness and fear. A high-pitched squeal comes out, like a dump dog shot with a BB gun. The sound frightens me even more, and I roll over onto my stomach and curl up around my pillow. My body shakes and quivers as if in battle with a high fever. I have to pee badly, and I think I still can, but I don't want to go outside.

It just drains out of me, spraying backward, between my legs. I hear it hitting the wood wall behind me and bouncing off it. It soaks some of my blanket, but the warm relief only makes me sob harder, my breath moving too quickly, out of control.

Jackson's breath is like a mosquito buzzing violently in my ear.

'You're my pretty baby doll, pretty baby girl,' he says between gasps and pants in my ear.

His hands run up and down under the white baby doll quickly, like a dog digging in the dirt. He covers my face in hard, hungry kisses, coating me in the film of his beer-fogged mouth. He lifts me off his lap, my arms encircling his neck. He carries me past the divider to their side, to their bed.

'Sexy baby, Daddy's hot little girl.'

'Am I pretty?' I ask.

'Mmmm-hmmm,' Jackson says, lying next to me, pulling the silver zipper down the middle of his orange jumpsuit like he's ripping himself in half. My arms are still wrapped tightly around him. I feel his hands working in the dark, and I hear the snap of his underwear.

'Do you love me?' I ask.

'Ready for Daddy?' He takes hold of my arms and pulls them off his neck.

'Nooo . . .' I reach back, but he pushes them down.

'You're chokin' me, baby doll . . .'

I put my arms out again. He slides on top of me, pinning me down.

'Ready for Daddy?' He reaches over to the nightstand, and I hear the fart noises of a squeezed container.

'I'm your pretty baby girl,' I say.

'Uh-huh, OK, baby, jus' relax, I'm gonna lube you some.'

I feel him searching, down there, his wet and sticky finger inside the white ruffled panties he bought especially for her.

'What's this?' He presses on my glued-backward thing, ignores it, and moves past.

'Am I good?'

'OK, baby.' His wet finger slides inside of me.

'Am I good?'

'Oh yeah, nice and wet.' Another one slides in.

I stare at the shadow his huge head makes on the ceiling.

'OK, baby . . . just relax it, OK, baby . . . ? Relax . . .'

'I am good, right?'

'There, baby . . . open for Daddy . . . I know you done this be-fore, so open for Daddy.'

His thing starts to press in on me. He exhales deeply and quickly so it's hard for me to get a breath.

'I'm good, right?'

He bends down and kisses me, his beard scratching my face, covering my nose. His tongue gags me as I open my mouth for air. He pulls up onto his elbows, his head is tossed back.

I try to put my arms around him, but I can't move them.

He grunts and pushes himself into me. I feel the tearing and remember the feeling from the last time. He was a cowboy, she was passed out, and I had to get stitches from a local doctor he knew.

I swear I can hear the tearing, hear it filling my ears, covering his moans and gasps, and I'm losing him. It's blurry and I can't see him, just a giant burning sun being smothered.

I try to tell him to not let me go, that I need to stay with him, to know what he knows, what my mom knows, what that cowboy knows, so after, I can lay in their arms, laugh, and curl up so peacefully I could die.

But I'm split apart inside, and it's all I know and all I can find.

I stand in the bathroom looking at the stain in the middle of her white ruffled panties, the ones he had special-ordered from Victoria's Secret.

Afterwards he pulled them back up my legs. He said nothing, I said nothing.

I wad up some toilet paper and wipe at the sore, throbbing wetness. I bring it back damp with blood and mucousy stuff.

'I'm split apart, and she's gonna leave me,' I say out loud to myself, and try not to cry.

I hear him turning on the TV and snapping a beer open. I stare at the red stain on the panties again, just like the panties she hand-rinses and hangs over the shower door when it's her time. She bleeds because men are thinking evil thoughts about her, including, and especially, me. So I have to walk to the canteen and buy her Tampax with the plastic applicator to stop the bad thoughts. They sit on the back of the bamboo shelves above the toilet, pink and thin and ready to absorb all evil.

She came home from cocktailing.

She saw me, looking like her, wearing the white baby doll Jackson bought her from Victoria's Secret, standing on a red metal folding chair, washing the bloodstained white matching panties.

She went looking for Jackson and found him asleep on their bed, laying next to a wet, red splotch on the white nubbly bedspread we got from the Holiday Inn.

She screamed so loud that Jackson himself woke up yelling.

She screamed at him for cheating on her. She screamed at him for fucking that little fucking cunt behind her back. She screamed at him for letting me wear the special things he bought her from Victoria's Secret and which are now ruined.

She saw that I had ruined everything, and she's gonna fucking kill me!

But there are worse things than getting killed.

I shine my flashlight onto the red-haired, freckled-faced boy waving at me to come and eat peaches. Even though my thing is glued backwards and there's a Tampax stuck inside me, he's waving me into his treehouse, where we can hold each other as tightly as possible and be split apart together.

We practice like we usually do on the way to the clinic, driving in Jackson's fire red pickup truck. My mom's not taking me to the local hospital; instead we're going on a long drive to the backwoods clinic in the Virginia mountains with all the retired doctors that don't like to do paperwork.

'Now how'd this happen to you?' she asks, smoking a cigarette in one hand, driving with the other, and staring straight down the highway, occasionally turning her head to blow smoke out the window.

'Did it to myself,' I mumble, my stomach feeling tight and sour. I swallow a gag.

'Louder, gotta be louder! You look 'em right in the eye, too, understand?' She tucks a piece of loose hair into her French braid, her cigarette almost burning her ear.

I nod my head.

'Now what happened?' she asks again.

'Did it to myself,' I say louder, and look up at the squashed-bug-filled windshield like it's the evil face of the Inquisitor.

'Anyone child abusin' you?' Her eyes are still a little swollen, but her fresh makeup covers it.

I watch her red, glossy lips clamp down hard on her cigarette.

She's wearing little Fairy Stone cross earrings. The tears of angels from when Jesus died. Jackson bought them for her at the Fairy Stone Park gift shop.

'Well, did they?' She slaps my thigh.

'No, no, ma'am or . . .' I stare back at the windshield.

'Or sir . . .' I glance up at her. She nods halfway for me to continue.

'Did it all myself, sir, or ma'am.'

'Say it loud.'

'All myself, ma'am . . .' I say louder.

'Why'd you do such a goddamn stupid fuckin' thing?'

I turn to her, she's staring straight ahead, blowing smoke, not even out the window like she usually does so she doesn't smell like a barroom slut.

'Well?'

'Umm . . . I wanted to be a pretty girl,' I mumble.

'No, no, no.' She hits the wheel after each no. 'You want them to arrest you? Lock you up in a mental hospital like they did before?' She blows her smoke straight into the windshield. 'Or put you in jail?'

'No,' I whisper.

'What?'

'No, ma'am . . .'

'You make sure you're not rude to them, you show them I raised you correctly.'

'Yes'm.'

'Now why you'd do such a goddamned stupid evil fucking thing?'

''Cause I wanted to know,' I say too loudly.

'Know what?' she says louder, and hits the wheel again.

I don't answer.

'Know what?!' She slaps it again, lighter.

'What?!'

'What it feels like to be good.'

'What?'

'Ma'am.'

'What? I think you need to be locked up in a loony bin for quite some time.'

'Stop!' I yell.

'What?' But she pulls over to the side of the two-lane highway.

I jump out and dry-heave into the dark green ivy growing along the black tar road.

But there's nothing inside me to come out.

'You about done?' she calls from the truck.

When everything was over and done, the white-haired nurse shook her finger at me and said, loudly enough for everyone else in the waiting room to hear, for me not to be doing fool things like I'd done. She gave us two orange bottles of pills. One was to keep my stitches from getting infected, the other for pain and discomfort. The nurse gave me one of the second ones, and when we got to the truck my mom swallowed two of them.

We say nothing on the ride home. I must have fallen asleep because I wake up in my bed, under the blankets. I wonder if my mom carried me in or if Jackson did. I wish I'd been awake but only faking sleep when someone held me in their arms and put me to bed. I rub my forehead and check my fingers to see if there are any lipstick marks from when I was tucked in. There aren't. They probably rubbed off already anyway.

My blankets are up around me, and a little pink stuffed bear that Jackson won for me at a fair is next to me. A bigger bear he won for her sits on their bed, but it's too big to be held and is thrown on the floor at night anyway.

They're fighting.

'Please, baby doll,' he says again and again.

'I'm sick of you,' she tells him.

'I'm so sorry, baby doll,' he keeps saying.

'You make me sick.'

I reach over to the window ledge and pick up the perfect brown angel's tear stones I found in Fairy Stone Park.

'Lookit what I bought ya, sugar, please, honey, it's real pretty.'
He sounds like he's gonna cry. I know it's hopeless. I know she's
going to leave. I hold my stone crosses and pray she takes me
with her.

'Please, baby, I'm sorry, please, baby.'

I didn't really find the stones in the forest.

'You can't just leave me, baby!'

I stole them from the gift shop, where they sell the perfect
ones that others had found. I pretended I found them, pretended
that only I could find something so perfect, so blessed, and so
special.

'Please.' He's crying now.

I pull myself up with difficulty, like trying to run fast inside a
dream. I lean out the small window over my bed.

'Baby doll, it won't never happen again!'

I inhale the sweet decaying smell of autumn and look at the
yellows and reds spreading down the mountains, like wildfire in-
fecting all the other trees surrounding our trailer.

'I thought he was you, I really did, looked just like you,
I swear . . .'

I reach out my balled-up fist and toss my crosses out through
the window into the dirt.

'He was all over me, talking like you, lookin' like you, baby
doll . . .'

I will wait for them to grow, like Jack's magic beans, transformed into a beanstalk growing up to heaven. I'll climb it, even
though the raindrop-shaped salt water cuts me.

'You can't do this to me, baby girl! You can't!'

The sky will open like slit skin, and the rope will shatter like
glass.

'Something ain't right with him, baby, just not right.'

And millions and millions of angels' tears will shake and pound the earth and solidify into stone crosses.

'I won't let him get me like that again, baby doll, I swear!'

And they will wait hundreds of years for me to return and reclaim them.

'We'll go away, baby, just you and me, somewheres nice and fancy.'

I will reclaim my tears petrified by the terror of loss.

Coal

I've spent a lot of time searching for Canada Dry ginger ale. Many stores don't carry it. Canada Dry doesn't have poison in it. I'm not sure about other sodas. Pringles potato chips with ridges don't have poison, either. You need a big chain, like Safeway or Piggly Wiggly, that sells fancier items. Whenever things feel out of control I know the black coal is doing it, and I know what to do, my mom taught me.

I watch all the walls in the supermarket and tell her as soon as I think they move. One time we leave the cart half-full of Pringles and Canada Dry at the checkout. I tug on her black raincoat, lightly; you don't want to be obvious or they'll see. She doesn't notice my tug the first time. I look up at her face hidden in a shadow of tangled dyed black hair. The pale blue whites of her eyes dart round and round, watching the suspicious faces, mostly at the couple in pink sportswear laughing ahead of us.

They're buying a lot of poisoned foods: Land O'Lakes butter, Mr. Paul Newman's salad dressing, Sprite, Burgers 'n' Buns, and way too orange carrots and Cheetos. I try not to stare, unlike my mom, who's trying to figure out what they are. If they're secret agents of the coal, trying to tempt and trick us. They might be innocent victims hypnotized by the forces of black coal about to be poisoned accidentally, but their pastel pink outfits match too exactly, so my guess is they are forces of evil.

I tug again at her sleeve, so long her hand is buried in its protective sheathing. It was $15 at the Salvation Army, just bought today soon after we discovered the black coal was active. We tried to find a black raincoat for me, but in my size they were all yellows and greens covered in bunnies and turtles. She said after the dye I'd be safe even without a raincoat.

The dye is in our cart, buried under six-packs of Canada Dry and the red Pringles cardboard canister with the vacuum seal, and I wish it weren't. I could slip it in the waist of my jeans, even though stealing only fuels the judgment of the coal.

I hear the *swoosh swoosh* of my mother's nails scratching up the inside of her vinyl raincoat sleeves. Her barefoot heels bounce inside her black rubber boots. I'm still in civilian clothes. My T-shirt is dirty white, as are my Keds, even my socks. My jeans are dark blue, not black. The Laundromat is next.

I'll lie naked in the backseat, staring up at the stained cheese-clothlike interior of our Toyota while she dyes my clothes in the washer.

The pink sportswear spy couple is next in line. She keeps grinning down at me, catching me staring at their Cheetos. It's poison, all poison, I chant silently to myself, louder than my rumbling stomach. Then, like a true demon, the woman reaches for a Hershey's bar from the rack above the conveyer belt, opens and bites into it. Hershey's can be safe sometimes, but now I know it's a trick because the chocolate smell sinks into me.

I look up at my mom to see if she's noticed, but her eyes are switching to the walls, judging their distances, measuring the inches of movement; she doesn't trust me to that job completely. I tug lightly again at the frayed sleeve.

The woman catches my eye and smiles hugely, her lipstick

lines extending way beyond her actual lips, her eyes narrowing to Chinese slits with wrinkles like cat whiskers racing from the outer edges.

I hold on to my mother's sleeve; the woman leans over so her face is near mine. I smell the sugary chocolate on her breath and look up into the dark patch of nose hairs with snot strands caught inside.

'Would you like a piece of chocolate?' she asks.

My mother shakes herself as if trying to pull her body from a trap. The woman looks up toward my mother, her smile disappearing as she speaks. 'He's standing so quiet and good . . . I thought he might like . . .'

My mother's head sways like a caged horse's, long swoops back and forth: no. Her eyes are focused on the checkered floor.

'Sorry . . .' the woman starts, her face contorting into a grimace. She steps back. 'I just thought . . .'

The hand clamping my wrist makes me jump. My mother says nothing to me or to the lady in pink still holding out a Hershey's bar; she jerks my arm as we hurry down the aisle, trying to find the way out. I can hear her panting, and my heart's booming.

All lines are filled, there are no clear checkouts to escape through. Her nails are digging into the skin inside my wrist. I crash into her. She's stopped dead still and is staring at the wall directly in front of us, stacked with cigarettes, logs, and charcoal, framing the way out.

It had moved.

'I tried to tell you,' I whisper, but I know she can't hear. I look down the row to the entrance turnstile and an empty aisle with a closed chain gate across it. I jerk my arm a few times till she follows, still gripping my wrist. She walks sideways, staring at the wall, her mouth hanging open in an O.

When we get to the gate I lift it as high as I can.

'Drop under,' I mumble. She stands frozen, staring at the wall. I shake my arm hard. 'Go under.' She only stares. A man with a nametag puts down the apples he's stacking and starts crossing the floor toward us. I drop the chain and push her as hard as I can. She turns down to me, anger flashing across her face, tightening my stomach.

'Duck under,' I order, and lift the chain rope again. I bite my lip so she won't see it shake. She bends her head, leans down, and crouches under the chain, still gripping my arm, pulling me under with her, as if we're in a sudden game of limbo.

'Excuse me, miss,' I hear. 'Miss?'

My mom walks out, oblivious, almost running through the front door; I gallop to keep up. The heat from the parking lot blasts up at us, making the air visible lines that waver into shapes. 'Miss . . .' I hear from right behind us, before I see a thin white hand reach out for her. It barely touches her black padded shoulder when she spins around, her teeth bared, her eyes too wide.

'What?!'

'I need you to open your coat . . . or come back inside the store . . .' He clears his throat, looking around, but not at her.

'You think I fuckin' stole? At a time like this? You think I fuckin' stole?!' Her hand clenches tighter with each word, around my wrist, like a tourniquet.

'Uh . . . miss?'

'You will be very, very sorry . . .' she starts, and without releasing my arm unbuttons her raincoat.

I turn away and watch some kids in the back of a station wagon stick their tongues out at me.

'OK, OK, OK, ma'am. Thank you, thank you . . .'

'Wanna check my cunt?'

I turn to see my mother holding her coat open, her naked body sheened with sweat and exposed. She drops my wrist and turns her pockets inside out. A small lump of coal falls with a thud to the ground. Her neck stretches out like a turkey's over a chopping block toward his red face.

'Ma'am?' He looks into her protruding grin with a mixture of fear and sadness that frightens me more than when he wanted to arrest her.

'Are you OK?' he asks softly.

A man driving past in a pickup whistles, and I follow his stare to the bristly blond clump of hair between my mother's legs. She takes a deep breath to respond, her face a dark scarlet. I reach up to grab the ends of her raincoat where she holds it clamped open with her fists. I tug gently but firmly, and her hands follow mine, pulling the coat closed like a curtain.

'C'mon,' I whisper, feeling a strength I treasure and dread.

'Is she all right?' he asks, talking to me for the first time.

'Just tired,' I say into my mother's raincoat, which I hold shut over that dark yellow curly patch. I hear him take a breath to say something, but he only releases a sigh. I look up into my mother's face, afraid she's preparing to say or do something, but all I can see is the tip of her chin. She's looking straight up into the sky, watching, waiting.

'She'll be OK,' I say to the man behind me.

'You sure?' he asks, and I hear him take another step back. It's always easy to convince people it's OK because if it isn't, they'd have to get involved.

'Yeah.' I nod, looking up at her, and squeeze her coat closed tighter.

'OK . . . uh . . . thank ya . . .' he says, walking away fast.

'Sarah?' I tug on her coat. 'Sarah?'

'The sky has black fire coming,' she says, her neck strained up.

A pretty woman in tan shorts pulls her cart up next to the car in front of us. A little boy is in the baby's seat. She starts to unload brown grocery bags into her trunk. She glances at us.

'Hot,' she says, and smiles.

'Ice cream,' the little boy says.

'Soon as we get home, Billy,' she tells him.

'Fire's gonna come down from the sky,' my mother says, staring up.

'Pardon?' she says, lifting Billy out of the cart seat. I can see the colorful tops of food labels sticking out the top of the bags. It's poison, I tell myself.

'You're gonna burn, you traitor!' my mother says, and I look up fast to see if she's talking to me, but she's turned toward the woman. The woman blinks at my mother a few times, shakes her head, and turns away. I watch her strapping Billy into a baby seat. My mother stares back up at the sky.

'Mom . . . let's go . . .' My throat is dry and I can hardly swallow. I watch the woman give Billy a bottle. He sucks on it with his eyes half-closed. Poison, I think.

'Mom . . .' I turn back to her. The sun is blasting down on the black tar, and I see the sweat running down her neck. My scalp feels wet. 'Sarah?' I let go of the raincoat she's now gripping closed, and I tap her hand. She doesn't move.

'Please?'

The woman in the car starts the engine. She doesn't look at us. I watch them drive away. I try not to picture the baby bottle filled with milk, filled with poison.

'There's another store down the road.' I poke at her hand beaded with sweat. She doesn't answer for minutes. I stand waiting, squinting at her face in the sun. Suddenly she looks down and around us. 'Where are our supplies?'

I look around, too, like they're missing. 'I don't know,' I tell her.

'It's all black!' she screams, pointing to the tar.

'It ate everything,' I say, and nod at the ground. And suddenly she drops down, grabs up the coal piece that had fallen from her pocket, and runs. I start running to catch her, past our car, out of the lot, onto the sidewalk. She runs down the broken concrete sidewalk to a little thatch of bushes behind a deserted nightclub. I see her crawl inside it. I catch up, panting, and follow her into the bushes. She's curled up, the jacket over her head. She's rocking.

I know I lied about the supplies and them getting eaten, but I was hoping she would forget; times like these she forgets things easily. If she remembered what happened in the store, she might say it was my fault the walls moved, my fault we have nothing to eat or drink, my fault we have no dye and I'm still in a white T-shirt and blue jeans. She might start thinking I'm the traitor. She might decide I'm the evil. I need to be very careful. I hope my lying doesn't raise the punishing wrath of the coal, but I had just witnessed its destructive abilities. It had burned our house to the ground, maybe killed my stepfather, and maybe burnt up my best friend.

I climb into the bushes and reach under her coat that's draped over her head. 'It's OK . . . Sarah . . .' She shakes her head no. I walk cautiously next to her.

'I'll protect you,' I whisper above her, and slowly slide the jacket off her head and down to cover her naked shoulders and body. I lower my hand to her matted hair; she whimpers. I stroke her hair soft and wet with sweat.

'It's coming . . . we're gonna get it . . .' I feel her trembling under my hand.

'Shhh . . .' I whisper, 'I'll protect you.' I pat her shoulder, and she leans her head into my legs. Standing, I'm a little taller than she is sitting, so I crouch down some and wrap my arms halfway around her.

'Gonna get it, gonna get it, gonna get it,' she mutters.

'It's OK . . . nobody can get us here.' I lean around her and gently kiss her tearstained salty cheek again and again.

'It's OK . . .' I whisper. 'It's all OK.' I reach down to her hands, black and sooty from the chunk of coal she dug out from her raincoat pocket. Under her nails it's grimy black as she scratches and scrapes at the black coal while turning it round and round. I pry the coal from her fingers and bend down and place it in the pocket of her bunched-up coat lying behind her.

I wrap my arms around her, squeezing her tighter and tighter, feeling like Atlas with the weight of the entire world inside my heaving arms.

When the sun goes down I get her back to the car.

'Should I go get some supplies?' I ask, feeling my heart beat in my empty stomach. She shakes her head no, lowers her seat back, and goes to sleep.

I wake up with a jump, not sure of where I am. The parking lot is empty, and a dim street lamp flickers above us. I open the door quietly and sneak out.

I walk over to a small green Dumpster next to a dark Burger King and piss. The thick greasy smell from the Dumpster makes my mouth wet. I turn back to the car and see my mother curled up in her raincoat. I lift myself in and start slashing with my nails into the white plastic bags. Fries, soft creamy buns, cups with soda still in them, I cram it all into my mouth so fast, I can hardly breathe. I find more and more as I dig, even unopened ketchup packages I rip open and squirt right into my mouth.

I don't know how long I am in there eating or how long she is standing behind me watching. All I can think about is eating more. The starchy smell of it is overwhelming, and I can't inhale it fast enough. I have no thought of being poisoned and dying.

When I see her, she has a half smile on her face. It gets bigger as I drop the doughy mush in my hands.

'Temptation has claimed you,' she says quietly.

I swallow the crusty fried piece in my mouth and try to speak, but only air comes out.

'You're lucky you have me,' she says, walking away from the Dumpster. I pull myself out and follow her to the car, my shaking hands wiping crumbs off my face. She gets in the front and opens the passenger side for me to climb in.

'I'm sorry.'

'You've just been poisoned,' she says solemnly. 'You're weak and you gave in to temptation . . . Now you're gonna die.'

The grease smell is all over my jeans and shirt, coating me like a film, making it hard to breathe. My eyes fill up, blurring everything. I wipe at them fast, hoping she won't see; crying would make it all worse.

'I don't want to die,' I whisper. 'Please, please, do we have any antidote?' I wrap my arms around my stomach and feel it ache.

'You ate poison, you ate poison, you ate poison,' she chants, her face in a huge smile. The tears start falling. I look down to try to get it under control.

'You ate poison, you ate poison,' she says like a taunting child in a schoolyard. I push my panic aside and look up at her grinning face, her teeth gleaming a diamond white in dim fluorescence.

'If I die, who will watch the walls?' I say as calmly as I can. Her mouth slowly closes.

'If I die, who will warn you if the earth cracks and swallows the car?' I hear her swallow.

'If I die, who will be there for the coal to destroy in flames first?' She says nothing, only turns in her seat and stares out at the Dumpster.

After a few minutes she reaches under her seat and brings out the small plastic bottle. I watch her unscrew the top as I swallow down a greasy burp. She hands me the bottle and I try to hold it steady, but my hands are trembling, probably from the poison starting to kill me. I bring the bottle up to my nose; the cherry smell of it makes me calmer. We just bought it yesterday at the pharmacy in Wal-Mart. In case we get poisoned, this is the antidote.

It took up a lot of money, so we only had enough left for a six-pack of Canada Dry in cans—bottles are poisoned. Even when I brought in the empty cans I collected for the deposit, there still wasn't enough for Pringles.

But being hungry is purifying and keeps evil from getting into you.

'Drink some,' she says.

I hold the bottle to my lips and sip some of the sweet bark-colored maple-cherry liquid down.

'Not all of it!' she shouts, and snatches the bottle away. 'Just bought it and now it's half-gone.' She holds the bottle up to the light coming in through the windshield to see what's left. I read the white block letters on the label.

'Did I get enough?' I ask.

'I should think so. Damned thing's near gone!'

'It works, though?'

'It should,' she says, putting it back under the seat.

'Thank you, ma'am,' I say, leaning back in the seat, secretly feeling warmed and filled by the food, comforted by the syrup, and how easy antidote is.

She leans back her seat and rolls over in it. 'The poison's gonna battle it out in you.'

'OK,' I mumble, drifting into sleep, dreaming about other Dumpsters and the cherry syrup antidote I can buy with my bottle deposit money on the sly. No more Pringles and Canada Dry, 'cause it's there in Wal-Mart waiting for me, that brown bottle with the green label and big white letters. Sweet like candy, my antidote: Ipecac.

I haven't slept very long when a violent retch jerks me awake. Vomit spews out of my mouth with such force, it hits the car windshield. It's followed by another retch, and more lumpy undigested food from the Dumpster flies onto the dashboard in front of me. My mother screams, reaches past me to open the door, and shoves me out. I fall onto the parking lot ground, my arms wrapped around my stomach, the automatic retching continuing. I try to take a breath but only puke up more, inhaling food pieces up into my nose until burning vomit comes out of it.

She's standing behind me, screaming. I hear her muffled shouts beneath the blood pounding in my ears and the nonstop spasms. She's screaming about the car, about the coal punishing me, the mess, the horrible mess in the car.

I feel myself suffocating, gasping. I reach out for her rubber-booted foot, but she steps away, still screaming. I heave once more, and everything goes black.

I had brought on the Black Coal Times.

A little coal-burning stove sits in the corner of the $75-a-month shack on the outskirts of a small town in West Virginia. The house has no electricity and a pump out front for the rusty water.

But I have a battery-operated TV Chester let me have. Chester married my mom two days after they had met at the pool hall bar in town. I keep my TV on day and night. Chester doesn't mind, though, he just gets me a new battery every week.

They work in the basement: Chester, my mom, and his

friends with motorcycles. They'll be down there all day and out all night. I'm not allowed down the creaky wood steps that lead to the cellar. I'm not allowed anywhere near it. I'd gotten a whipping from Chester for tugging on the padlock when I thought they were gone, but even after my whipping I'd run down the stairs to the door and tug on the always locked padlock, to try to see what all the secrecy and excitement were about.

My mother doesn't talk to me much. Her eyes, like Chester's, are ringed red like someone drew marker circles around them. I lie on my stomach on the dirty yellow shag rug, looking at my TV but watching my mom pace the living room. She scratches at her face constantly and chomps her jaw back and forth even though there's nothing in her mouth.

When I speak to her, all she'll ever answer is, 'Huh?' even if I ask her again.

Chester always brings me a TV dinner and Cap'n Crunch from the grocery store in town which he gets on the way home. He wakes me up four or five A.M., lights up the coals, and puts my tin tray on the little rack above them. In thirty or so minutes it'll be done enough so I can wolf it down while I watch morning cartoons. The cereal I eat later.

My mom stays away from the stove; it's mine. She stays away from the coal. When I need more I ask Chester and he brings it up from the cellar, where there seems to be an endless supply.

'Here's some coal,' he'd whisper, away from my mom, and toss it into the squat black iron stove, his red-ringed eyes large and rotating too quickly, like a squirrel's.

When Chester isn't in the basement he paces, like my mom, the shadow of his long, lean body hunched down by the weight of his head and shoulders, passing like a black cloud the grinning faces of magazine models and race cars pasted up as wallpaper by some long-ago tenant.

I enjoy watching the shadows his always busy hands make. Six-headed dragons, ferocious bears, multihumped camels as they attack and destroy entire happy, catalog families. Back and forth his waving empty hands slice and mutilate.

I wait as patiently as I can till he disappears again down into the basement, and I take out my red pencil I keep in my back pocket. I spit between my fingers and squeeze them close together. Then I slide the red lead point between them. I turn the pencil till it begins to leak red in my bubbly spit. I go to the wall, to the shiny blond lady smiling down at her redheaded, freckled child that Chester's flying dragon's tail has sliced across her mouth. With the wet pencil tip I gash blood through her lips and pour it down her chin. I spit on my fingers, bleed the pencil more, and continue the blood gushing down her face and onto her child's head, splattering into his eyes. I watch Chester's dragon carefully. I'm pretty sure that's all that happened to her, though just to be sure I gash her arm, the one that's around the boy, but I only bleed it some in case I'm wrong. They're surrounded by black-and-white racing cars, and though I know some damage was caused, at the very least a smashed windshield flying into the faces of the passengers, and I am within my rights to bleed them, I savor my mercy and my self-control.

I step back and examine the bleeding woman and boy. It's perfect except for the finishing touch, what I always do. I don't lick the pencil for this; if it's too wet, it won't work. Around her eyes I draw faint red rings.

I wake up in the backseat, my stomach churning with broken glass. Before I lift my head I smell the stench of vomit. I peel my face off the backseat, my cheek glued to the vinyl with drool. The windshield and dash are still coated in a clumpy liquid sheen. My mother isn't in the car, but I call her anyway. I feel my stomach heave, and I pull open the door that feels suddenly heavier than I'd ever felt it, and I spit up sour water. With my arms wrapped around my stomach, I look around. We are still in the empty lot, the sky starting to lighten and painting the white concrete parking bumps a veinlike pink as they rise like exposed arteries from the sealed black pavement. A light from inside the closed Burger King flickers, casting a grayness of winks and flutters in its tinted windows. My Dumpster stands open, its small dark green metal lid flipped over like a hatch into the underworld. I cross the parking lot hunched over, walking like a drunk to the Dumpster I'd been inside of, the greasy smell of it causing me to gag. I cover my nose and push the lid closed, erasing my entry inside.

The fluorescent street lamp switches off with a loud hum that makes me jump. I make my way back to our car, avoiding the puddles of vomit surrounding the passenger's side like a moat. As I climb in the backseat, leaving the door open, a large green car with its headlights on pulls into the lot. I sit up and watch it come closer, my heart beating hard. It stops near the Dumpster. I squint to catch the first glimpse of my mother coming back with help, with someone, maybe my grandfather; even though he'd be furious, he'd know what to do. He knows how to cut through and pull out the pure soul from the temptations and conflicts of sin, especially when it's black coal evil.

I strain to see a man, alone, get out of his car, slam his door, rattle keys outside Burger King, and enter. She isn't with him. My stomach lurches, and I puke some spittle up. I'm thirsty, so thirsty, and I'm freezing, and I need more antidote. I didn't take enough to counteract the poisonous food. I need to be better so I can clean up the car before she gets back, but I bet she's at a bar trying to find a replacement for Chester, someone that's good at cleaning insides of cars.

I climb over the front seat, my stomach sliding on wet piles stuck on my T-shirt. I lean down on her seat, retching and spitting nothing up. A loud ringing is starting in my ears, and my eyes feel bathed under a heat lamp. I push my fingers around the metal bars under her seat, searching for antidote. My fingertips graze the smooth plastic, and I lean my arm under farther, deep into the guts, until I grasp the bottle. I sit in her seat holding the bottle, watching the lights flicker on in Burger King. Another car pulls up to the back, and more people enter. None of them my mother. I unscrew the lid. Singing birds are competing with the high-pitched squealing in my ears, and it all sounds like guitar feedback.

The sticky smell of antidote makes me gag. I'll clean the car, I'll get wipe-ups and napkins from Burger King. I'll tell them my little sister got sick, I'll tell them I'm a girl, I'll be pretty, I'll pretend I know nothing about the coming evil of the coal destroying the world.

I close my eyes and drink the Ipecac.

It finally happens one morning, after months of trying the lock. My mother and Chester run out screaming at each other about the money, about the delivery, about the ashtrays. Well, that's not what they call it, but I figured it out what they do down there. They make ashtrays. Special ashtrays. Like the one in my grandfather's study, a small round crystal bowl, with smooth dents like rivulets cut by rain in its walls. Every now and then there'd be a faint gray dust of ash clogging its bottom, but never the smoky scent. Tobacco, he always said, was a sin, a tool of Satan.

So my mother, Chester, and his friends hide their sinful creations, but I hear their fights and the words thrown around: smoke and crystal.

Chester had given me a glass ashtray to use as a cereal bowl when mine disappeared down into the cellar and came back blackened and cracked. I know they tried to use it for the crystal, I heard Chester say the crystal needs water and my mom carried my bowl outside, I heard her pump the water and carry it down the squeaky wooden steps. I guess the ashtray I got was not one of their fancier, more enticing ones. Probably it was the 'Shit from the Competitor's.' When Chester would pace and make flying sea monsters and machine-gun shadows, he'd also mumble about the 'Shit from the Competitor's.'

'Nobody's crystal is better than mine!' he'd shout. Before I filled my ashtray bowl with my Cap'n Crunch, I'd spit in it loud so he could hear. 'Stupid, fucking crystal!' Sometimes it'd make him laugh.

They're in such a rush, they don't even close the front door. I listen for the car pulling away down the dirt road, and I run for the cellar door. There it is, the padlock hanging open, the door closed but not locked.

The black wood door squeaks as I push it. Even though I know what is down there, I want to see for myself the rows and rows of rainbow-colored diamond-cut crystal ashtrays, the containers of sin that my grandfather forbade but also possessed: the crystal ashtrays created in secret revenge despite the horrendous danger.

The darkness glares up at me, and an acrid, curdling smell burns my nose. I run up and grab my flashlight and return to the blackness. I shine my flashlight into it. Lightbulbs hang from the wooden beam, with wires crisscrossing them like a freeway, and a switch dangles down past the door. Before I can think, I reach up and click it. The cellar lights up. My mouth drops at the electricity I was told we didn't have upstairs, though I'd never tried 'cause there were no lights to flick, no plugs to plug in, not even on my TV. There is no real stove or refrigerator; a flashlight Chester gave me is my only protection to chase hungry ghosts away at night. I keep my flashlight on and walk down the wobbly stairs into the cement cellar. I shine my light on tables, slate on wood horses covered in burners. Tubes, vials, containers, scales, plastic bags, and razors cover the rest. Even though it is incredibly bright, I inspect it all with my flashlight; sometimes things can hide by being too exposed.

There is a beat-up uncovered mattress in the corner with blankets and pillows and, a little past it, a fridge as tall as me. I go over to it and run my hand over its smooth, round door. I press my ear up against it to listen for breath or a heartbeat. All I hear is its steady, electric hum. It has a silver handle lever across it, and I tug hard, pulling the heavy door open. It's dark inside, no fridge light. I shine my flashlight on the contents, lots of plastic containers and beer. I yank open the freezer, which is almost frozen shut. Inside, sitting in an ice-filled window, are more plastic containers and a stack of the TV dinners Chester always gets for me. I slam the fridge and freezer doors closed. 'We have no fridge,' he's always reminding me, so I can't get anything that'll go bad, 'cept he's been nice enough to stop off every day and pick me up my frozen dinners.

'Liar.' I spit on the fridge, hook my flashlight onto my belt loop, and continue my walk around. But there are no ashtrays or crystal anything, just stuff steaming and bubbling. They probably took it all to sell.

In a corner is a burlap-covered pile. I know it's the coal. The coals in my stove are almost all sooty ash, and I hate asking Chester for more 'cause it's a big secret, and he has to sneak it out past my mom. I reach over to the brown potato-sack-type cover and lift it off the pile. I jump as a huge spider scuttles under the coals and away from me.

Staring at the mound of coals makes my heart thud. I've never actually touched the coal myself; Chester puts it in the stove. He usually lights it, though he showed me how to use the newspapers all twisted up. But I'd just as soon wait for him to do it. If I stare too long at those red eyes glowing in the black heart of the coal, it starts talking to me, hypnotizing me just like my mom said it would.

I once burned my hand badly because the coal wanted me to touch it. I had told my mom its evil thoughts. She held my hand, pressing it to the hot stovetop until I screamed. 'The coal has to be fed,' she said. That was my lesson. I never stared at it again.

But unlit it isn't really bad, I think. Unlit it doesn't seem alive and I don't feel too afraid. I grab a couple of coals from the side, but I decide I might as well take more and hide them under the house so I don't have to ask for them. Chester won't notice. He always says, 'Goddamn, I just gave you coal yesterday. You eatin' the stuff?' I reach over and start filling my pockets. I'm taking them off the pile, grabbing the loose ones off the side, stuffing them in my jeans. I pick up one big chunk and another spider jumps as if he's been thrown at me. I scream and hurl the coal at the pile. It hits the side, knocking loose coal, making it slide in a small avalanche. The spider scurries over my Keds and under the new pile on the floor.

'Jesus Christ,' I whisper. The stairway door creaks behind me and I spin around, but it's empty, just the morning sun sliding in bars down the stairs, dissolving into the overly lit brightness of the cellar. Coal lies all over the concrete floor. I want to run up the stairs and hide in my bed with my blankets over my head. I take a step back toward the door and feel a lump of coal crumble under my foot. I look at the flame glowing blue from a burner on the tables and then down at the coal. 'The flame can't jump out,' I tell myself and the coal. 'I'm not gonna feed you,' I tell it, and kick a piece. 'You're not gonna get me.'

I wipe the sweat from my hands on my T-shirt, painting black sooty streaks on it. 'Goddamn it!' I kick some chunks; they

bounce off the pile, causing more to roll to the floor. 'Fuck . . .
OK . . . I'll get you . . .' I swallow hard, bend down, and start to
collect the spilled coal. I imagine how I will torture the tarry,
charcoal pieces. I'll smash them with rocks behind the house,
bleed them with my red pencil, drown them in water so they'll
never have hope of burning. I smile, biting my bottom lip, as
I decide which pieces get put back and which I will put to
death. I pull off my T-shirt, lay it on the ground, and toss the
coals I condemn onto it. I hold a baby coal up above my head
in the sour-smelling cellar air. 'You're gonna die,' I tell it. I get
ready to smash it but stop and pick up a grown-up coal that had
been next to the little one.

'Look, it's your momma.' I wave her in my left hand, taunting
the baby in my right. 'You want your momma, don't you?' I spit
on the baby coal and smear its lumpy face with my finger. 'Oh,
look at the crying baby . . . you think you're gonna get what you
want by crying?'

I bend down to my hand, tilt my head side to side, and smile
in the baby's face. 'If you didn't cry, I would have put you and
your momma back home, but you was a baby, so now see what
happens.'

I hold the momma close to the baby. She's trying to scream
for help, but I've got her mouth covered with my finger, plus,
without fire or my grandfather, none of her family can do anything.

I spit on her. 'See?' I tell the baby. 'You even made your
momma cry, now she gets punished.' I raise her back above my
head, like I'm throwing a pitch, and slam her into the brick-
exposed foundation wall next to the coal pile. She splinters apart.
I run over, gather up her body parts, take out my red pencil from
my back pocket, and hock up phlegm and spit it on her. I wet the

lead and press it to the wet goo on her body. I bite my lip in an excited grin as I hold the baby over her cracked body.

'See!' I shout at it. 'And it's all your fucking fault.' I shake it hard.

I put my pencil back in my pocket. 'What?' I ask, raising him to my ear. 'You wanna go home?' I look at the baby and caress him gently. 'Hmmm . . . OK, baby, you can go home, it's OK.' I pet his little head. I walk him over to the pile and hold him over it. 'Uh-oh.' I turn to the baby coal shaking in my hand. 'Listen to that.' I hold him close. 'They don't want you.' I put my hand to my ear, like they do in cartoons, to listen. 'They say you kilt your momma so they don't want you.' I hold him over the pile so he can plead and cry to them. Finally I pull him back. 'Now all you have is me . . . don't worry, I won't kill you . . . only if you're bad.' I scratch his head, caking his black soot under my nails.

And suddenly the sobbing of my baby coal is drowned by the faint revving of a motorcycle coming toward the house. I'm frozen, my legs like concrete pillars bolted to the foundation. I hear the small explosion of a backfire echoing through the holler; it's Buddy on his Harley. Chester convinced me Buddy is a giant; his head scrapes the ceiling of our house, and he has to duck through the door.

'One day Buddy is going to grow right through the roof,' Chester said, and laughed, pointing at him.

'I'm not gonna grow through the roof,' Buddy said in his slow, lumbering way, his mole-covered face squeezing like a lemon as he walked over to me in his thick leather boots, causing the floor to vibrate with each step, and sat down with a boom.

Even though he is a giant and I know his foot will one day be large enough to crush our entire house, I'm not afraid of him. Unlike the others, he doesn't run down to the basement to play with their crystal first thing. He always sits down next to me and watches cartoons. Usually he brings a box of Fiddle Faddle hidden like a flat shoebox under his too tight shirt that pulls up, showing a hairy round belly, little white lint pieces nesting in the black fuzz.

'Whatcha got there, Buddy?' I would ask, not turning from the cartoon.

'Me? Don't got nothin'.' He would shake his huge head back and forth.

'Nothin', huh?' Without looking at him, I would reach sideways and tap the raised rectangle of his stomach.

'Knock-knock,' I'd say, smiling, still watching the TV.

'Who's there?'

'Fiddle.'

'Fiddle? Fiddle who?' he'd squeal like a little piggy. And I'd jump up quickly in front of him, grab his shirt, and pull it up, exposing the colorful box of caramel corn stuck to his folded-over stomach.

'Fiddle Faddle all mine!' I'd shout, and grab it off his belly and start to run. He'd always grab a belt loop on my jeans and hold me still while I'd try to escape.

'You look like Road Runner running in the air, not goin' nowheres,' he'd say, laughing.

'I'm gonna eat it all,' I'd taunt, and laugh, ripping the box and foil inside and plowing handfuls of Fiddle Faddle into my mouth, as he'd lightly pull me back and I'd push forward. This would go on till Chester or someone'd tell us to shut up and for Buddy to get his slow ass downstairs, or we'd just get distracted by the cartoon, the Smurfs getting in danger, and slowly he'd let go. I'd sit down more or less in his lap, and we'd silently watch the TV, stuffing the sugary, sticky corn into our mouths.

I can tell by the backfires it's Buddy on his beat-up, loud-

as-hell cycle, and I wish I were an Indian so I could put my ear
to the ground and tell by the sound if he's got someone on the
backseat. Another loud bang echoes down the stairwell. My body
moves automatically, and I toss handfuls of coal on the pile, but
it only seems to cause more to roll down. Now the coal is getting its revenge on me. I can hear their throaty, dusky chuckling.
I squat down to throw as many off the floor and onto my T-shirt as
I can. The roar of the bike surrounds the house, and I scramble
under a table, gathering up the coal, trying to escape.

'Fuck you, fuck you, fuck you,' I tell them as I chuck them
onto my shirt. But suddenly I realize past my panting, the silence
has closed in again, no engine rev, no nothing. On my hands and
knees I quiet my breath. Maybe it wasn't Buddy, just a joyrider
going to ride out the ramps and bridges past the house.

I strain to listen. I turn my head back to the stairwell, just
dusted lights and particles twisting and turning as if in a slow-
moving blender. I look back at the coal scattered beneath me,
and there, staring up at me, is the mother, crushed and bloody.

The footstep on the porch is heavy and almost sounds like
the foot broke straight through to the ground. Then there's more
up to the front door, and the rusted screen door screeching open
makes me twist my head back to the stairs like a rabbit, hypnotized and paralyzed by the sound of its stalker creeping up.

I can feel the loud boot in my chest stomping into the house.
I can't tell if there's a lighter step beneath it. I look up to the cellar ceiling and can see the indents on the wood boards as Buddy
walks into the living room toward my TV.

'Hey, where are you?' Buddy calls. I watch the depression
move around the living room above my head.

'You hiding?' I see only his steps, no one else's. I slowly
stand up.

'You by your lonesome, Buddy?' I call up, my voice wobbly.

'Where you at? Quit hidin'.' He stomps to the kitchen, closer to the cellar door.

I gather up the coal in my T-shirt, make it into a bundle, and carry it over to the stairs.

'I'm down here, Buddy.'

'Where at?' But his voice is louder, and his steps head toward me. I step into the light shaft and squint at the brightness of it. At the top of the stairs his huge outline appears, blocking the sun like a gigantic redwood.

'Down here, Buddy,' I say softly. I hear his lumbering thud as he climbs down the groaning steps. He stops and ducks through the doorway and stares at me, his large pink lips hanging open.

'You ain't supposed to be down here, I don't think.' He swallows loud, and his mouth flaps open again.

'I needed coal, Buddy, I was out.' I squint up at him to see his face.

'Chester's gonna be mad at you.'

'He's not with you, right?' I lean against the stairwell.

'Nope, coming, though. You really ain't supposed to be down here. You break in?'

'The door was left open, Buddy. I don't got no superpowers.' His stomach heaves a big sigh. The rectangular box stuck under his shirt rattles its contents with every breath.

'He's gonna whoop you bad.' He shakes his head, making the dust whirl around him like a cyclone.

'We don't have to tell, Buddy, we can just watch our cartoons and not say nothin'. If you tell, he'll take my TV and we can't watch no more.' Buddy stares at me awhile, then rolls his giant eyes side to side and grunts.

'Chester'll find out.'

'Please, Buddy, he won't. I swear, Buddy, I didn't do nothin', just got coal. I was gonna do us Jiffy Pop.'

'You don't got that!' His head shakes hard.

'Look in the refrigerator down here.' I point to it behind me. 'I swear, Buddy, I was gonna, but I got no coal and I wanted to surprise you, so it's your fault I'm down here!'

He rubs his face. 'For real?' He shifts his weight.

'Check and see and nail me up as a liar if it ain't, Buddy.' I wave him down, and he follows into the cellar to the fridge, his head hitting the hanging lightbulbs.

'Why's the coal all over?'

'Just fell out when I taked some.' I bend over and pick up a few. 'Buddy, Chester coming now?' I ask, trying to keep my voice calm.

'Said he'd meet up here with me.' He opens the fridge door and leans inside. He spins around. 'Jiffy Pop's in here!' he half shouts.

'See, I told ya!'

'Yes, you did.'

'Ain't no liar to ya, Buddy.'

'No, no, you ain't that at all.' He smiles widely.

'But if I get whipped, we won't get to pop it, Buddy.'

'Won't we?' His smile fades.

'No, Buddy, no cartoons either.' I shake my head and listen in the silence for Chester's car.

He stomps his foot on the concrete. 'I wanna watch TV with ya.'

'Well, Buddy, you can fix it for me.'

'The Jiffy Pop?' He turns to open the fridge to get it.

'No, no, Buddy!' I take hold of the fridge door and close it. 'If you can clean up the coal, say you were down here . . .'

'I don't got the key.' He shrugs, and his shadow looks like giant mountains collapsing.

'Tell Chester it was open, he won't whip you, Buddy.'

'That's lyin', though.' He shakes his head.

'Buddy, it's not lying 'cause you're down here now. Right?' He nods. 'And I came down here to pop our corn just for you, right?' He nods again. 'So all you have to do is leave out the part of me bein' down here, too, and there ain't no part of any lie.'

Buddy stands there thinking for a minute and laughs out loud.

'You're a smart one,' he says, and pats my back with his over-size hand.

'So are you, Buddy.' I smile up at him, and I knock at the box still under his shirt. 'When you are all about done we'll eat this right down, OK?'

'OK.' He nods fast.

'So I never was down here no matter what Chester or my mom says.'

'OK, that's right.' He nods even faster.

'OK, I better get upstairs, just put the coal back.' I point to the pile. 'I'll take this so we never run out.' I point to my T-shirt bundle. 'Bye, Buddy.' I lift it against my naked chest and start up the stairs.

'See you soon.'

I look over my shoulder and watch him picking up coal one at a time and placing it gently on the pile. I sprint up the stairs with my bundle and run out and hide it under the house just as my mom and Chester drive up.

I turn on my TV but keep the sound off to hear Chester yell, 'Why was Buddy down there?' and my mom screaming about the coal spilled all over. Finally Chester shouts at my mom to shut up about the coal, which only makes her yell louder. Buddy comes creeping out finally and sits next to me to watch TV with the sound turned down. Silently he pulls out the Fiddle Faddle, opens it, and hands the box to me. It's wet from his stomach sweat. I dig in quietly and eat and listen to my mom let out a horrific scream.

'The coal's bleeding! It's bleeding!'

I reach out for the sound knob and drown my mother out.

The retching returns with an unbelievable force, like a facial tic that just won't stop. My whole body gathers up and jousts forward as if every limb and organ were trying to collapse itself and be born again up through my stomach, throat, and mouth. There is nothing coming out but watery spit. I picture myself a swimmer only allowed brief turns to come up for air, and I try to take breaths between heaves, but my racing panic and the cold make it impossible.

I sit in the driver's seat clutching the wheel, throwing up on my chest and down between my legs. I lift my head between gags, and I see her entering Burger King. My mother's dyed black hair is swept over her face, reflecting almost a rainbow in the morning light. The black metallic raincoat is clutched too tightly around her, and her rubber boots covering her bare feet instead of shoes almost fall off with each step.

It's her. I push the car door open and run, my stomach rising into my throat. I pull open the glass Burger King doors and run in half-speed, past the children in cardboard crowns staring with their parents, as I run toward the woman in black at the counter. I hear her order two French Toast Sticks.

'It's poison! It's poison!' I gasp between retches. I grab her coat, somehow no longer black in the fluorescent light, and I fall down onto the tile floor as her coat comes off her shoulders into my hand.

A face I don't recognize clouds what should be my mother's face leaning above me, calling for help. She kneels down and puts the jacket under my head. I raise my hand and hit her again and again, like hitting a TV to make the picture stop jumping, to stop her face from changing like it was doing. Someone grabs my hand and holds it still. Faces spin above me, and I fall into the comfort of nothingness.

Chester never did find out I got into the cellar; Buddy told him he'd gotten the coal for me and that's why it'd fallen all over the floor.

My mom never felt easy about having the big pile down there to begin with. It had come with the house. As long as the pile was covered and stayed in its place, well, she could ignore it; but it had moved and even bled. No one could explain that one. Chester said she was seeing things, trick of the light, but my mom knew. She'd seen a piece come apart and bleed from its evil red heart.

She knows and I know. There will be revenge. Even though Chester and everyone, even Buddy, got rid of the coal from the basement, the black stain memory of it is there on the gray concrete. Even scrubbing it with bleach, which my mom made Chester do, couldn't remove it.

My mom hardly goes down to the basement any more. She paces and smokes, moving in jerky fast movements like a marionette, talking quickly to herself. Chester often gives her special vitamins to ease her mind and calm her down.

She has Chester remove the stove. I feel relieved and keep meaning to get rid of my small pile under the house. It hangs over my head, the coal waiting for me, plotting how to burn me up alive. I keep the baby coal whose mother I had destroyed; I keep him with me at all times in my back pocket as a hostage.

I jump when the big explosion comes downstairs, but I can't say I'm surprised. Me and my mother have been waiting and expecting something. And it happens like we knew it would without knowing we did. She is standing in the kitchen on one side of the cellar stairs, I'm walking toward the kitchen to help her open a beer can, her hands are too shaky.

'It's the crystal,' she says, and laughs too loudly. I ask her why would ashtrays do that, but she only says, 'Huh?'

In a way I feel happy it has finally come. Lately I'd catch her watching me under a haze of sour smoke, staring at me while she paced; I'd turn the sound on the TV lower, but she never said anything, just watched me, hardly blinking. She'd ask me to do things like to bring her the wine bottle from the cabinet as she sat outside on the car tire porch swing. When I'd do something wrong like drop the wine bottle, smashing it all over the floor, she said nothing, did nothing, didn't even tell Chester. I took a piece of the glass from the shattered green bottle and ran it lightly across my stomach till I bled, just to keep everything in balance.

When she screamed and hit, it was Chester that got it, not me. She'd take off her shoes and throw them at him and call him 'stupid fucking cunt' because he didn't get enough for their crystal. He would cover his head and slink down to the basement. She didn't threaten to leave, though. She never said, 'Fuck you, that's it.' And she left to go to town less and less. She stayed at home upstairs with me, pacing or rocking in the tire, figuring things out aloud I couldn't understand, and waited.

And I, like she, started eating only Pringles, drinking only Canada Dry ginger ale. When Buddy would bring out the boxes from under his shirt, I'd shake my head no, until he stopped bringing them. My mom and I watched Chester and the others take their cheeseburgers downstairs, trying to hide the bags past my mother's wide-eyed glare. 'Poison,' she'd hiss.

We stand almost facing each other, ten feet on either side of the cellar stairs as the basement explodes. The floor below us jumps and bangs and roars like a river-flooded waterfall. It's followed by synchronized popping like a fireworks display. And it's Buddy that comes out first, fire running up and down his clothes like some fire-eater's trick. Then some other guy I didn't even know, on fire like Buddy, screaming, followed Buddy out the door, out of the house.

I look at my mom slowly and deliberately smiling, and I understand. She stares back at me as more glass and miniexplosions break from down below us. A big tongue of flame leaps out of the basement toward us. I follow my mother out the door.

The man I don't know is rolling in the yellow dirt, screaming for help. I don't see Buddy. My mom walks to the car that had been our car and then became Chester's. He'd fixed up the broken-down Toyota Tercel a used-car salesman had given my mom, turned it into a 'souped-up, super-JAP bitch, ready to outrun any sheriff's cruiser.' He'd even painted it demon red, his favorite color.

She gets in and opens the passenger's side for me. As I climb in, another man comes stumbling out. I slam and lock my door. He runs in circles, patches of fire sprouting like grass on his arms, back, and legs. My mother starts the car. Another small blast that makes the car shake breaks the upstairs windows; little red orange flames dance inside.

The man beats wildly at himself as if a swarm of bees is attacking him. My mother backs up the car and the man suddenly turns and lunges toward us, his skin a rusty, puckered brown, flaking off him like autumn leaves. His blue eyes stare out too wide from his blackened face; his lids seem to have melted away.

He waves his pink-and-black arms, chasing us as she accelerates backward. The wheels spin in the dirt and the car lurches forward, almost hitting him as we pull out of the driveway and ride past him. I turn and watch him try to run after the car. I don't need to tell him it isn't his and my mother's car any more. It is

my mom's and mine again, the way it is supposed to be. I swivel
more in my seat and watch Chester give up chasing our demon
red Toyota and just stand still, howling.

At first I thought it was my mother's voice floating in the air
around me.

'He's finally coming to.' I force my eyes open to try to find
her, but the bright lights only make a blurry halo of the woman
standing at the foot of my bed. I open my mouth to speak, but my
throat is swollen and sore.

'Just you lay still,' she says, sounding half like my mom and
half not. 'You go drinking down poison, now you want to go
jumping out of bed.' Her tongue makes clucking noises. A different woman with a soothing voice leans over me.

'You're in the hospital,' she tells me. 'There's an IV in your
arm and a little tube in your nose to help you breathe. Just relax
and let them be.' Her hand rests on my forehead. 'OK, sweetie?'
I nod, my head stiff and ill fitting on my neck.

'Your grandma's here,' she says, petting my head softly.

'Momma?' I whisper in a croak.

'In a hospital, same as you. Fitting, isn't it? Gone from us not
six months.' I strain my head to see my grandmother turn to the
nurse. The nurse takes her hand from my head and turns toward
my grandmother. 'Not six months and he ends up half-dead here,
and she half-crazed in the mental ward.'

I drop my head back down and run my tongue over my
parched, cracked lips. I suddenly feel very thirsty.

'They hauled her off middle of the Memorial intersection,
stark raving naked, preaching the doomsday.' I hear the nurse
make 'mmm, mmm, mmm' sounds.

'Well, she didn't learn that false preaching from her father,
that's for sure!'

'You never can tell,' the nurse says, and I drift under the hum of machines buzzing like prayers.

We drive on in silence, saying nothing, as if nothing happened—it felt as if nothing ever had. We had passed Buddy running halfway to town, not on fire any more and not black like Chester, but sooty and red, his hair on his head seeming about gone. We hadn't even slowed.

We drive, stopping once for gas, my mom paying from a small bill roll tucked inside her bra under her T-shirt.

We drive till we get to some bigger town I don't recognize. I'd fallen asleep with no dreams. I wake up as she stops the car outside a Salvation Army used-clothing store.

'Wait here,' she says flatly. And as she gets out, 'Keep the windows shut and your thoughts pure.' Then she disappears into the paper-mirrored doors of the Salvation Army.

The mothball smell of the clothes fills the car when she returns. I look in the bag, all the clothes are black.

'Nothing for you, didn't have your size, we'll have to dye your clothes so the coal can't recognize you,' she says in monotone, and drives on.

We stop at a pharmacy. She buys black hair dye and antidote. She reads from the label. 'For accidental poisonings . . . antidote,' she says, tapping the plastic brown bottle, then pushing it under her seat. We pull into a Mobil and go into the ladies' and lock the door. She pours solution and covers our heads with the cold wet dye. Someone knocks on the door. 'It's broken,' she shouts. 'Go away!'

We sit on the bathroom floor while she counts the time till we wash it off. 'One Mississippi, two Mississippi, three Mississippi, four . . .'

We leave the Mobil bathroom with black-ringed sinks and black dyed hair. She leaves her pink T-shirt, jeans, white sneakers, and white bra and panties in the Salvation Army paper bag under a toilet stall. She puts on the black shiny raincoat and black rubber boots.

'Now we'll get supplies, dye your clothes, and the coal won't recognize us.' She smiles and we walk toward the car.

'Maybe we can paint it black,' she says, pointing at it.

After a few days I was released from the hospital. One of the alternate preachers from my grandfather's church drives me home, his peach-colored hair glued tight to his skull like a swim cap. He preaches psalms to me during the long three-hour drive, taking a break to tune in my grandfather's radio sermon. 'Why we will burn in eternal hellfire unless we are truly saved' is the topic.

I stare at the white plastic band stapled around my wrist, my name printed in purple. When I first woke up it said John Doe, but a hospital worker knew my grandfather, recognized me from services, so now I was another me again, my hair oiled, combed back, and parted, wearing blue slacks, a button-down white starched shirt, and a blazer.

Before we get out of the car to go into Piggly Wiggly to get our supplies of clothing dye, Canada Dry, and Pringles, the only food not poisoned by the coming black plague, I reach into my back pocket and enclose the baby coal in my sweaty palm.

I pull it out and place it on the dash in front of my mother. She says nothing for a long time, just stares. I want to confess about the coal under the house, how it was my fault, but all I can say is, 'It's the baby,' and she nods and closes it inside her hand.

Her eyelids closed but flickering, she presses it to her heart and then buries it in her pocket, still clutched in her hand.

'Thank you,' she says in a whisper.

I stand still in my grandfather's antique-filled study as if in a dream, remembering again the smells of lemony wax and baking bread, the sounds of oxfords clicking on hard wood, clocks ticking off seconds, and the rules of felt-covered Bibles and leather straps hanging on hooks.

I listen to hear if he's coming, and in the absence of his footsteps I walk slowly across the wood floor to the small black coal stove, its opening like a barred jail cell or blackened teeth. Its mouth would glow behind, a demon Day-Glo red when lit.

I place my hand lightly on the smooth coal stove like I had on ours when it was hot; my mother's hand had covered mine, pressing it down.

In the car she turns to me and speaks very solemnly, her hair slicked back and hanging like a worn leather shoe tongue.

'You and I will be the only survivors. Everyone and everything else will be burned, crushed, or poisoned.'

From the corner of my eye I see people chatting and laughing, pushing their shopping carts, unaware of their coming fate.

When she tells me the story it's always around Christmastime, after she comes home early in the morning smelling like beer, lipstick, and smoke. She flicks on the light, pushes me over to sit down, and tells me what used to happen at Christmas.

It's a German custom, German like my grandfather's father, like the throat-spitting words he shouts at my grandmother late at night.

The stockings are hung over the fireplace for all ten children, their empty shoes under the tree. On Christmas morning they line up fully dressed, excited and silent in the hall, until my grandmother allows them in. They walk to the fireplace, and from the weight of how their stockings hang their faces fall or lighten.

'I knew what was inside, I heard my brothers whispering what they found in theirs,' she slurs, and slaps her leg. 'They'd gotten theirs filled bad before, but not me, I'd always . . .' She raises her hand up and lets it fall sloppily onto me. 'Always was a good girl.' She shakes her head too widely, her hair flapping and sticking in her eyes. 'I was a good girl,' she whispers.

'My sisters all had treats in their stockings, only me . . .' Her fingers run through her smoke-filled hair. 'Everyone went to their shoes next: treats or a switch, or more black . . . Jason and Joseph got switches, Noah and Job and me, just like in our stockings: coal lumps.' Her voice rises in a half shout. 'Fuckin' coal!'

'Now . . .' She gets up and paces drunkenly beside my bed. 'I'd learnt my verses, my psalms, my chapters, I'd done my sidewalk preaching, Bible studies, done it all . . .' Her hands wave out like she's smoothing a tablecloth.

'My sisters stuffed down their cakes and counted their Christmas money from inside their stockings and shoes while Jason and Joseph went in to the preacher to get their whippings . . . I went, too, bold as lightning!' She wobbles into a wall. 'I carried my stocking in my left, my shoe in my right.' She holds out each empty hand.

' "What's this for?" I asked him before he'd even turned around, old fuck!' She snorts a laugh. 'He says nothing, right? Tells me to leave his study at once!' Her voice imitates his.

' "What's this for?" I yelled again. And know what, know what?!' She slaps a wall, laughing. 'He didn't answer me none, so I dumped it all out, the stocking and the shoe. That coal all over his fancy antique Persian motherfuckin' ugly rug. And I stomped on it, too, ground it right in, crushed it all in the rug!' she says between laughs.

She holds on to the wall and slowly slides down it, laughing. 'And you know what he'd said I'd done? You know?' She slaps the floor, tears rolling down her face from laughter.

' "You have evil and sin in your heart," he told me!' She snorts, then starts to choke.

'You were born less than a year later, so he knew what he was talkin' 'bout!' She lies there laughing until she falls asleep.

Sometimes, though, she'd have a needle still hanging in her arm and I'd slide it out, wipe it dry with toilet paper, and she'd mumble the rest: how he had her gather the coal up off the rug, place it in the stove, and light it. She stood, still seething, waiting for his apology. Waiting while he whipped her brothers. Stood and waited hours while the family went to services, her hands rolled into fists, watching the red coals burn and pop like her rage, while her father preached in his church. Waited till he returned, took off his jacket, hung and smoothed it. She would take her whipping and not cry. She would still ask what she had done.

She took off her blouse like he ordered, covering with her arms her newly formed breasts. He towered over her, grabbed her by her hair, and dragged her to the squat, cast-iron stove.

No one came when she screamed as he pressed her back to the door of the stove.

No one ever said a thing about the raised, welted lines like jail bars or thick red teeth that still line her back.

• • •

'We can outsmart it,' she says, staring out at the shoppers rushing past. 'If we become as black and as devious as the coal, we won't ever burn.' She points to the people entering in the automatic sliding doors. 'They all will.'

Her face pulls back in angry disgust. 'We'll survive because we know the power and the evil of the coal.'

She gets out and I follow behind her.

Viva Las Vegas

Along the deserted topaz-colored mountains, under the crowding of trees, our car cruises in its separate world. No lights from bars or clubs penetrate or distract, there's just thick, unbroken wilderness. So, life changes to adapt. She survives, and I treasure it.

I sit next to her in the front seat. My power surges as if I were a liquid constellation. I am the keeper of the maps. I measure the veinlike lines against my thumb. I remember the names of upcoming towns, villages, and stations, like a relative searching a crash survivors list.

'You sure this is right?' she gnaws on her fleshy lips.

'Trust me.' I clear my throat and sit taller in my seat. I can't help but feel she's a caterpillar squirming on my arm. I like the way that feels.

'Watch for Tawnawachee!' I order. She leans forward and squints. Her yellow hair is breathing back the three o'clock October sun. She's so pure looking, I ache.

'Help me here!' She bounces on the seat, glancing at me. I laugh.

'You ain't passed it.'

'I'm sick of goddamned trees and fuckin' mountains!' She

slaps the wheel. I'm not. I like to pretend we're runaways together, like Hansel and Gretel abandoned in the deep growth of
ancient woods.

'Tawnawachee . . . left, here!'

She turns sharply, tires squealing.

'You almost made me miss it!' she whines.

'Did not.' I blink at her.

'Did too! Damn, I need a drink, smoke, Valium, anything!'

My stomach tightens. 'OK, keep goin' straight for a whiles.'
I look out the window. The trees are thinning out.

'Vegas is so great, gonna refill on cash . . .' She pats her jeans
pocket.

'Are kids allowed?' I look at her.

'Oh, I have my ID.'

'I mean . . .' My throat starts to clamp. She interrupts.

'I can't hardly wait! How far?'

'Far, go faster.'

'Men just dying for hot young blondes . . .' A deer scampers
out of the way. She doesn't notice.

'I have the luck of Satan on the dollars slots, I swear, too, the
men are so easy . . .' I roll down the window, and the cool air
blowing through my hair makes me squint and fills me with a
strange excitement. I imagine birds flying in to steal my maps,
like bread crumbs, losing us forever.

'Now what?' She turns to me with such an open, trusting expression, her eyes a wide translucent pale green, that I can almost see the world through them.

'OK, now you turn left . . . yeah.' My confidence is reflected
in her full moving lips, silently and absentmindedly repeating
my directions.

'Here? Here?!'

'Yeah, now after the creek you turn left.' The complexity of all possible outcomes of each turn, each direction, are stored inside me, filling me with strength.

'Faster,' I grunt. I imagine the Dart on a runway, sprouting wings and taking off.

'You can win cars, too, I'll try to do that.' She flutters her hands as she talks, almost forgetting the wheel. 'And get rid of this piece of shit.' A stomachache is making me lean forward.

'Faster,' I order, my heart racing.

'What?' She looks at me.

'Olive juice,' I mouth to her, and close my eyes.

'What did you say?'

'Faster, faster!' I almost yell, the wind howling in my ears.

'Don't you order me.' She speeds up anyway.

'Let's never ever stop!' I laugh hysterically.

'What?' She laughs. I rub my hands over my face and hair like I'm scrubbing myself.

'Oh, you'll love Vegas . . .' She thumps the wheel.

'Faster,' I whisper.

'I can't wait, I swear!' She wets her lips.

'Don't stop.' I pump my knees up and down.

'Hey!' She starts to slow down. 'Hey, we miss it?'

'No!' I shout. Her hand flies out quickly and, like a magic trick, transforms into a fist and pounds once, hard, on my thigh. I become very still. She slows down some more. The trees are giving way to rocks and shrubs.

'Now where are we?' Her voice is controlled, not like Gretel any more. Despite myself I unfold the map.

'The turn is still a whiles up,' I mumble.

'Don't you fucking try it!' She shakes her fist at me.

I carefully fold my map into its neat rectangular shape. 'Try what?' I smooth it against my jeans leg.

'Don't you'—she glares at me—'ever try to lose me! You fuckin' hear me!'

I turn my face to her, smile slightly, and inhale.

I won't ever lose you . . . I promise.

'The turn is still a whiles up,' I mumble. I roll up my window.

Now it's passing us by too fast; there is nothing solid to grab on to or hide inside of, even if there were more than just sage-brush, tumbleweeds, and flat sand blazing by.

I've slid down behind her seat where it's curved as a cradle. But I can't get small enough 'cause the sky's too smooth and open, without a cloud's shadow to move into. This is God's mag-nifying glass.

'See the lights? Way off there . . . oh, some high roller's gonna get lucky, so lucky . . .' She drums on the dash.

I curl up smaller, clutching my neatly folded maps no longer needed.

'Oh, not some drunk cowboy, like Duane, 'member him?' She laughs. 'No, I'm gettin' me a married professional!' She smacks her lips. I wrap a fist around the metal bolting her seat down.

'Gonna get another daddy! Time for some pampering,' she mutters. ''Bout that time, I think.'

I lean my skull into the fake leather seat back, and I can feel the press of her spine.

'Bet you're hungry!' I push my head into the nauseating smell of Naugahyde.

'Did you gobble up your doughnuts?' I smile to myself and reach under her seat. I hold up a greasy smooshed jelly roll as if for target practice. My stomach growls at the sticky scent of it.

'Why didn't you eat it? You must be hungry.' I hear her adjust-ing her mirror to find me. I keep the doughnut raised.

'You hungry?' I shake the doughnut, no.

'Bet ya gotta go.' I shake again, no, and feel my gut cramped and aching.

'Well, I'm starvin'! Big juicy burger is what I need, fries, lotsa ketchup . . . how's that sound?'

I close my eyes and savor the attention like a soldier standing on a land mine before his battalion, and just as quickly, it's over.

'Sit up, c'mon, get up!'

She's not asking permission any longer.

I climb up onto the seat and stare out at the too bright sand sea like an overexposed photo. And there is nothing to anchor on to, to stop what's happening.

'Mile up's a diner,' she says, detached. I stare at her eyes in the mirror, looking straight ahead, filled with Vegas. I part my legs. She switches on the cassette play.

'Oh, I love this song,' she says. 'Dead Kennedys, yeah!'

She starts singing. 'Bright lights city . . .'

I raise my hips up off the seat.

'Gonna set my soul . . .'

I watch her in the mirror, rocking her head, looking like a child lost in a dream.

'Gonna set my soul . . .'

I loosen my bowels.

'On fire . . .'

I wait, unblinking into the mirror.

'Viva Las Vegas, Viva Las . . .'

She sniffs the air. 'You fart? . . .'

She glances at me through the mirror. I smile. 'What the . . . ?'

She snorts loudly. 'You fuckin' didn't!'

I remember a scene from a movie where a man places his bare palm over a flame to prove he will endure whatever neces-sary out of loyalty.

'You motherfuckin' evil fucker!'

I slide my hands under my thighs as she half turns toward me, still driving, her free arm reaching over the seat.

'Try to ruin everything, everything!' she sobs as her fist bounces off my legs, chest, stomach. 'You always have, always!'

I keep grinning as I feel something solid dropping, capturing us both, holding her to me.

'I've sacrificed so much for you.' Tears stream down her face. I lean forward so she can reach me better. I bite my lip through my grin.

'You shitty bastard!' She keeps driving, snot and tears flying as she swirls her head back and forth, from me to the road, her hand flailing at me.

'I've tried so hard, I've lost so much.' A giggle escapes me, and suddenly the white neon of Dolly's Diner is flashing through the windshield, filling the car and catching her fist, midstroke, like a projector burning through a film frame.

Silently she turns back in her seat. She wipes her nose on her sleeve and pulls into the parking lot. The crunch of the driveway sounds too loud in the silence. I'm still grinning. She parks in the shadows.

'I bet you're hungry.' Her voice is sweet but cold, ironed of any previous wrinkles.

She gets out, opens the trunk, digs around, comes over to my side, and opens my door.

'Honey, you go clean up.' Her hand pats my head, each touch too swift, too brief, to be caught. She hands me my bag.

'Here's ten dollars, get us burgers, sweetie?' She sniffles, wipes her nose again, and reaches her hand out to me. She looks away. I put my hand around hers, she leaves hers open. I step onto the gray gravel and look up quick to her eyes, staring toward the lights of Vegas.

'I'll just go get gas down at that Chevron.' She motions with her head. Her hand is gone from mine, and she pats my back with little pushes forward.

'Go eat.'

Robotically I walk away. She's humming as she gets in the car. I keep moving forward, still grinning. The ignition turns. I see people talking, laughing, eating through the yellow-lit windows. The smoosh in my pants travels down my leg as I walk forward.

Tires turning, gravel popping. A kid stuffing in a big forkful of cake. The bump of wheels hitting tar.

I spin around, a frozen grin plastered to my face, and watch the car pull out with a screech.

I wrap my hands around my ribs like I'm gripping a cliff ledge as the orange taillights pull away. And suddenly I'm running to the road edge and I don't breathe as the glowing lights approach the Chevron and quickly float, like a disembodied spirit, past it.

I watch the red orange glow grow smaller and smaller until it's all gone.

Meteors

'Are you trying to get hit by a meteor?'

I nod yes and take a few steps to regain my balance, because my face is turned up parallel to the planetarium-looking desert sky.

'I said, are you trying? I don't think you're trying.'

I hear her shift resentfully against the car. I keep myself from looking for her solid black silhouette against the shifting darkness around us.

'Sarah, I'm trying. I swear.'

'He won't marry me if you can't just do this.' She adjusts her body with a bounce.

'Will you wear a white dress, Sarah?'

'Hmm?'

'Last few weddings you wore regular clothes. I think he'd fancy you in a white gown, don't you think?' I hear the familiar dull scrape of car keys digging into her flesh.

'A gown? What, like a wedding dress?'

'He strikes me as the type.' I kick at the dusty sand around me.

'He'll carry me over the threshold, too. I know just the suite at the Mirage.'

As the keys scrape faster, I imagine I can see her arm skin curling up like shaved chocolate.

'Oh, I saw something streak in the sky!' I point up with my whole arm.

'Try and get it to hit you. You should lay down,' she says. 'Then there's more of you to hit.'

I take big showy steps around, my body tilted upward to expose more of me to the sky.

'See it?' I can tell she's looking up. 'It's coming, I think. Maybe I should get in the car so it don't hit me by mistake. It's gotta hit you.'

I hear her open the car door, slide into the back, and slam the door. She leans out the window. 'If I'm unconscious, how'll he fall in love?'

We'd pulled into the tourist station in the middle of Death Valley to get water and use the facilities. We were heading back to Vegas. She was going to be a showgirl with her own dressing room, and cherry tomatoes and ranch dressing laid out after every show.

He was in beige shorts—the longer, more dignified ones. His back was to us. The golden fuzz on his legs shimmered when he moved, as if someone had colored outside the lines. His shoulders were broad and worked as he talked warmly about meteors. Sarah jerked nervously and joined the tourists hearing his lecture. Her eyes went round and dark when she saw his face, and I knew she'd chosen another one. I watched his hands as they flew out while he spoke—tan, blunt fingers, no rings. Her lips parted in awe.

'Just like snowflakes, you won't find any two meteorites that'll be completely alike, even if you're dealing with the most common L6 class.'

His head bobbed rapidly as he spoke. 'We gather clues and more information from every new meteorite, about the beginnings of our solar system.' He drew a broad rainbow in the air. 'I never tire of seeing new meteorites.'

A few folks in the back of the crowd turned to watch Sarah. She flipped her hair back over her shoulders like a horse whipping its mane. He didn't seem to notice. 'If any of you'd like to hold a real meteorite,' he said as he started uncovering shoebox-size crates lined with a cloth napkin sitting on a glass display case next to him. 'They don't bite.' He gave a little chuckle.

Sarah pushed her way to the front, and her hand was in the box before he'd finished.

'Oh,' he said, 'here you go.'

'This is the most beautiful rock I've ever seen.' Sarah's voice echoed painfully.

'Not a rock—you have yourself a chondrite, one of the most common subtypes of stony meteorites.'

'Common?' She raised her voice a little.

'Well, yes, but there are chondrules contained within, silicate inclusions.'

'Please hand me an uncommon meteorite.' She thrust her open palm out, the rejected meteorite in the center. He paused, tilting his head like a dog in confusion.

'Can I have one?' A little girl's hand reached up.

'Yeah, sure.' He took the one from Sarah and plopped it in the girl's hand. Sarah left her hand extended, gave it a shake to remind him.

'Uh, OK, well, no meteorite is really uncommon.' She shook her hand again. 'But, OK, well . . .' He turned to a box. 'Pallasites.' He carefully placed a shiny metallic rock with yellow green crystal cubes in her hand.

'Rare.' He swallowed. 'Considered one of the most beauti-ful.' She nodded approvingly. 'This one is polished,' he said, then cleared his throat and announced to the group, 'Olivine mineral makes the green yellow. Here, everyone help yourself.'

He carried on about meteorites, even as the children who had crowded up front dropped their meteorites back in his boxes carelessly and started running around, screaming about dead pioneers' bones. He didn't stop, though there were only a few people left in the group yawning loudly. Sarah never left her spot, even as little kids pushed around her. When one kid got in front of her, she put her hand on his shoulder and firmly pushed him aside. During the lecture, Sarah turned her head abruptly to find me standing off to the side. She signaled for me to come take a meteorite. I crept slowly into the thinning crowd and worked my way up to the boxes. I cautiously reached in for a rock and kept one eye on her. She usually doesn't like me around when she's casting.

'Cats don't like to be pet when they eat, now, do they? I don't like you rubbing around me when I'm casting. Besides, he might not like kids.'

I glanced up at the ranger. He had a composed look that would've seemed solemn or aloof if it weren't for a nose that was too pointy and upturned. It offset his face in a friendly way. I knew if it weren't for his nose, Sarah never would've cast for him.

When he finished, only two white-haired retirees were left, besides Sarah and me. They thanked him, and before he could stop them, they pitched their meteorites in the box. Sarah glanced at me again and deliberately wiped her finger across her mouth. The shoplifting sign. The nobody-is-looking-so-put-it-under-your-shirt-or-in-your-pocket-now look. I wasn't sure at first what she meant for me to steal. I looked around for a wallet someone had put down. She wiped her mouth again, but it looked more like the slit-your-throat sign. All I saw near me on the glass display table were a few small meteorites that some of the bored tourists had replaced. I put my hand over them. Her face was turned toward the ranger, but she gave a small nod. I closed my hand around them and stuffed them, plus one I already had, into my pocket.

Sarah ran to the facilities as soon as he finished. Our ranger lovingly wiped down each meteorite with a cheesecloth and placed them back in assorted wood boxes. I kept my hips turned so he wouldn't notice the bulge of my pocket.

'Death Valley was given its name by the gold seekers, many of whom died crossing the valley during the 1849 California Gold Rush,' another ranger's voice boasted from the next room. When the meteorites were almost all packed up, Sarah burst out of the bathroom, the pink lines around her plump lips redrawn, and I could tell she had dampened and remoussed her hair, blowing it dry under the hand dryers to maximize its volume. She'd rolled up the denim legs of her shorts as high as they'd go, until they were cutting into her thigh, and her T-shirt was slightly damp.

'It's the wet T-shirt trick,' she once told me. 'No guy can resist a girl that looks like she just won the contest. Did I squeeze my nipples enough? Are they out?'

'Do you think we will get hit by a meteor?' she called out before the bathroom door had even swished shut behind her.

He turned and looked surprised, then pleased, that someone had anything to ask him. It took him a few seconds to realize who was asking, and when he fixed the voice to the rapidly approaching body, he blinked like someone was waving a hand too close to his face.

'I'm afraid I'll get hit by a meteor.' Sarah had chosen the Southern ladies' society accent. She fanned around her head with her hands, making the gelled hair clumps flutter like tentacles. He stopped blinking and turned to a box and fished around inside it. 'I have a Mbale chondrite in here somewhere.'

'Oh, good,' Sarah sighed, and ran her finger under her lacquered lashes.

'Here, here.' He pulled out a small gray black rock. 'We've recovered over one thousand specimens, it was a huge fall!' He stared at the rock.

She moved in close, pressing up against his shoulders to look at the rock. 'Umm,' she moaned, and licked her lips. He took a small step away from her. She stepped forward.

'In Uganda, a boy got hit on the head,' he said, looking into his box. 'I have more from that fall somewhere.'

I pressed my hand over my pocket.

'Hit on the head?' Sarah gasped. 'Lord have mercy!'

He stepped back, quick little steps, and put the rock out in his hand to show her, or to stop her from moving in. He nodded down onto the rock. 'Well, the specimen was slowed down by a banana tree, so the boy wasn't a casualty.'

'Thank the Lord for the wilds of Africa,' Sarah sighed. 'But out here in the desert, without any banana trees, I fear for our safety.'

He took another step back. 'Oh, I assure you getting hit by a meteorite is extremely rare. I would love to have met the boy.' He stared from the rock in his palm to the box of rocks. 'I often dream of visiting Uganda to examine him.'

'I would like to go with you to Uganda.'

He looked up at her quickly, his eyebrows raised, then took a quick breath to say something but blew it out like a deflating tire; he gave a tight laugh.

She shook her hair and smiled and stuck out her hand. 'My name is Caitlin. Is there a place nearby we can go for a drink?'

He looked like he'd been punched. After a second of hesitation, he shook her hand. She kept shaking it.

'Caitlin,' I said to myself softly, so I would be sure to remember. I wished she said what my name was, so I'd know if I was going to be a boy or a girl and how I would be expected to move.

He abandoned his hand to her and fixated on his rocks.

'I would love a cool beer, wouldn't you?' She giggled.

For the first time he looked at me, as if for help.

'That's my brother, Richard.' She waved at me with her free hand. He nodded and smiled warmly at me. I nodded back.

'Richard,' I whispered. Been Richard a few times.

She cleared her throat, and I knew she resented our exchange of nods.

'I—uh—I have a tour to give soon.' He tugged gently at her grip on his hand.

'Great—I can't get enough of meteorites,' she said, strengthening her grasp.

'Oh, oh, it's out in the field.' He pulled his hand away with a little effort. 'Got to pack these up.' He gave her a strained smile.

'Here, let me help you!' she exclaimed as she picked up various rocks and tossed them.

'No, no,' he said, putting his hands out over the boxes. 'Thank you. Thank you. I can do it. But thank you.'

'OK.' She laughed as if he were being silly.

'We're camping tonight.' She started tapping her pink nails on the glass.

'Good.' He fished out the meteorites she'd thrown in and started polishing them.

'Well, what if we get hit?'

'Pardon?' He glanced at her with such a bewildered expression, I knew she would misread it.

'Oh, you!' She giggled, threw her hair back, and did a fast twirl like a ballerina. 'You know we might just get hit!' she said sexily, and slapped her hand on the glass next to his boxes so hard that he and the meteorites jumped. He grabbed his boxes to keep them from falling, holding tight. He kept his red face tucked in close like he was saying prayers to them.

She leaned over him and did the cascade in his face. She learned that from stripping.

'You lean back, lift your long hair, and let it cascade down the back. That'll get you a man's paycheck faster than his ex-wife!'

When she was gone I'd put the mop head on and practice my cascade.

He wiped hair from his face, piled up his boxes, and without looking at her said tersely, 'Ma'am, if you get hit by a meteorite, I will be very impressed. I have to run now. I am very late. Have a great stay with us in Death Valley.' Before she could say a thing, he lifted his boxes and hurried for the employee exit. Sarah stood there for a minute, looking puzzled. She shifted from side to side and stared at the employee door. After about twenty minutes she said, 'You think he wants me to wait here?'

I swallowed. 'I think this would be an OK place to wait.'

She didn't say anything. We stood for another twenty minutes until a short woman ranger with a face like a shovel asked us if we needed help.

'Where is he?' Sarah tossed her hair at the employee door.

'Who?' the ranger asked.

'The meteorite man!' she said, annoyed.

'Jim? Jim left a while ago.' She smiled.

'What do you mean, left?' Sarah's bottom lip sucked in and out between her teeth.

'He has a tour at Scotty's Castle. He left. Can I help you with something?'

'He just asked me to stay with him here in Death Valley,' she stated, as if the ranger had said the world were flat or something.

The ranger smiled too widely and nodded. 'OK—well, we're closing, so if I can't help you with anything, I'm going to have to ask you to leave.'

I saw the rage flash over her face and I knew she was about to hit the woman and I got ready to run and grab her fist, but she shook her head violently like you do an Etch A Sketch and smiled at the ranger. 'OK.'

She turned and left the station. I followed.

There's a way that still warm air can make me feel incredibly lonely and small. Just the silence of it allows me to hear the world completely and how exposed I am in it.

She squinted at the yellow orange beginnings of a sunset and just stood there.

'Good thing it's fall,' I said suddenly. 'In the summer it once was a hundred and thirty.' She nodded and I felt myself get all excited. I continued, 'See, pioneers were dying of thirst, after going so long without anything, and then they saw all this water and they thought they were saved.'

She turned and watched them lock up the station.

'But when they got up to the water they found out it was all salt water.'

The shovel-faced ranger gave us a good-bye wave as she climbed in a jeep.

'That's how it got the name.' I felt out of breath.

'You'll see,' Sarah muttered toward the woman. She turned to look at me.

'Badwater,' I blurted.

'You're going to get hit by a meteorite,' she said.

I nodded. 'A lot of folks drank the water.' She turned and walked toward our car.

'And they died.' I followed her.

The first meteorite grazes the side of my face and kind of tickles, but I stay asleep sitting up against the car tire. I dream I am getting hit in the face with the burnt-up testicles that fall off a blackjack oak.

'Those would be the petrified balls of the crank master,' Sarah had said as she pointed at the light brown hairy acorns scattered beneath the tree.

'That's their innered organs,' she said, pointing to the leaves under our feet that resembled flattened livers. 'Look up.' The twisted split branches spread out like a highway of veins in the see-through human body dolls I've always admired. I nodded at the gore of it. She nodded and made 'tsk-tsk' sounds with her teeth.

'If you run across a blackjack, you know there was once a crank house that exploded. That's where they grow in these parts. It's a warning, and if you don't pay it,' she said, narrowing her eyes like a fortune-teller, 'it'll curse you when it could be protecting you.' She walked up to the black twisted tree and started petting it. 'See, if you were a girl, you could now be assured you would never die in a crank house fire.' She pulled down her pants and rubbed her bare crotch against it as if she'd wiped with poison ivy leaves by mistake. I ran up and started to pull down my pants to do it also. She waved me away.

'No—these fuckers ain't got their crank no more. These fuckers got burned alive and their eyeballs boiled and now they're stuck here in this tree! You think they want you? You'll piss 'em off! I'm satisfying their need for pussy, and in return the spirits will make sure I never burn up alive in a crank house fire and have my eyeballs boil!'

'I don't want to get burned up alive and have my eyeballs boil,' I said, trying to rub against the scorched-looking skin of the blackjack.

'Forget it.' She pushed me away with a hard shove. 'You missed out.'

The second meteor hits me on the head with a loud thud, jerking me out of my dream. I wave my hands around my head to protect it from the falling testicles.

'Are you bleeding?' Sarah says. I can make out her vague form standing a body length away in the dark. I put my hand in my hair and search for wetness.

'I don't think so.' I rub my eyes.

'Shit, can you find one of those meteors? It just bounced off your head. Don't think it went too far.'

'I got hit with a meteor? I thought it was balls!' I excitedly run my hands in the cool sand around my splayed-out legs. Suddenly a loud *thwack* cracks against the car door next to my shoulder, making me jump.

'Fuck!' she yells.

'You're throwing them again?' I ask quietly.

'You fell asleep. You don't really care to get hit with a meteor or you would've tried harder!'

I listen to her huffing in between the spooky desert night noises of clicking bugs, scurrying rodents, and crying coyotes. It all sounds too loud and contained and the star-pocked sky too rounded and low above us to be anything else than some small weird bedroom we're stuck in.

'Meteors don't work,' I say too quietly into the room. 'They're too small to hurt me.'

'What?' She stomps.

'Find a big rock. I can get hit with that. He'll never know what it really was. It'll be just like in Africa.' I listen to her thinking, biting her nails, making little paper-tearing sounds.

'You think it'll work?'

'Better make those reservations for the bridal suite at the Mirage,' I tell her.

We decided it was better for me to get hit in the car so she wouldn't have to carry me into it if I got knocked out. She spread out a beach towel to protect the vinyl interior. I lay on my stomach with my head almost hanging out of the door. It was a pretty good-size rock we found. Little bigger than a baseball. It took her a few tries, cracking the windshield, hitting the seat and my back before she nailed me.

'Oh,' I said. And everything went black.

The ceiling is white. Like in a hospital. There is something gooey in my eyes clouding everything. I try to move and can't. I look around for a nurse.

'You shouldn't wake up yet.'

I try to lift my head, but I can only roll it to the side. I want a nurse. A nice one with short, unpolished fingernails, because those are the ones more likely to hold your hand and pat your forehead.

'Go back to sleep,' Sarah whispers furiously.

I want the nurse to tell Sarah to wait outside, like how they do on the soaps. I twist my head to find a nurse.

'Close your eyes again!' Sarah yells.

I rub at the goo in my eyes to see better.

'No, no. You're wiping away the blood! You look better with it. Stop!'

Her hand grabs mine.

I look past Sarah's panicked face and see the mountains of Death Valley.

I roll my head the other way and see my filmy metallic reflection in the tinted door of the Death Valley Visitors Center.

'He'll be here any minute. They open any minute! Wait till he sees you! Lord, I can't wait. He'll be so impressed.' She drops down next to me and whispers even though no one is around as far as I can tell.

'Remember, we were camping and then, bam,' she yells into my ear, 'this meteor hit you.'

She unfurls her hand and waves one of the little meteors I stole in front of my face like smelling salts. 'Got it?'

My head feels bloated inside, and I can see my heartbeat. The goo is still oozing into my eyes and burning. I wipe at it again.

'Stop it!' she screams. 'Are you gonna ruin this, too, after all my hard work?'

I slowly shake my head no. The concrete under me is freezing, but I'm grateful it's not hot. What if I was wounded by a runaway wagon or scalped by the Indians in the mountains and I had to wait on burning hot concrete outside the visitors center and had only badwater to drink?

'Thirsty,' I say.

'You'll be impressed, too.' She puts the meteor up in my face. 'See it?' I blink at the blurred rock. 'That's blood! I stuck it in your head to get it like it hit you. You didn't even think of that.'

She closes her fist fast around the rock as if I were going to try snatching it from her. I stare off at the hazy mountains and watch a flock of dehydrated pioneers struggle to cross the range.

'We got hit! We got hit!' I hear Sarah yell out enthusiastically. I don't try to open my eyes. 'C'mere! C'mere!'

A car door slams with that metal clink that sounds so final. 'We got hit! See, I knew we would. I tole ya, didn't I? Didn't I?'

I hear the soft pad of his boots, hesitant like a deer, coming toward us.

'Look here. See? I got a meteorite for you!' she calls out teasingly. 'And it hit him! Bam! Just ask him.' Sarah's foot pushes into my side. 'Tell him. Go on, Richard, tell him what happened.'

'Jesus,' I hear the ranger say.

Sarah nudges me again harder. 'Tell him.'

'I got hit,' I mumble, and open my eyes halfway.

'He got hit,' Sarah boasts.

'Did you get the car license plate?' I hear him tread closer to me.

'License plate? What're you, kiddin'? Ain't no license plate on a meteorite! I told you. We got hit with a meteorite!'

'You got hit with a meteorite,' the ranger repeats, and leans in over me. I try to smile at him, nod, wave, but my head just kind of wobbles and my arm flops on the concrete.

'Here. Look at what came streaming down from the heavens above and knocked him on the head.' She reaches out and hands him the rock.

She hops around to get closer to him. 'That's his blood on it!' I can make him out standing over me, turning the rock around in his hand. 'Just like in Uganda,' she says. 'It bounced off a cactus instead of a banana tree.'

'This is an L6 chondrite,' he says.

'Exactly,' she says.

He wipes it clean on his khaki pants, and a brownish streak is left on him. 'This isn't fresh.' He shakes his head.

'Now you don't gotta go to Africa!' Sarah says and nuzzles closer to him.

'There isn't molten material.'

'Sure there is.' She giggles.

'There would be a fusion crust.'

'I can get us a suite at the Mirage,' she whispers loudly in his ear.

'This has been polished,' he says.

'I'm gonna be a showgirl with my own dressing room,' she says.

'I'm going to radio for assistance,' he says.

'I'm easy to carry,' she says.

'I'm not going to move him,' he says.

'Over the threshold, silly,' she says, and gives his ass a little slap.

He walks away quickly, and she follows after him. I close my eyes and dream of hemorrhaging banana trees falling at the speed of light.

'Can you open your eyes? Richard, open your eyes.' The voice is very stern, kind of like an angry teacher when you fall asleep in class. I blink my eyes open.

'Very good, Richard.' A man is leaning over me. Not the ranger. 'Try and stay awake with me, OK?'

'I'm Dr. Peterson.' He's speaking as if I'm standing a mile away from him instead of lying right in front of him, and he smiles too wide, his mouth like a cartoon coyote. His eyes are little yellow lemon drops behind thick, fishbowl glasses. 'You have quite a little scrape there, got a good number of stitches and what looks like a concussion.' The doctor nods at me; I nod back so as not to appear rude.

'Want to tell me what happened?' he says.

'I got hit by a meteorite,' I say, surprised by my own voice.

'No, you weren't, Richard. A meteorite didn't hit you. You want to tell me what happened?'

'It fell and hit a banana tree first,' I tell him as he shines a bright penlight in each of my eyes. I try to remember who Richard is. I think it's the ranger.

'Do you know where your mother is?' he asks, and keeps the light shining on me, like in a spy interrogation movie, moving it from one eye to the next. Dull panic starts seeping over me.

'Where is my mother?' The words run into my blood like an IV line and make a rusty taste in my mouth.

'She was in the waiting room, but she left and hasn't returned. We'd like to talk with her. Do you know where she could have gone?' He switches off the light, and little blue and red dots swim like aquarium fish through his big glasses.

'She's with Richard,' I mumble. He nods.

'How many fingers am I holding up?' He waves three fingers that look like a gun.

'Bang,' I say.

'Richard!' He snaps his fingers and sounds like the angry teacher again.

'How many fingers? Hmm? Can you see it?' He holds up the peace sign.

'OK,' I say.

'OK what?' he asks.

'OK, truce,' I say.

'Do you know where your mother is?' he says.

'Is she with the ranger?' I ask.

'No,' he says.

'She's all alone?' I ask.

'I don't know,' he says.

'He's not marrying her?'

'Get me Social Services on the line,' he says over his shoulder. 'You don't know where she is, do you?'

I shake my head no and close my eyes against Dr. Peterson, acting like he's in some jazz concert, snapping his fingers frantically in my face. I lay back into the bleach of the pillow under my throbbing head. The bright, garish lights of Vegas begin to flash around me like an ambulance. I feel cold as people stream past me, but then I see her. Sarah, smiling. She dips an L6 meteorite into ranch dressing and holds it out to me and waits for me to bite.

Natoma Street

It's like I'm pushed from behind, pulled down the slope of Natoma Street like a ramp down into another world. All the buildings are low and tight huddled around me. Heavy-gated sweatshops, sunken-down tenements, windows filled with dusty laughing Santas and graying fake snow and ancient slaughter-houses with rusted metal beams jutting suddenly out above me. I watch my shadow slip underneath them, sharpen under the piss-colored street lamp, and slide unsliced over the green and white pebbles of glass worn smooth from streams of urine. And behind me somewhere is the rainlike sound of a car window being smashed, and in front of me the crunch-crunch under my boots, pulling me forward. I tilt my head to listen to the blood in my own ear, and all I hear, and all I feel, is my cold ache. The sheet metal door glistens in front of me like an ax on a fire blade, and the sound of my pounding fist on the door echoes through me and down Natoma Street. Each split second of contact with the frozen metal is like a jolt trying to wake or stop me, but all that's racing in my blood is too old and too known and too me-chanical to be turned back. I stand and wait and watch delicate white puffs of air float out from me. And it's amazing anything can come out of me. Soon nothing will. I bang the door as hard as I can, bruising my knuckles, and wait a few seconds.

'C'mon . . .'

My teeth are clamped. I kick at the door with my boot. They're gonna find me collapsed here as drained and as empty as if a vampire had fed on me. I kick the door again and again, and it shudders. I feel the panic and desperation in my stomach spread as my blood roars away, feeding on itself.

'You're supposed to . . .'

I kick and hit the metal door.

'Be fuckin' here!' I yell. From behind me a window slams open.

'People sleeping, people sleeping!'

I turn and look up to see a bald Chinese guy, his face so chubby and squished, he looks like a smiling Buddha. Christmas lights flash like a strobe around him.

'You go 'way, go 'way!'

From behind me I hear heavy latches and bolts moving, and I twist around, and it's like an opening in the world, with cars, lights, and people passing the mouth of Natoma, and they have no idea I'm here, and waiting to be.

'Goddamn, you're eager . . .' The door pulls open like a bank vault, and blue light reflects onto the sidewalk.

'It's just eleven-thirty now, I don't start early,' he says in a deep radio announcer tone. My ears pound and I look back up to the Buddha man, but he's gone, just the empty flashing space of his gaping window.

'Let's go,' he orders, and I turn to face him, but he's gone, too. I climb into the blue lights and the door that's framed in steel, and it slams behind me.

'Bolt it,' I hear from ahead of me. I stare at a puzzle of red-

and-black-painted locks and bolts. 'The bottom,' he says. It's a lock that will need a key to unlock. I feel it clink in my stomach as I watch my hand seal me in.

I walk down an unpainted narrow Sheetrock hall with bare blue bulbs poking out like lights in an arcade. The ground is concrete and cracked.

'C'mon!' he says impatiently. 'Off to the right.'

The hall opens into a huge warehouse with two giant Harleys parked in the middle and a maze of other halls, lofts, ladders, and doors surrounding it. I follow the blue lights into a smaller room that smells of rubbing alcohol and something else I recognize but can't recall.

'Over here.'

He's sitting in a director's chair in the middle of the room, holding two Fosters. He holds an open one out to me. I watch my shadow like a black fog moving toward him. My shadow head hits his feet, black in engineer boots, and I trace up faded Levi's to a leather vest half revealing shining silver hoops through his nipples. His arms are like air-drawn traces of a woman's figure. I avoid his face. I reach out for the beer.

'Uhh, thanks.'

'How old are you?'

He crosses his legs.

'Eighteen,' I say automatically, and sip some foam. He laughs.

'Try again.'

His boot wags.

'Fifteen,' I mumble.

'Fifteen?' he repeats. I follow the floor to a brick wall to my right. There are things hanging, attached, from the wall. A warm wave rushes over me; I swallow loudly.

'Fifteen, I like that.'

I nod my head.

'But I have ID in case.'

'In case of what? . . . Huh?!!'

I look up at him. His cheekbones are cut too sharply, his lips are small, tight, and curled up like old newspaper. His hair is black and slicked straight back. His eyes are the reddish brown of dried blood.

'This is between you and me, got it?'

'Mmm-huh.' I feel awkward and stupid. 'I got your money!' I say too loudly, and start to reach back to my pocket with my beer hand but spill some. He laughs, shakes his head.

'Sorry . . . shit!'

It takes me a few seconds to figure out how to maneuver my money out with only one free hand.

'Blonds,' he sneers. 'Fuckin' geniuses!'

He takes a big gulp of beer. I hand him $100.

'So, how's it feel being on the other side?' He smiles, crooked little teeth.

'Huh?'

He holds the money up and shakes it, eyebrows raised.

'I had to borrow it.' I look away.

'Jesus you're quick,' he snorts. 'And stop rocking.'

I didn't know I was. I feel like my eyes are telescopes I'm peering through, somewhere far away.

'Uhh, sorry.'

'You will be.' He smiles sarcastically.

'Huh? Oh.' I nod. 'Yeah.' I feel my face getting hotter and hotter.

He nods, grins, and says, as if I don't speak English, 'You are paying me . . . how does that make you feel?' He starts fanning the money.

'I dunno . . .' I sigh. His foot taps.

'Umm . . . weird.'

'How?' He leans in.

'Uh . . .' I rub my face, it feels red.

'Embarrassed, I guess,' I mumble.

'Would you be, humiliated, if your friends knew? . . . Hey, hey!!' He snaps his finger. I look up.

'Stop rocking!' He puts his arm out and waves his hand like he's trying to move something aside to see me.

'I dunno . . . yeah . . . I guess.'

I can't explain it. Paying for it does humiliate me, and I want that, I need that part, it calms me in some way. You can't trust people you don't pay.

He sighs loudly.

'Just, just sit down.' He leans back. I look around me.

'Right there.'

'Yeah . . . sorry.' My left eyelid starts twitching. I sit on the cold concrete and chew on the inside of my cheek.

'I've heard about you,' he says with a little laugh, and stuffs the money away.

'Uh-huh.' I nod. My blood swirls around faster and faster.

'No limits for you, right?' His beer clanks on the wooden chair arm. My eyes shift from side to side, back and forth.

'No safe word, right?'

'Mmm.'

'You can take it all, huh?'

My head twitches in a nod.

'Coz you'—he points at me and laughs—'don't give a fucking shit, right?'

'Well . . .' My voice sounds too high. 'I'd like, umm, I'd like it if, uh . . . I'd like . . .' I twist my mouth from side to side.

'Sssay it,' he says, singsong.

'Ummm . . . . I'd like it if you would . . .' My head jerks.

'Would what?' He leans forward again.

'Um . . . give a shit, I mean, ya know . . .' I swallow hard. 'Sorta like, care um, ya know.' My bottom lip starts to quiver.

'Yeah.' He sighs. 'You know I care . . . shall we get going?' He gets up. 'I don't got all night.'

I take a few huge gulps of the beer and rise up like I'm pulling myself out of a pool and follow him to the exposed brick wall.

'So what do you need?' He waves his arm like a model on a game show at the collection of belts, paddles, whips, and crops displayed on the wall. He smiles proudly.

'I dunno,' I mumble.

There's a jungle gym–looking metal thing, with wrist restraints hanging down, in the middle of the wall.

'Whatta ya think of this?' He reaches for a short whip and starts fondling it. I'm starting to feel nervous-sick.

'It's cool, but uhh . . .'

'Not into whips, right?' He replaces it gently. I shake my head. My eyelids twitch nonstop. 'No cats?'

I shake my head again and notice that under the metal bars there's a drain.

'Look, I know talking is a drag,' he says, like I won't eat broccoli or drink my milk or something. 'But you'll be happy for it later.' He pats my shoulder.

'I'm not a mind reader, you know. I haven't heard everything about you.' I want to ask him what he's heard, but I'm afraid it'll hurt too much.

'C'mon.' His voice is soft. He moves over to me and places his hand on the back of my neck and massages it lightly.

'Let me help you,' he whispers into my ear, and I feel it all start to melt. 'Let me help.'

'That one,' I say softly, and motion with my head.

'That?' He points to it. I nod and stare at the drain.

'Good boy!' he says enthusiastically, and I should be embarrassed, but I feel sort of proud. He goes over to it, I hear him take it down, and it's all starting.

'Take your clothes off, you can put 'em on that chair.' A chill jerks my head, and I close my eyes. 'Yes, sir,' I whisper, and start to undress quickly.

'That's right, you call me sir,' he responds. I hear him moving things, setting things up. 'Any other special words?'

'I dunno.' I lean down to unlace my boots. He comes over to me and I feel his hands sliding along my naked back, down my open jeans and underwear.

'You do take a lot, huh?' he says.

'Fuckin' knot!' I pull and slap at the tight knot at the top of my boot.

'Dad? . . . Stepfather, right?' He's running his hands across the little gullies and streams lining my back and ass.

'Can't get this fuckin' knot!' I yell, and punch my boot top and stomp.

'Hey!' He grabs my face between his hands and leans over me from behind. I keep stomping. 'Hey, hey, hey, not yet, stay calm . . . it's OK . . .' His voice is soothing. I hear a moan escape me. 'It's OK, it's OK, it's OK.' Like a lullaby.

'Please . . .' I half whisper, and reach one of my hands up to his holding on to my face.

'Tell me,' he says into my ear. His breath smells like warm beer and saliva. I bring my other hand up around his other hand, cupping my face. I feel him leaning into me from behind, and I release into containment.

'Tell me,' he whispers. We breathe together, him leaning over me, in-out-in-out.

'Fix me,' I murmur. 'Fix me.'

'What's it say?' He points to the words cut on my stomach, ass, thighs.

'Bad boy,' I pant, 'evil . . .' I feel like I've hooked onto a train that's speeding away from me, or with me.

'You are a bad boy, aren't you,' he says above me, squeezing my head.

I feel it loosening.

'Sinner, aren't you.'

I close my eyes and my stomach cramps and a chill runs through me. He wraps his arms, crisscrossed, around me. I moan.

'Tell me, now,' he says quietly.

'Punish me,' I pant.

'How hard?' His chin digs into my shoulder.

'Till I learn . . . please? I need you to, please?' My body is shaking.

'Safe word?' he whispers.

'No, no, not till you're done, OK?' I pant. 'Just, OK, please not my face, OK?'

'It's a very pretty face.' He pats my cheek, and I try to lean my head into his touch.

'Yeah, yeah, tell me that,' I gasp, and he rubs against me through his jeans. 'Tell me I'm beautiful . . . please . . .' I can't stop.

'You are, and that's why I need to help you,' he whispers, like a kiss.

'Save me,' I groan, and he squeezes his arms tightly around me, and I hope he'll never let go.

'I will, you beautiful, conceited, bad evil bitch.'

'Yes . . . please . . . yeah . . .'

He reaches down between my legs and grabs my thing. 'Call me sir!' His voice becomes throaty and harsh. He twists me hard and fast. It's all coming back, like being lost in waves of wheat, just rolling by, rushing me, soothing me, caressing me.

'Make me cry, I need to . . . cry . . .' He twists his hand, harder.

'Sir!' he shouts in my ear.

'Sir,' I whisper, and I feel the tears swelling in my gut. 'Sir . . . hold me after, please, I'll pay extra, please, after hold me.' He says nothing. 'I'll pay extra . . .' I sound pathetic, but I can't shut up. 'Please.'

'Let's go,' is all he says, and reaches behind to bring out a long switchblade. He flicks it open. I suck in air.

'You like this?' He leans down, slices open my laces, then helps me kick off my boots and step out of my jeans. He presses the switchblade against my thing, and I'm spiraling away inside myself.

'It's a dirty, evil thing,' I whisper. 'And I hate it! I hate it!' The blade presses harder, I feel my skin ready to slit gracefully, like a paper cut. 'I hate it, I hate, I hate it!' I'm hyperventilating.

'Well, we'll take care of it, don't you worry . . . C'mere.'

I feel suddenly embarrassed, exposed, stupid.

'Get over here now, now!' He stands by the rack contraption. I walk as if in a dream and face the bricks. I hand him my arms and watch him Velcro the restraint cuffs around my wrists so they hang above me spread apart on the bar. I look down at my chest heaving up and down, too quickly from my heart or my breath, I don't know. He stands beside me, the thick black leather belt unfurled, swinging back and forth like a pendulum. He steps close to me and raises the belt to my face. I panic.

'Please not my face!' I plead. 'Please!'

'Shut up.' He brings the belt closer. 'Kiss it.'

I look at him. He grabs a handful of my hair. 'Kiss it!' He shoves the belt up to my mouth. It smells faintly of bleach. I begin to kiss it. I feel relief and excitement surge through me.

He knows. He understands.

'You're a nasty cunt, aren't you?' He pulls my head back by my hair. The belt disappears.

'Yes, sir.' My eyes roll up. He drops my head with a shove, and I hear him pacing an arc behind me. My body hangs limp like a swing wanting to be pushed.

'You're a very nasty, evil, bad, sinful boy, aren't you?!'

'Yes . . . Yes, sir,' I correct myself and moan, my butt muscles flexing in anticipation.

'Say it!' he orders loudly from behind me.

'I'm a bad, disgusting, evil boy.' I hear him pace.

'Again!'

'I'm an evil faggot, sir!' I can hardly swallow. 'Please punish me . . . severely . . . sir.' The heat spreads down my legs, into my toes. No sound, not even his breath. 'Oh, God . . . please!' I yell.

'You need it, don't you?' His voice is heightened and tight.

'Yes, please.' I'm starving, ravenous.

'You're a pig.' The word someone once carved on my stomach. I freeze and taste sour spitup. I nod my head. 'Say it!' he screams in my ear.

'I'm a greedy pig, sir!' I shout breathlessly. He laughs.

'So beautiful,' he whispers, and caresses my face. 'Beautiful.'

I gasp, it's perfect. He moves back behind me, and I watch the shadows. The strap is hurled back, like he's throwing a football, whole arm into it, and I hear the familiar sound of air being thrashed through and the cymbal-like crash across my ass. My body rocks.

'Thank you, sir.' My mouth hardly moves.

'I have to punish you, don't I?' I nod. It crashes down again. My body sways in disagreement, and my butt skin puckers. How can you crave something your whole body rejects, and even increase the cravings the greater the protest from the body?

'I bet you're a fucking cocktease, aren't you?' The strap slices into my ass.

'Yeah.' My head rocks backs.

'Sir!' he corrects. The strap lands on my upper thighs. I lift my head.

'Punish me, sir . . . teach me.'

'Beg.' He walks behind me.

'Please, sir . . .' He laughs, I hear the belt drop.

'You're not worth my fuckin' time.' I hear him walking away.

'No! Please! God, please! Don't leave me, I can't take that, please, God!' I hear him open drawers. 'Sir, punish me!' I howl, and shake my arms rattling the jungle gym thing.

'You don't order me, spoiled cocktease brat!' He's next to me.

'Yes, yes, yes.'

'What?!'

'Sir!'

He's jingling something in his hand. My stomach hardens.

'Close your eyes, cunt.' I stare down at his closed hand. 'Now, you bitch!' His open hand slaps hard at my thing. Air spits out of me, and I can't fold over. My eyes clamp shut. He laughs. 'You're not too fuckin' bright, are you?' I sort of swing, letting my arms hold me. I feel something cold against my left nipple. I hold my breath.

'You want me to fix you? Discipline you?' I hear it snap down around my right nipple, and it feels like a needle being driven in. 'You have to learn obedience.'

'Yes.' The heat rushes through me. 'Please, sir, I want to be, yours . . .' My left nipple erects next to the open clamp. 'Please. I'll do anything!' He snaps it shut on my tit. I grunt.

'I know you will, you fucking nasty, spoiled brat, cocktease, bad, bad boy.' Cold heavy chains hang from the clamps, and he gives them sharp swift tugs as if in a bell tower. I feel his hand caressing my cheek, and I push my face into it like a dog searching for scraps. I kiss his palm, lick it.

'Say it, beautiful.' I feel the cold metal by my thing. My mind swirls away, and I feel his hand slap hard across my cheek. My eyes jerk open at him, surprised. He's inches in front of me.

'I won't scar your pretty face,' he says flatly. '. . . If you're lucky.' My face stings. He caresses the other cheek. 'Close your eyes,' he whispers. I hear the metal chink-chink, and his other hand snaps a clamp on my thing. I jump and whimper.

'Tell me what you are.' He snaps another one on but continues to caress my cheek.

'Uhh . . . a dirty whore . . .' I want to bury my face in his palm as his other hand begins to twist the clamps and snap more on. How can I explain pain that burns like torture but soothes and excites more than a caress or kiss? His finger traces my lips and dips in and out of my mouth. The rest of his fingers tap on the outside. I suck his finger as it slides in and out of my mouth.

'You fucking cocktease!' His hand pulls away and slaps my other cheek loudly, and it feels like a punch. I blink away the tears rimming my eyes. He pulls at the chains. 'Tell me! You faggot whore!'

'I'm a fucking dirty whore cocksucker . . .' My chest tries to curl up against the pain like warped plywood. He walks behind me.

'It's time for you to learn.'

'Yes.' I ball my fists in the air and open my eyes wide to the brick wall in front of me. 'I need to repent.' My blood throbs.

'Yes, you do, 'cause you've been a very naughty boy, haven't you?'

'Make me pay, sir,' I whisper. I hear him pick up the belt.

'It's time for you to cry.'

'Oh, he'll cry!' My mother squeezes and twists my wrist.

'Never done seen a thief, young or old so bold-face remorseless,' the white-haired security guard says, and wags his finger at me. The steak and beer six-pack from my knapsack sit on the table in front of me. 'See all the trouble you put your poor mother to?!'

The young frizzy blond checker that busted me shakes her head at me.

'Steals it for his no-good gang friends.'

'Oh, we don't let gang members in this store, ma'am.' The manager quickly shines his shoes on the back of his pants legs.

I feel my mother smiling at him. She fans herself with her hand. 'Well, that's a good thing, sir . . .' She crosses her legs.

'We have special services for them at our church, the Virgin of Perpetual Love and Mercy, but all in vain, I reckon.'

She sniffles, and I can't help but laugh. Her hand reaches out fast and slaps my cheek. I keep my grin despite myself; I know I'll pay later.

'Yes, ma'am, the police won't do a thing to help you, ma'am, 'cause his age . . . he is amazin'.' The manager leans down over my face. He smells of tuna and pickles. 'Have you no shame, boy?'

My mother clears her throat. 'He's been a bad boy since his father passed, few years back, that big blaze? Was a firefighter, over Tallahassee.' Murmurs of sympathy. 'Thank you, Lord rest his soul. Boy hasn't had the father he badly needs to give guidance and discipline.'

I spurt out a laugh at the thought of her being married to a firefighter. Her hand smashes across my face again.

The manager clears his throat. 'Well, I think this is the best way to handle this, ma'am.'

'Mary.' My mother nods.

'Mary, Howard.' He reaches out and shakes my mother's hand a little too long.

'Howard, sorry we meet in such a way, but I'm sure it will help save my boy more than police or I can.'

I roll my eyes and groan. My mother's nails dig into my wrist. 'You're an evil boy, you thank Mr. Marsh.'

'Thanks,' I say flatly, and grind my teeth.

The checker girl flashes her braces and flips her hair. 'We should whoop all the shoplifters like him.'

'Way it used to be, and hardly anybody thieved,' the guard grumbles. I look up and see two bag boys, a little older than me, peering in wide-eyed through a broken, small, one-way mirror. 'Well, no time like the present.'

My mom stands and pulls me over to the table. My heart pounds louder. 'Please,' I whisper.

'Oh, now we see the remorse,' Howard gloats. He opens his belt. 'Soon you'll see the tears.'

My mother jerks me forward. 'Take down your pants.' I look up at her, and her eyes flash a private message of rage. She didn't tell me to get caught.

'Excuse me,' Howard says to my mother as he pulls the belt from the loops.

I stare at the checkout girl biting her lip. 'Oh, I'll leave . . .' She starts to get up.

'Oh no, darling!' My mother waves her back. 'He stole in front of you, so he'll pay in front of you.'

I look over to the boys in the mirror and point. My mother shakes her head and smiles slightly at me. I feel everyone's stares, and it's like heat, my body shivers, and like Batman sliding down his tunnel, I am suddenly transformed to endure the impossible. I am able to lean over the table and pull my pants below my underwear. But I pull as much as possible of my jeans in front of me, and I pray and pray. At some point I feel Howard's belt beating me, as he will almost every other day as my new loving father, till we move out of his trailer three and a half months later, stealing all his cash, gold cuff links, and school ring.

I pray during my punishment. I pray so hard, I drown out the horrible whipping sound. I pray that God, or Satan, or whoever, won't let them see how sinful and repulsive and bad I truly am. I pray something won't let them see what my mother knows and has tried to punish me for but which only worsens. And the tears that eventually come burn through me and only heighten it all.

For hidden in my bunched-up jeans is my erection, like a gleaming badge of guilt, waiting to be discovered and ripped from me.

The belt is slamming into me all over, my back, ass, and thighs, and the tears are streaming, and confessions of every sin and every evil thought or action I ever did or almost did pour out from my mouth. But I cry harder and harder as the truth washes over me. Even as he takes the belt to between my legs and the pain is unbearable, I'm like an opportunistic mosquito, sucking blood down from the punishing hand of God, reaching down from heaven. I am still excited even though my thing has long been cured of its ability to have erections. I beg for it harder and harder so perhaps I can outrun it, but like my shadow, it is always next to me. It follows me.

As I hang from the gray bars, swaying, wet, and throbbing, I recognize the scent from earlier as blood. His switchblade at my crotch slices like I begged him, to try and help save me. One hand caressing, one hand cutting.

I remember when I saw Peter Pan when I was little. After all the other kids wanted to reenact the battles of the lost boys, pirates, and Indians, all I could think about was the part where Peter Pan sits still while Wendy takes a sharp needle and, with concern and maybe love, sews his shadow onto his feet. And I wonder if the pain excited him as much as it excited me to watch.

I hang here, the voices still bleeding in my ears. I watch my shadow, solid like a murdered body's outline, and I pray. Maybe one more slice, just one more, will sever it forever.

Other JT LeRoy
Stories

Balloons

It was something I always knew. Heroin coming in balloons was a special message to me, that heroin comes in balloons. The Mexicans keep it in their mouths, little knotted balloons, spit it into your hand if you're for real, swallow it if you're a cop. Crayon used to joke that I bought the heroin just for the damned balloon, 'cause I never cut the balloon, only if I'm on a run and getting sick. But even then I feel like this guy in some movie I saw where he slices open his loyal dog and puts his hands in it just to keep warm.

I sit there and pick at the knot on the balloon, drive anyone with me crazy waitin' for me, but they know better than to snatch it from me and rip it open.

I save all the balloons. I save them because the truth is I do buy for the balloons. Yeah, I smoke, shoot, the dark tarry clump inside. I have to do that; like buying baseball cards, you gotta chew the crappy gum that comes with them. But the balloons are the only thing that's really going to save me, and they know it and I know it.

I keep them hidden in a cigar box under some bushes in Golden Gate Park. As soon as I get 10 balloons, I dig up the box and carefully place the new ones inside. I like sitting alone, in

the silence of the park at night, shining my flashlight on my collection. I bury my face in their sticky, damp hollow bodies and
inhale their rubbery glue-like scent, then I lie on the grass with
the torn balloons that were my mother's draped over my closed
eyelids like coins on a dead person, and I'm so comforted and
soothed, I drift right to sleep.

One Mexican on 16th and Valencia sold for-crap smack, but
he had Day-Glo silver balloons, so I bought from him instead of
the Mexican with good-deal in black balloons.

No one knows about my collection, and I won't tell until The
Time. I've had my plan forever, and I can't just go buy balloons;
they have to be special magic balloons, baptized by saliva, made
holy by the fear of getting busted with them, and transformed to
the sacred by all the desires floating in the tension surrounding
them. Our sweat, our fear, and my love. In my box I still have
some of the red balloons my mother would slash apart with her
long red nails. When I would try to open them my way, picking
the knot apart slowly, she'd scream for me to fill up the goddamn
works or she'd die, and I'd slash 'em open too. But one day I knew
I'd buy my own balloons.

I go to sleep at night and dream of my balloons; I try to decide
how many I will need. I put my hands between my legs and rub
where it feels good, and I imagine them filling the sky, as they
will, like a leaking gumball machine in heaven.

The heroin inside, to tell you the God's honest truth, is just to
tide me over until it is The Time. It will be a clear day, no clouds,
no wind, just blue buttermilk sky. Crowds will gather, smiling
and joyous. A clown with oversized shoes with yellow pompoms
on the ends will breathe life into my balloons with helium-filled
red lips. People will surround me and slowly attach one filled
balloon after another—my silvers, my blues, my greens, my
yellows, tying them to my outstretched arms and legs. I will an-

nounce to them all that it is finally The Time. They will cry and tell me they will miss me, but they know this is a miracle—this is the plan, as it always has been and must be.

I feel myself getting lighter as branches of balloons spring from every limb. I tell them not to cry; I must rise for their sins. I am the Lord's outcast and will face him for all outcasts. I will refuse to leave heaven, and I will offer up the black heroin I once hid from my mother and wouldn't return to her, even as her fists beat against me, even as she lay shaking and sweating, howling like a trapped fox, and I sat, ignoring her, watching TV. The sacrifice of my gift shall cause Jesus to weep at my feet. I can barely feel the ground, and with one more dark red balloon—repaired from my mother's fingernails—I am released. I fly like I do in my dreams, the cheers below becoming distant, up into the blue, up to God and Jesus . . .

I am the Holy Ghost coming for their redemption, whether they like it or not. This is the plan and always has been, since I saw it done years ago on TV, on 'Sesame Street'—a little boy lovingly encased by balloons, flying out from the cheers below, while his absent mother dies somewhere below.

The Astounding
Flying Scarberryies

The shafts of sunrise reflect off the truck's chrome into blazing flashes pitching through my hidden nest in the scrub and serving as a laser beam of sorts, burning through the sleep glue of my sealed lids. The night voices of the lot are tenuously rasping and easily overtaken by the newly minted daybreak assertions of truck lot commerce. Like an army awaiting the dawn to attack, the shrubs encircling the lot begin to morph to human forms, a leg sprouting here, an arm poking there, as the economy of the lot rotates with the earth. Mourning cloak butterflies tremble off the spirited bushes, their dark maroon wings pumping in the air like congealed blood suddenly made weightless. The thick leaded diesel smog fractures over the damp sweet grass scent as trucks make their escape before the morning assault.

I crawl quickly out my sleeping bag the six feet to the end of the hollowed-out scrub. I grab hold of a branch and lean out as far as I can without falling into a deep drainage ditch framed by a cracked muddied concrete embankment. I unzip my pants and pee quickly before the gaming begins. I still make a noble effort to hit the wall over the gully with what feels to me must be a strong current of torrential pee.

'What ya got a swarm of yellow jackets dribbin' down ya legs for?' Sheriden's laugh is sufficiently self-incriminating as to soothe any accidental wounding of egos.

I lean out toward Sheriden, his leathery face looking like an old cracked red rubber ball from a jacks game, squeezed up in all its concentrations on the concrete embankment wall.

'Naw son, you want to see a piss that shovels coal, you place your money on this one.'

'Sheriden, won't you put that tired old cod down for his mercy killin'?' Drasco leans out from the bush aside Sheriden and tips the black shiny top hat perched atop a frosting wave of his shoulder length brown hair, barely allowing for his green eyes to poke out like rectangular sprinkles. 'I'd rather be herdin' cats than watch you flail that thing out in the all of doors!' He rolls up the flannel arms of his shirt and claps his hands like he's ready for a pitch.

'That ain't a no count thing to say to your elder.' Streetrodder peeps his alternately haggard and adolescent face from a thicket of laurel up the bank some. 'Sheriden done hit higher on that wall than you Drasco, last few weeks in a tow of rows!'

'Maybe when you take-up young'ens are better off pissin' in the brush and not walkin' before folks you'll a'stop losing your wages to me.' Drasco smiles and tips his cap.

'Well knock me down and steal my teeth why don't ya!' Drasco exclaims, his face a smooth mask of sly incredulity. 'Drema, you gonna do that count or you hoping to go Johnson picking later, mines about to freeze clear off the vine!' He wags his hips fast so it sounds like a basketball hitting the court.

'Tis true about that!' fellows say down thc line.

'I'm gonna do my count. I was just letting y'all have your little to do,' Drema's abrasive voice echoes through the brushwood holler. On the far end, she stands on a bridge of felled spruces piled up so thick they're as strong as any metal frame overpass. Drema's small body looks misleadingly available cast in the welcomingly overt flowers spattered across her mail-order housedress. The fog reveals her in segmented veils, making it seem as if thick microscope slides were being pulled back and forth across her.

'Oh, it's gonna be runnin' like a sugar tree from what I drank of last night,' Streetrodder says warming up his pelvis, tapered, flat and vaguely green like Gumby's.

I lean out towards Sheriden's bush. 'I almost hit the wall,' I whisper to him. He squeezes off a fast wink with his sleepy lids, then narrows his eyes even smaller towards the wall five feet in front of him. If it weren't for the peek of disquieting white blues of his eyes, you wouldn't suspect he could still see a God darned thing.

'Had me some of Indian Peach mountain dew!' Streetrodder boasts licking his cracked lips.

'Briggity Britches ain't ya?' Sheriden says without turning from his focus in front of him, his legs bounce in a half-squat gunfighter style. 'But sweet peach shine aren't givin' you but a peach fuzz piss.'

'On yer set . . .' Drema sings out. 'Give her mark—' All the men take a deep breath and lean their hips forward. 'Get Go!'

And with that, huge semicircles of urine arc high through the heavens with a good number splattering against the concrete side with the force of a thrown china dish.

'Great day in the morning!' Sheriden calls out after seeing his pee mark, as usual, blacken a good three feet higher on the wall than anyone close.

'Not so quick on that!' Drasco yells out while flogging urine drops with an irate vigor from his member. 'Have you a look see yan side!' He stuffs himself away and points with both arms at some dripping spray on the side of the wall across from his perch.

'Durn Drasco!' Drema shouts out. 'Your watercourse is all turkey tails out, what didn't ya hit, except Sheriden's set point, bless your young heart!'

Covert laughter disperses from the hollow, quickly transforming to clearing of throats and the quick rip of zippers being yanked along their task, as Drasco leans out trying to catch any faces that might be caught mocking him.

'That there!' With a sporadically sinewy arm looking like a clown's balloon, untwisted into little bubbles from its former shape of perhaps a dog, he points to a dark spot on the wall. Branches all rustle as everyone inclines forward to look up at the small globule that hangs a good foot above Sheriden's utmost pee droplet.

Gasps echo around the gully.

'Drasco, if my eyes do not deceive me, I do think you got a squirt higher!' Drema stomps and swipes her leg as if she were to bust out square dancing.

Drasco tips his hat towards her and pulls his smile in high and tight so the deep sockets of dimples hollow out like a snake charmer's pit.

'Drasco, I do might've think you a'had yourself the winning urination of the day!' She claps her hands like an amused child.

I look over at Sheriden, trying to prod his hefty lids up in disbelief, like a sleepwalker trying to come to. And before I am aware my mouth has even spoken, I shout out, ''twant nothin' but a buckshot!'

'Mind you,' Drasco hisses in a crouching voice to me.

'What'd you say thare?' Drema motions like she's trying to swim through the fog to see me.

'You need to be put a good quietus on your behind,' Drasco snarls quietly.

Everyone's attention is turned toward me, even Sheriden has directed his vigilant gaze at me and despite Drasco's threat to punish me, my vocal cords keep propelling words out of my mouth.

'I saw him shoot buckshot,' I mumble into the silence of the gully. I'd seen him in the evening while everyone was still out drinking. I'd crawled into my bed early, tired from a day's full work. I heard the shot, sounded like an exploding tire down the embankment. I crawled over and I peeked out. I saw Drasco with his rifle. I figured he was hunting coons. They can make as good a dinner as any and their penis bones been well known to help a feller in the love department. But I saw no coon or coyot' or anything 'cept a smoking hole in the concrete. And before I could ask Drasco why he was shooting straight into a wall, he did it again. I heard him laughin' to himself. Figured he had himself a pint bottle company, and it's better to leave a man alone that's taken to shooting at concrete walls.

'Any plain could see that ain't no buckshot, why'd I shoot at a concete wall?' Drasco yells out.

'I agree Drasco, can't see why you would be wanting to shoot at no concrete wall,' Drema cocks her head like a hunting mutt. 'But it's been a questioned and if I don't check it out now, you win this pot, and later I hear it's but a buckshot, well, and I ain't saying yours, well, I might lose my officiating job and that's a whole lot of sweet tea I can't buy. Can't afford to let that lie on ya tender conscience. Somebody put a boy up there, I'll recompense ya for your troubles.'

And out of the bushes, tumbling up the brush, past Drema on her bridge, leaping to the other side of the gully, come some of The Astounding Flying Scarberryies. They were a renowned

Appalachian circus act known for soaring like flying squirrels using their hanging underarm skin the Scarberry clan was partial to. For generations they performed till Juliussen Scarberry, the patriarch of the family, lacking in substantial underarm drape so was more known for his crock-pot still that toured the circuit along with them, fed shine mash to the dancing elephants that as a consequence took to highstepping in the audience. Now the Scarberryies give exclusive engagements at truckstops and are the bravest roofers anywhere. The four youngins are up on the wall before anyone can blink. The mist dampens the Day-Glo yellow of their satin unitards, causing them to look like monstrous banana slugs as the elder Scarberry brothers clutch the smaller by the heels of their feet over the wall.

Everyone watches as their fingers work the spot like basket weavers. One of the boys pushes up on his arms and holds up the round BB. 'Buckshot!' His voice rings out clear.

Sheriden turns and nods at me and the pleasure I feel wash over me is swiftly doused by Drasco's pitching over to me, running his nails over the short stubble of his meager beard so it flutters like a pack of playing cards and uttering, 'We'll be talkin' at you.'

'Drasco, you takin' credit now for shootin' bullets out that thing?' Drema's arms wave like she was beset, but her voice betrayed a placid satirical tone.

Drasco brings out his dimples and tips his satin hat again. 'Thought t'was my mark,' he says grandly, pushing a grin. 'Boys, I'll pay ya for your trouble, and Sheriden,' he turns toward Sheriden's hedge, 'let me take your thirst from ya later, all ya come on too.'

Everyone cheers and branches ripple round the holler like a crowd doing the wave at a football game.

Sheriden swooshes his mouth. 'Drasco, you could throw a tub to a whale.'

'I'm a-callin' the rightful and most lauded urinator in these lands to get yourself here and take these winnings from me 'fore any more dramas of the day give me cause to go a'drownin' my heavies and out piss all and every last of ya!' Drema calls out.

And I look around at the mouths peeled back in laughter and I know not a soul has seen the silent gun Drasco crafts with his fingers in my direction, holds it low to his hips, and fires with the rapid see-sawing of his thumb in my general direction, and after he blows the invisible smoke off, half his face breaks in all its pre-ordained lines that run counter to wrinkles in a fast and intimate wink before his face disappears back into the thicket of Climbing Bittersweet.

I climb back in to the little domed room inside the brush, and fall on my sleeping bag. I try not to think, only to listen to the sounds of men pulling on their coveralls, heading to the spigots with their cans of Red Devil Lye to make their cleaning solutions for the day. I hear Sheriden's measured saunter through the dust outside on his way to claim his prize loot. And as soon as Sheriden's past I locate the slicing click Drasco's boots somehow always make, as if he were walking on hard mahogany instead of soft red dirt. The sound pauses outside my shift. I raise my head and watch his form, like a varying puzzle beyond the leaves. I hear him raise a match. My eyes go to the fallen leaves collected outside my pitching, near his shined black leather boots sculpted with yellow unbroken stitches looking like treacherous do not pass roadways. The boots rotate like a ballerina on a music box to face my hedge.

And there are the times you are stuck in an abandoned amusement park, in the fun house, and they've all been killed gruesomely, all of them, the friends that convinced you in the first place that spending the night in an abandoned fun house would be a valuable adventure. And they are all undeniably dead. Guts ripped out like spaghetti squash hanging upside down swinging in your face dead. And now the ogre is coming after you.

'What do you do?' She is leaning back in the comfort of the plush couch and the knowledge that she would unequivocally know what to do. Her thighs squeeze around the beer warming between them. Are you the type that curls up in horror, crafting a safety zone via the fetal position and scrunching of eyes? Or the sort that runs, runs no matter what injury. And fights when it is time to, when you cannot get away. To the death. 'What make are you?' Her skin gives way with a fleshy suction as she pulls the beer up. And as she sips, a seductive smile shadows her lips, as if you are a spy she must bewitch information from.

Then her laugh that follows your silence burns as hotly as your immobility in your dry throat. 'How can you be from me?' she says rolling her eyes, unpausing the VCR. And there on tape, the last survivor unfolds from her crouch to behead the creature in an acrobatic feat of violence that leaves you breathless.

The match tumbling down from his hand glints like light refracting from a mirror. And as the cone-shaped flame, small as a pilot light, pops up in the oil-soaked straw and vegetation, I pull the open sleeping bag over my body, zip it up tight and roll over into it. I watch upside down as the flames form a suddenly sprouted low grass line.

'My-my-my,' Drasco says quietly, squatting crossways to the fire. 'You see what a'caught out of here?'

She is still running, she's still out there, waiting her chance to rise like a wild beast and end him before he dispatches her.

Drasco's face wears the unplagued rage of a carved pumpkin. The smoky sweet perfume of charring hay-scented ferns seems like a useless appeasement against incineration, and so they release squiggly rescue plumes of white smoke like a peace pipe offering.

Firemen always come round the trailer parks and let the kids scamper across their trucks, try on oversized rubber boots, ring the big brass bell. And they always make you repeat, 'in a fire you drop and crawl out, in a fire you drop and crawl out, in a fire you drop and crawl out,' and then they scan all the small dirt-smeared faces, locking eyes, and raise their yellow raincoat sheathed arms to conduct the recital chorus of, 'YOU NEVER HIDE IN A CLOSET! YOU NEVER HIDE IN A CLOSET! YOU NEVER HIDE IN A CLOSET!' And all the kids disclaim their allegiance to closets. And then they strain their heads up to get patted by those thick, gloved hands that smell like old tires. And but two days later there is another mishap whilst producing a fine batch of kitchen crystal meth and the same fireman shouts, 'I told you ignorant sons of bitches not to hide in the goddamned closet!' as he lets slip the white sheet covering the charred black small bodies that were carried out of the shell of the trailer closet. 'When y'all ever goin' to listen?!' And as all the small heads bow down following the shrouded remains as they are wheeled into the ambulance, nobody ever explains to the fireman, hiding in the closet is a habit as hard to break as breathing. The closet is a world of safety and to undo that you need a whole heck of a lot more than a sticker promising deputy firefighter status.

And I am breathing the soothing oxygen of my sleeping bag closet as little nannyberries hanging low off my bush begin to turn black like chocolate chips. I reach up to pull the zipper to seal off the horrible tapping of the black boots that waver in the smoke like a tarmac road in a barren. And suddenly a hand reaches in from above and latches on to mine, pulling my arm along with the rest of me out of my bag like hair being tugged from a drain. I am towed up, through the bushes above the fire and into the startling morning. I see faces attentive to me with the low eyes reserved for the well-cooked as I am laid out on the ground. The fireman's chastisement echoes in my head, drowning out the moving mouths above me. Cold droplets of water from the sloshing buckets splatter on my face as men pass them over me to douse the fire.

I wait for the white sheet to be draped over me.

'How many times we tell you?' Drema's leaning over me, her watery red mouth looking like a twisted smile being upside down as it is. 'There ain't no smoking in them brushes! What you smokin' in there for?'

I turn my head to watch Sheriden standing over me putting a plug of Mail Pouch into his expanding cheek.

I don't feel any pain yet, but my limbs feel vague and faraway. I swallow the parched sootiness and manage, 'How burnt am I?'

'My lashes get more singed from chew!' I hear laughter from above me.

I raise my head confirming my body in all its un-blackened form. I drop my head, humiliated by my lack of combustion.

Drema leans her glowering face directly over mine as I stare off into the horizon of her set wave puff of hair, the shadings of dye looking like far off mountain ranges. She shakes her head over me. 'Ain't ya got no grace to give?'

'Thanks,' I sputter up to Sheriden. I cough, surprised the bit of smoke got to me as I realize it did now that I'm in fresh air.

Sheriden blinks at me, words finding their way out between chomps of chew, 'Drasco the one that was a'saving you!'

'With no thought to his own person getting burnt to a sapling!' Drema continues. 'Nor t'werent a grudge held for you costin' him the bet pool neither or you'd be blackened Corn Pone.'

'I don't get het up over that sorts,' Drasco's voice comes down at me, the silver tip of his boot touching cold on my ear. 'Just glad I shot an eyeball on it, as I saw him a'tossin' that match out, younglings don't know no better half times, bless they hearts.'

'Aint ya got no senses? We all coulda lost everything, not just youself,' Drema quakes the landscape of her tresses.

Against the side of my face, Drasco's boot swivels some as if he were snubbing out a butt. His shadow falls over Drema and covers me in its elliptical darkness. The smoke of the put out fire wafts over me and I choke again. Drema sucks her lips in disgust of me not offering up a proper apology.

I look to Sheriden but his Eeyore-like countenance sways like a bough at the lack of my remorse. And with all the man-hood I can summon I look into the shadows of Drasco's face. And there is no message of furtive wrath in his eyes as I had expected. His eyebrows, burgundy thick and uneven as a red-tailed hawk, lay drawn up as a theater curtain over the clear absinthe green self-possession of calm eyes. The thin track of his mouth is puffed in a Betty Boopish pucker. At first I think it is his trepidation that I will expose the truth of the fire that lets hold such an affable expression.

'Wilder than a plum orchard boar,' Drasco says and reaches his hand down to me. And I recognize with the astonishment one has when one discovers they are as easy to read as My First Bible, he knows of what sort I am. I will not rise up, a deathly screech emanating as I point at him like a pod person from *Invasion of the Body Snatchers*: 'Liar liar pants a'fire!' He knows an invisible zipper has crossed my lips as surely as he had ordered me to do so.

I reach my hand up and he closes his, smooth as striped tree bark from all the lye he's soaked in. He pulls me up hard to stand next to Drema. And with his heel he jabs my bare foot, and I know what it is meant to knock loose in me.

'I apologize for smokin' in the bushes,' I mumble, avoiding both their faces.

'Wall-eyed, can't even but look for ground worms,' Drema huffs, standing, brushing her hands hard as if the dirt of these dealings will never come clean.

'Yup,' Sheriden says and stuffs another wad of Pouch into his cheeks. I want him to disagree with me accepting a blame I should not own. I want him to state he can testify for the conscientious standing of my character and for the known fact that I do not char or smoke tobacco, he being the one that apprenticed me when I arrived at the Conduit Truck Stop just some time over a month ago.

I had set out with a driver to head to California, but being overly eager to prove my trustworthiness, that I would shell out my share of diesel and what not for incidentals, I showed him my little fold of cash from inside my boot. And I thought it was lovely he wanted to camp outside instead of sleeping in the cramped smelly insides of the cab. And I thought the cocoa he brought me back from the diner did have the distinct tang of burnt rubbing alcohol, but I thanked him for his trouble and drank it anyway. And when I woke up in the brush, way past noon, my hands holding my brains from slipping from betwixt my ears, it was to Sheriden leaning over me laughing with his rutabaga face, sniffing round me like an aardvark. 'You look a might youngin to be a'drinkin popskull!' He squatted down next to me. 'But maybe it'll learn ya for the next time.'

He only laughed his corroded warble, his mouth pulled back like a spongy red pepper as I raised my head to scour for my boots and the billfold in there.

'Yes, ya shoes is gone, and ya pockets turned out.' He squats down next to me. 'Now that explains the bust skull your highway cowboy bought up for y'all.' His face creases into its humored folds. I feel like a hand puppet as he slides his hands under my slicker and bends me up to sitting.

The vague memory of the astringent cocoa makes my mouth pucker and my stomach force up a dry heave.

Even though Sheriden's worn work boots are under my line of fire, he doesn't withdraw his feet, which strikes me as a sacrificial kindness I am grateful for. He reaches down his hand. 'After what with you drank, best you find ya feet right ons or like a new bore foal, you may never walks again!' He yanks me to standing. I am astounded to find I really can't seem to recall how exactly to walk. He hoists my limp arm around his shoulder and anchors his around my waist and under the low roof of the Rhododendron brush, he walks me like a loose strung marionette.

'I'll introduce to you as I am known myself as Sheriden,' he says, and takes hold of my floppy hand, which feels like a leaf that has yellowed and he is attempting to pluck off instead of shake. 'You at the Conduit Truck Stop.'

I nod my greetings and endeavor to tell him how I am off to California to find my momma. 'Well yee boots and notes done about rode out with ya ride onto the four lane, so you might think on staying for a dance or two.' Sheriden spits a big black bubbling glop like roofing tar. 'Have ya any skills about ya?'

I nod but then think better of enlightening him on my former proficiency as a lot lizard, and would like to shelve that as a skill that is best locked in the in-case-of-emergency-break-the-glass box. 'What ya skills?' he asks again as slowly the crackling electrical synapses reattach in my brain, finally guiding my ligaments on their motory course.

The only skill I can think of besides the unmentioned, is what I just know my mother must be doing and, from what everyone tells me, must too be my awaited fate. 'I can be famous in Hollywood.' But I don't need to finish the sentence to realize I just gave tongue to one of those things you say to yourself in bathroom mirrors, and you shucks folk when they tell it to you, but to say aloud is akin to being tricked into uttering the secret name of the bogeyman, unleashing the probable destruction of whatever fragile kingdom you may reside in.

'By godlings, that is an enviable skill!' Sheriden shakes back a long flowing multi-hued gray mane, like Moses in Technicolor. 'I should like to learn that skill.'

I look down at my dirt-caked socks and feel a heat rise in me.

'I've no skills,' I try to announce as strongly as I am able so he knows I am in on the joke.

We circle the small perimeter of the brush before his voice slides into a yodelish, 'Eeeehhh, I don't know.' He spits again and with a quick card-trick-like flip of his foot covers the mess like a cat. 'My Momma used to swook the cows with a voice fellas said she'd a'win the bank down in Nashville. But she ain't had a big-feelin' bone in her.' He rubs a raw knuckle between his teeth, 'Didn't think but the cows should get wind of her. Knowin' you got a patina to you is a skill not to be played with.' Sheriden looks at me, the skin around his eyes curling like split ends, he bows his head in an eloquent way that fills me with an unbridled current of hope.

Lattice

The come waits on his fingers in its gooey thick ropes. 'Why does it have to string like that? I mean I really think it has some invisible ligament in it. Must be a designated molecular thing.'

'I dunno man . . .' Mick strains his neck scanning the sparse room again. I admire how the worm-like muscles on his neck resemble the corded come draped over his fingers.

'I mean, don't you think come would be less a bitch to swallow if it just, like, splat out, more like piss?'

'Don't compare it to piss man.' He swivels his head in the other direction like a weather vane.

'I mean, it's not like piss. It has texture, like snot . . . It shouldn't, is what I'm saying.' I want to trace the cords on his neck, instead I reach for the cat's cradle of come held out in his fingers.

'Don't!' He pulls his hand away. 'Just don't. And don't compare it to snot either.'

'I fucked up.' I look down at the linoleum so worn it has the translucence of protective paper inside an old book. 'I shoulda just swallowed it man, I just . . .'

'Whatever. I don't care.' His eyes blink rapidly, as if a fist swooped too close to his face.

With his hand he makes a slow-motion movement as if he was going to fling the goo. 'I'm just sort of fucked now.'

'Just put it in the garbage, just use the roll there . . .' I point at the toilet paper on the three-legged table by the door.

'Look at the garbage, man. Remember what he said?' Mick points with his head to the small empty yellow plastic pail. In the dimness of the room I can see a few ants circling the rim, like sharks. 'He made a point of saying throw nothing in there. I put this in there and the ants will be over it like Twinkies, man. I don't want ants eating my fucking come anyway.'

From out in the hall, slamming doors, slurred Spanish cursing.

'I wanted to swallow. I wanted to.' I collapse on the floor. 'I just suddenly pictured the invisible adhesive in the come.'

'You're whacked man.' Mick looks up at the ceiling, the paint hanging down like shaved cheese.

I put my hand on the soft leather of his boot. 'It's not like I'm grossed out by it. Fuck, I've been eating that shit since I was like nine.' Under the leather I can feel the hard outline of the protective steel toe. 'I just suddenly realized the message in it.'

'Now you're fucking hearing voices in jizz, man?' He steps back so my hand falls away. 'Whatever, I gotta get this shit off!' He moves to wipe it on his shirt. I jump up and grab his hand.

'Don't! He'll fuck you up. It's silk.'

'Like I don't know that.' He pulls his arm away, but doesn't try to wipe it again.

'If Kamal comes back, sees come stains on the outfit he got you, he's gonna think you pulled a trick with some other pimp who marked you and he's gonna fuck you up.'

'We're locked in here! How the fuck could we have let someone in?'

Mick pushes at me with his forearm, shakes his shoulders in a tough swagger, but his eyes are blinking too fast again.

'If he's tweaking, he won't think of that, man. You know he can fucking smell come a mile away and if he don't, his Dober- man will.' I hold on to Mick's forearm.

'Bring me the toilet paper, man,' he motions. 'I'll just put it in my pocket.' With his elbow he pats the small slit at the top of his leather pants.

'He'll find it when he searches us for scamming on his hid- den stash, man.' On Mick's arm, my finger tips Braille along the tight raised punctures. I'm the only one Mick ever lets tie off and shoot him. I'm the only one that can hit it just right. And I'm the only one that knows that when it does hit he always puts his head on my chest and cries for his home.

'When he gets back, I'll just tell him I gotta piss and I'll run to the hall bathroom.'

'He'll think you're running to shoot. He'll search you first, you know that.'

Mick turns away from me, dropping my hands. 'This is stu- pid. Fucking stupid.' He goes over to the unmade futon on the floor.

'I'm just wiping it in these sheets.'

'Oh, like he won't find it there later.'

Mick stares at me, his eyes narrowing and opening like a cam- era on automatic focus. 'What do you want me to do, huh? You getting off on this or something?'

I let myself slide to the floor again. A sharp nail poking out of the linoleum digs into my legs. I don't move to avoid it. 'I gotta tell you something Mick.' I look up to see him staring at the locked door. 'I gotta say something.'

'Say it.' He doesn't look at me.

'I never charge more for a date . . . to let him not use a rub- ber.' Mick doesn't say anything. 'I can be sick and needing the money bad, but I don't. No matter how much they offer.'

'Good for you,' he says and turns to look at the ants scaling the garbage.

'But I do it, sometimes, without . . .' I move so the nail stabs into me more.

'He's gonna be back soon.'

'It's those threads in it, Mick. All those sperms, I know they string like that 'cause they're looking to grow into something more. Inside somebody, something permanent.'

'You're not a fucking girl. You don't got eggs.' He looks down at me. 'Try and remember that, right?' He squats down next to me, his hands out like a little boy stringing taffy. 'OK?'

'It doesn't matter Mick. It still sticks.' I lean toward him. He stands quickly. 'It holds inside me. At night when I sleep, I see them all . . .' I want to tell him how the come moves, releases from the web it's wrapped around my insides. A big toothpaste ringworm. 'It threads through me, and I see them all. All my mom's drunk boyfriends, tricks . . .'

'You're the one that wanted to suck me off . . .' I can see Mick's lip crushing under the bite of his teeth.

'It's the married ones, with their wallet fold-out pictures of their fucking kids . . . I always do it for them. They touch me like I'm their wife or their kid.'

'You are not their fucking wife. You're not their kid.' He stomps his boot close to me. 'They don't give a shit about you. And I can't believe you don't charge them more. You never give anything away for free, stupid . . .'

'See, I always thought it was enough. I mean just to have their come. Inside me, searching to create—'

'Fucking create what? You ain't gonna get pregnant any time soon, idiot!'

I close my eyes and can sense the streams of come floating inside me like phantom jellyfish held up under an ultraviolet light. 'But I realized, while I was sucking you, how I couldn't, I just couldn't . . .' I feel the words choking.

'You can swallow some fucking pedophile's come, but not mine. Not your best friend's. Whatever man.' He moves away and walks to the barred window, his webbed hands held out like burnt limbs.

I roll my eyes deep up till all I see are bursts of bruised light. 'I wanted it more than anything. You know that,' I whisper.

'Just shut up OK?' He turns to me. 'I'm jonezing too hard to think clear. I gotta figure out what the fuck to do.'

Mick abruptly starts to reach through the bars to the windows, then stops and turns to me. 'Open the window for me man, I'm just gonna fling this shit out, hit some lucky fucker in the face.' A bitter smile passes over his face. I watch his hands trembling like pages fluttering in a book. 'Open it!' He stomps.

'It's nailed shut,' I say calmly. I suddenly feel I could absorb his trembling into me, like a faith healer. 'Can I hold your hands?'

'What? This is not the fucking Girl Scouts!' Mick moves around the sparse room like a haunted house ghost. 'I don't want him beating me. I knew we never should've gone with Kamal. This was a bad idea. I just want to go out tonight, make his money, get fucked up and sleep. I don't want any shit.' Mick bangs his head against the black bars that look like an ornate monkey chain. 'Why'd I listen to you. I knew not to let you, knew you'd get fucked on me.'

I feel the air pushed out of me as if all the come strands have suddenly decided to choke my lungs. 'I'm sorry,' I push out.

Mick pushes off the bars and moves toward me, 'Let me suck you off . . .' Mick mimics me. 'You won't think about shooting . . .' He shakes his hips as if I hula danced at him. 'And when I'm getting my ass kicked by Kamal, I won't think about getting high either, was that the plan?'

'It can be like venom too,' I whisper.

'What? What are talking about?'

'If you get bit by a snake, you have to suck the poison out. Suck it, then spit, unless you want to take the venom in . . . you spit.'

'OK, next time I'm in the woods and a snake bites my ass, I'll know what to do. Thanks very much, you've been very helpful.'

'I'll clean you off,' I whisper.

'With what? He'll see or fucking radar the come on you too. With what?'

'My mouth . . . it's OK, I want to now.'

'It's OK? Now, it's OK? Fuck that! I'm gonna tell him the truth and if he thinks it was some other pimp Spidermanned in here, then let him whip me. I'll kick his ass back!' Mick makes an exaggerated punt with his skinny leg and looks so much like a little boy kicking stones I almost laugh. Mick catches my face and squares his thin shoulders but the rapid blinks betray him. 'I'm ready to quit his ass anyway. I can get my shit from that Mexican pimp. Fuck him! I don't really—' We both freeze hearing the familiar loud chirp-chirp of the car alarm being set from outside on the street.

'Fuck!' Mick shakes at the come on his hands.

I pull myself up, go over to him and grab his arms. 'Let me,' I whisper. I bring his hands to my lips and before he can say anything I place his fingers in my mouth and suck them clean. He says nothing, just turns his fingers inside the wetness of my mouth like a child washing off finger-paint.

We can hear Kamal in the hall, the heavy spiked chain of his Doberman clanging against the walls.

I finish swallowing and give Mick his hands back.

'You shoulda just swallowed before,' he says under his breath. 'I don't know why you had to fuck with me.' Mick turns toward the door and starts fixing his hair.

We listen as Kamal puts his keys in and unbolts the door. I watch Mick stiffen.

And as the yellowed fluorescent light from the hallway starts to spread into the room, I roll my eyes up tight.

'Ahh! Glad my bitches is still here! Now ain't you glad I kept you from getting all fucked up before you get your shit done,' Kamal says. I hear him moving over to Mick, patting him down, the Doberman sniffing along him.

'First date is waiting for you at the curb.' I hear Kamal slap Mick on the ass and push him toward the door.

As Kamal's hands frisk me and the cold wet nose of his dog plies over me, the ache inside me hits. I fold over gripping myself.

'Naw, naw, don't run that shit bitch. Your date is in the red Camry, get ya ass out.'

I open my eyes and force myself out into the hall. I catch a glimpse of Mick's boots turning the corner and disappearing down the stairs. I hold on to the wall as I feel the floating ligament of Mick's come drifting inside me, waiting to attach.

Trick Question

I didn't know where we were going as we drove through the park,
I just knew we were going somewhere that would be in black and
white. Even in old gangster films, dudes always get what's coming on gray dilapidated wooden docks that always catch the shadows of the angry surf surging in black and white beneath them.

Kamal says nothing to me, just hums along with the gospel
on his CD and nods his head yes, back and forth, more from
habit than actual agreement.

'Lordy lordy,' Kamal sings, barely moving his mouth while
patting the red leather steering wheel cover as if he were calming
an excited dog. I scrunch down in my seat to try to see my face in
the outside door mirror.

All I can see is my bruised mouth and trees.

'Park looks all spooky just drivin' through at night, huh?!'
I knock on my window with my knuckle.

'What?' He stares straight ahead.

'Uh, park's . . .'

'I'm listenin' to my music, do you mind?' He doesn't look
at me.

'Mmm, no . . . sorry.'

I try creeping my hand between my legs but everything there

is curled up into my guts and sitting there like a big lump of undissolved aspirin.

'Mehhersay-gee-sus,' Kamal sings out thunderously with the choir, making me jump.

'Amen,' I call back loudly.

'What?' He slaps the wheel.

'My grandfather's a preacher, see, and he says Jesus himself ordained him to . . .'

'Look, I don't give a fuck about your grand-mama or whoever the fuck!' He reaches toward the ashtray fast and jerks it open. I jump again. He pulls out a small plastic container. I watch him pour a bunch of Tic Tacs into his mouth and start grinding them down between his teeth.

'May I have one?'

Kamal shoots me a look. 'No, you may not have one.' He shakes his head. We sit in the silence of the music as the park moves past us.

'Umm . . . if that was a Certs . . . wintergreen, wintermint, ya know, it would spark, like, if ya bit into it.'

'What the fuck is wrong with you?' In a blur of his black and white Raiders jacket his arm flies out and his palm thuds on my forehead. My head bounces off the headrest. Getting hit on the head always makes me feel so retarded, like I'm that kid in 'Mask' and my skull is amazingly huge. It makes an embarrassing noise too, the thud—a smack or slap is way more sexy or sympathetic.

'OK, OK, sorry . . .' I adjust myself back into my seat. 'I just uhhh, thought you might wanna know, Certs are pretty more dangerous—Retsin, I mean, what's that? You gotta wonder, so I agree with you, Tic Tacs are probably . . .'

His hand swings out again and I snap my head back before he even gets to smack it. He pauses a second like a video game with a glitch, and then knocks my forehead so it bounces on the headrest again as if we were playing handball with my skull.

If you're a black and white gangster you never cough up blood no matter how many blasts you take. You can even sit up and say some cool shit like 'Top of the world Ma!' or 'You got me copper!' But if it's in color then you always vomit blood and your guts up. I inspect the car dash for the black and white switch.

'Tic Tacs probably safer,' I whisper, and a slap flies across my mouth backhanded. The choir sings His praises, 'Joy, joy, joy,' way too loudly. 'Joy, joy, joy.'

I turn to the window and watch the trees, looking like a forest in the dark, watching me. I lick at the blood around my mouth. When I'm living in the park the trees are my turrets, surrounding my castle penthouse, they are my bodyguards to disappear into. I don't feel afraid at night even if I am alone.

Suddenly BOOM! Glass shatters and sprays all over. Broken mirror-type shards splinter into his eyes, exploding them like Pop Rocks. A huge wooden spear suddenly descends, stabbing through Kamal's guts just like in *The Omen* when this priest ac-quires a flying tree bough sliced through him diagonally. My trees stoop down before me, helping me out, their leaves apologeti-cally sweeping the glittering glass chunks off me. I turn to watch Kamal projectile vomiting bloody intestines and crap while long bony branch limbs pull him out and I hear it—CHOMP. His legs kick helpless in the air, CHOMP, CHOMP!

'This is my park!' I scream as the trees eat him.

We drive on, the trees only making distorted darker shadows that reflect me more back in the car window. I keep wiping at the blood trickling down my chin in brilliant color and I watch as the trees open and the road spills out past the old windmills to the beach. I know I should be hearing my heartbeat, like in all those movies; at times like these, that's what's supposed to happen. But all I hear is the frenzied gospel of witnessing, singing it, crying it, screaming it, fast organ keeping pace like a hardcore punk song, all his glories coming together. I've been there, felt the certainty of His spirit. Even if you hold the viper cradled in your arms the devil will not bite, for your faith in HIS strength are beyond all fear and reproach.

I feel calm as we drive along the deserted stretch of beach and park overlooking Ocean Beach.

'Get out.' He unclicks the door. I know he carries a gun — Mick's seen it. I watch for it in the outline of Kamal's Raiders parka. 'Come on.' He's ahead of me, down the concrete sandy stairs leading onto the beach. Now my heart beats; I can feel and hear it and it seems like the appropriate soundtrack so I don't try to turn it off.

It's cold and my sweatshirt is wet with fog and sweat. I'm shaking and I feel the sand filling in my boots. I follow him closer and closer toward the ocean that's struggling to gobble up the sand, only to give up, slide back into itself, crash again, doomed to repeat it over and over.

I'm following him when I should be screaming for help or mercy, but there's just the smush, smush sound of us walking. I've heard about the shit he's done, the pimp special — heated wire-hanger beatings and all. There's this wax museum on Fisherman's Wharf and it's got all the tortures ever invented, the obvious ones like getting baked alive, and the real intriguing stuff like boiling lead poured down your throat, or the mummy case full of nails and they close the spiked doors and they meet each other through you. My favorite is this contraption they put around your neck which forces your chin straight up until finally your head just tumbles off under its own weight.

And as we walk through the dark toward the water, I can't

help thinking of all the time and energy people spent coming up with new and improved ways to torture, and the fact that people actually went through it, got tortured in all the wax museum ways and died—they died! They didn't get to survive and be on *Oprah*, they died and it was horrible and now all anyone cares about is seeing the machines invented to do it. I spent $5, I just had to go in, and I started wondering what it would be like to be the one pouring the hot lead or closing the nailed casket door. I wanted to know and I have, I have—I kicked and kicked. He was down covering his head, crying. 'Mothafuckin' faggot cocksucking faggot!' My feet jerked with my whole body, searching out the soft belly which my boot would just bounce off of. And I couldn't stop. I didn't want to, the more he begged the harder I slammed and screamed at him, 'You wanna fuck little boys! Fuck this bitch!' I screamed at him until Mick and Goatboy grabbed me. They had to pull me away shaking and sweating and laughing, proud and pissed at the bloodstains on my boots.

He stops walking at the ocean's edge, and I nearly crash into him. There's no moon, and the dim streetlights don't carry out here. Under the wind blowing in my ears and the ocean waves crashing, I think I can still hear the gospel choir from the car, begging and crying to Jesus, to Him, 'How much you own me.' I can see the whites of his eyes, he's staring right at me. Goatboy says Kamal's the fucking IRS, knows how much you should be making, down to the tips.

'I bought a jacket, that's all, I swear!' I cross my legs to fight the overwhelming urge to piss.

'How much?'

'$215.' I bounce in the sand.

'Plus what?' His hand tap-slaps against his leg impatiently.

'A few balloons.' There is too much saliva in my mouth and I keep having to swallow.

'So how much.' His voice is flat and calm.

'$300 tops! I swear on Him!' Then I hear it—pulled out from behind and under the jacket. I watch in slow motion and shadows. I recognize that click-cocked cold steel pressing on my forehead, and I feel it wet, warm and terrifying, sliding down my jeans leg. I can hear it drizzling like maple syrup in the sand.

And I am surprised I feel tears sliding down my face. I see the smile of his gold-rimmed teeth, Tic Tacs moving in the dark cave of his mouth, and he laughs.

'Please, I swear . . . I'll never . . .'

'You been showboating on my ass.'

'No, I, I . . .' My throat is doing convulsions and I keep hiccupping and burping.

'You playin' me muthafucker.' I feel the gunpoint slide across my forehead.

How did all the people beg that were placed on the rack or in the iron maiden? Is there some plea that is so uniquely moving the torturer suddenly says, 'Oh, well, in that case, never mind'?

I remember when I first met Kamal, some trick was picking up boys, cutting them up, tying them, burning them, maybe even killing them. The rumors got worse every day. This one kid I vaguely knew, Clementine, wound up in a mental ward because this dude held him for days and fucked with him badly.

Kamal guaranteed—or your pain and suffering cheerfully refunded—only dates he knew. Plus he rented a few SRO hotel floors you could rent from him. It snowed with peeling paint and the floor crunched if you walked it at night from waterbugs, but it felt safer than car tricking or going to a date's house. He got me a room that I shared with two others. It had a hot plate, a tiny fridge and a pet rat. The bathroom was in the hall, and usually clogged and flooded or filled with a junkie nodded out, works still stuck in his or her arm. I kept any valuables hidden in the park or at lockers at the bus terminal. Anything I left got snagged. If it wasn't too cold, the park smelled better.

Kamal was very friendly but businesslike—straight up and that's why everyone liked him. They were scared of him too, and I guess I liked that also. It was supposed to be just a business-type deal—no pimp crap, I was still an outlaw, worked for myself. But somehow that didn't happen. The rent kept going up, as well as the cost of the food in the fridge that I never really got my share of, the tab I had at the diner, and the cost of fake IDs or clothes Kamal bought me. Somehow it just started where I turned over all my money to him, because he was caring, keeping me from using too much, giving me only a little so I wouldn't OD. He was concerned and he'd compliment me, but he never had sex with me no matter how hard I tried. 'Chefs can't taste their own cookin',' he'd tell me. I worked harder than any of his boys, just to get those nods he would throw me. But then there was a new boy, younger and blonder than me. I didn't even get the nods any more. I had started stacking on him, holding back, and he didn't even seem to notice. I started tricking for drugs, a big Kamal no-no. I felt like the dog with a scratched nose from the half-open cans thrown into the yard. Can't even be bothered to take off the fucking lids.

So I bit back.

'I'm gonna blow your fucking brains out,' he says serenely.

What the fuck can you say to that except beg like fucking crazy—like that trick did to me—for mercy. And I had none in me, and I expect Jesus to have none for me and damn me straight to fucking hell.

I thought I'd be thinking about all kinds of shit, like in the movies the way your life flashes in front of you, but all I really can think about is the times I've sat numb on closed-lid toilets, scraping a razor blade across my wrist like a road grader, watching the vertical lines fill in darkly as I furrow through the translucent wrist flesh. And all the times I've run into traffic praying they will not be able to stop in time. All the times I've taken more money and let him leave the condom off. And here I am.

Just here in the sand, wet and crying with the sound turned off, completely wanting to live.

'Please!'

'Shut the fuck up!' The gun handle cracks sharply on my head and I almost fall over, but I am too afraid to even do that. I catch myself.

'Please, I'm sorry . . .' He pushes the gun back to my forehead as if he were decorating me with a bindi. I pant.

'Why should I not?!' Trick question. 'Who the fuck would care?' And I realize that is supposed to be the mercy they give you. It is the tormentor's way of anesthetizing. I sob and wait for the truth of his mercy to spread from my heart in a numbing freeze.

He gives a brief sarcastic laugh. I hear him uncock the gun and I see the flash as it disappears behind his back like a magician.

'Gimme your hand.'

'Huh?' Everything feels unreal, or more like I am in one of those dreams where I can control the outcome, I just need to will this to happen and I can't.

'Hand! Right hand, gimme.' I see his ring-festooned fingers demanding.

I sink down to the sand, my limbs deadened. I remember a game of falling off a swing, and She would reach her soft hand down. 'Give me your hand . . .' I would grab ahold of her hand and pop up into her arms.

I reach up my right arm. He takes my hand in both of his. He looks at me and pats my hand like I am a lost child. I wonder if my legs will let me pop up into his arms.

'Naw, you ain't gonna steal from me no more!' His voice is kind of singsong, like the preacher on his tape.

I nod like a dog wagging his tail.

'Oh, but you ain't gonna go saying you got over on me?' I hear his feet shifting in the sand.

My head jerks again but I am not sure if I should be nodding yes or no, so I just jerk it like an epileptic and hope he gets the drift. One of his hands moves to my wrist. I start to move my legs so he can pull me up. But like a bug leaf-hopping, his hand moves swiftly to my middle finger, and I feel it jerk out and back. It sounds like an eggshell cracked and torn apart—snap, snap. I fall back on the wet sand as far as his grip will let me. He still holds my hand. My eyes are clouded, my mouth is open and drool starts sliding out—no sound, just air trying to get in and out. His hand wraps around another finger and we wait. There is only the sky low with smeared cotton fog to stare up into. 'No, you sure won't,' he says and again, like he is working a slot machine, he jerks out and back—pop, pop.

I howl out and start throwing up. He nimbly steps out of the way. He still has my hand and strokes it gently like I am a virgin date. And finally I find words, it is the automatic core supplication of the hustler. Not 'Please!' or 'Help!' or even 'Mercy!' It is, 'OK, OK, OK!' My voice is so low and deep inside me I don't recognize it.

'You ain't gonna show on me now, are you?'

'OK, OK, OK!'

'Well, I've left you something to show off case you still havin' the feelin'.' He lets go of my hand and it just drops, hitting the beach sand, and bounces.

'Go to the clinic in the morning,' he says in a dead tone. He turns, adding over his shoulder, 'And you're lucky muthahfucker—but luck runs out!' My hand is an ornament hanging on my body, connected only by a string of blinking Christmas lights, shooting a steady throb up and down my arm. I sit on my knees and watch Kamal's black outline walking back to the car.

'Come back!' I scream, before I know I have. 'Come the fuck back!' My heart is racing so hard it hurts in my ears. He keeps walking. I hit the sand with my other fist. 'You're not done yet . . . come back!!!' I yell so hard my voice cracks painfully and snot flies out of my nose. 'You're not fucking done! It's not over already! You can't leave me!' I lean over my knees, bank the top of my head on the salty sand and shake my head back and forth. 'I'm still . . .' I moan into the hollow between my knees, and wipe some snotty tears against my sweatshirt shoulder. I raise my head and watch the lights of his car moving away.

'You didn't do your job!' I scream. 'You were supposed to fix me you stupid fucking bitch!' I fall backwards and the sand depresses around me, looking like a black snow angel. I stare up at the sky, a murky wipe of mashed potatoes, my blood and the ocean roaring.

I turn my head, trying to stop the tears from sliding down into my ears, and knock my head against the soggy sand. 'It was my . . .' I roll my head and stare at the ocean rocking the earth back and forth, back and forth. I extend my left hand and it slowly disappears under the incoming soapsuds surf until all it looks like is a mannequin's arm with a clean cut wrist. I twist my head to locate my throbbing right hand. It lies up and away from me, a crumpled bird, slingshot down and mangled. I focus past my fallen hand, beyond the beach to the start of the park. I can see the tops of the windmill sails that never spin any more, circled and protected by thick treetops. I can make out the wind sound slicing around the frozen sails that look more like over-sized spatulas, and the treetops like big globs of chocolate Jell-O, quivering to be scooped up and flung someplace far away.

The voices of the church choir are inside it all, chanting in Latin, like in *The Omen* when the demon child has survived his father's attempt to murder him, and all that's left is the certainty of destruction and death the little boy will bring. And he smiles bitterly, as I do now and listen to the voices chanting louder and louder. I close my eyes until he appears above me, in black and white. He stands in thick black buckled boots and a trench coat, calf high and the bottom part soaked black like a paper towel drinking up an ink spill. I squeeze my eyes up at him and blink, but his face is a hazy shadow under his old gangster hat.

He tips his hat and turns away.

'How much more?' I yell out, but he keeps going until he dissolves. I roll over onto my back and stare straight up. 'How much?' I whisper. 'How much until I'm saved?' I close my eyes and listen to the choir drowning under the waves.

Oliver

'They killed themselves all over your glass!' I yank the muslin curtain back to cover the window so he can't see.

'What?!' I hear his zipper jerk curtly in its tracks. He leans over me to get at the window. I am half over his desk, a wide plank resting on beige filing cabinets. The window is past his computer on the desk, edged by stacks of fraying old hardcovered books, the kind that are always in the half-off pile when an antique store closes.

'Didn't you hear the thuds?' I tunnel my left hand through a small space in the books, around the side of his computer monitor to the hem of the curtain. My face is pressed in the crushed-apple-seed scent of the particleboard in front of his keyboard, my right arm extended around the other side of his monitor. I can see myself in the black mirrorlike screen—a boy wonder, ready to fly away with his computer. I lean into my hands pressing them parallel, holding down his curtain so he can't easily lift it. Like straws my hands draw up the chill from the glass; the curtain beneath them is cold too and no insulation. He hoists himself over me, sucking his stomach up into a partial fetal position so his skin won't be forced to touch my back. I expand my torso the way a frog does its cheeks as he moves over me, curves himself higher above me and tries to snatch a portion of the drape from me. His chest refuses to make contact with me no matter how high I press up. The warmth of his body presses down on me like a blanket hovercraft, making the draft streaming in from the window frame all the more menacing.

I flatten the sheet under my palms, as if laying a print in cement so he can't lift it. As he tries one more time to get past me a pile of books crashes off. He lets out a disgusted grunt and backs away from me.

'You knocked them over, not me.' I look over my shoulder, he is shaking his head—a private note to himself, the swearing off a gambler makes, accepting he must now leave the table and never return. His jaw is set in bony resolve; all around his eyes the cheese strings of muscle plunge out in fine threads like twine on an overbound newspaper.

I elongate the window drape, make a quick peek, a mocking eyelash flicker, 'Oh, guts and blood are just oozing all over!' My voice takes on an extravagant tease.

He lunges swiftly over me, surprising me, like a jump-the-eight-ball trick. As he reaches an edge of the curtain I arch my back up, squishing it into his chest, slapping together a disassembled Oreo.

'Argh!' he grunts but still pulls up the curtain, snatching it out of my hands, and I let out a victorious snicker despite myself. I aim my chin at the rows of rectangular windows across the street, now exposed. 'They might see!' I taunt. Whenever I enter his apartment, he checks the curtains to make sure they're drawn, as if they could have been caught up on his dust-covered rubber-tree plant without his noticing; he even pats down the edges. He's careful and firm in this, as he is in everything, like tapping at a hypodermic to eliminate the bubbles.

The russet leaves are plastered to the window glass like decoupage. He splays out the curtain as if he were throwing a tablecloth, and I quickly contract my spine tighter up against him—I want him to notice the contrast of my body warmth and the abandoned gum between us. He swats the curtain down, against the possible spying eyes across the street, pressing it tighter as if those eyeballs had wings. I imagine flying eyeballs smashing against the glass, their wide black pupils leering in as they slide down the pane. I wish I had told him there were smashed eyeballs on his window glass instead of dead birds.

'There is nothing on my window,' he says beneath his breath, still above me. 'Birds have never and did not fly into my window.'

'Oh!' I say with shock. 'I swore there were.' I stare down at my hands, which look like camouflaged mushrooms growing on his desk. I want him to notice too how they just fit, necessary additions to the taupe stapler, the mosaic mash of colored files. Dirt maps the creases in my hands—two more of the crumpled sheaves of unbleached paper littering his desk. His palms are outside mine. His hands are pinker and smooth, like the inside of washed dog ear. If I spread my pinkies they will hit his thumbs. Instead I reach for a pack of green thumbtacks and plant them in the plank between my fingers as if tacking down a buffalo skin.

'They should stay here.' I turn my head and whisper it up into his chest.

'Let's not start that crap again.' His hands give a little push-up and he rises off of me. 'Urgh.' I hear him tearing off paper towels, scrunching them, wiping himself up. I don't move. I hear him finishing his zipper, latching his belt though I know he'll pull it off as soon as I am gone. 'Clean yourself off and let's go. Tomorrow is a school day.'

He clears his throat fast after he says that last line. I picture TVs switched off, pajamas laid out, pillows fluffed. 'Did I do my homework?' I want to sound sarcastic, but my voice catches.

I look down at the forest floor of his desk. He doesn't respond so I glance over my shoulder at him. I try to figure out what makes his face look like hardened wax, layers of it escaping and settling over one another. It's not fat—his face has the taut pull of a trampoline—it's the working of the facial muscles, which visibly skim over each other like the Earth's plates with every grimace he makes.

He splutters a detached sigh, 'I've got to teach tomorrow,' and shears the paper towels between their perforations. He draws a wad up my back.

'I can help you clean the windows.' I reach around and grab the paper towel ball sticking to my back.

'Are you on acid?' I hear him pulling on his undershirt. He knows I steal them. 'Come on.' He claps his hands to hush his class. It makes me jump. He sweetens his tone. 'I need you to go.' He reaches alongside me and the fine hairs on my arm magnetize toward him. He picks up his glasses, frail quarter-size lenses threaded like jewels on a silver wire. I wish I'd hid them. 'I've got to get up in the morning.'

I crumple the paper towels tight in my hand and toss them on his keyboard. Green tacks trace a vague outline of my hand. He clears his throat again as I stand. 'It's really fuckin' cold out . . .' I ignore my clothes, which he's dropped on the swivel chair next to the desk. I bend my knee on it and pivot my hips with its sway.

'There's enough there,' he says heading off to the bathroom, 'for you to get a hotel room.' I look at the money on his desk, next to my clothes.

'C'mon man, I was so good tonight. I memorized so much!' I whip the chair with my shirt. Dust jumps off the upholstery in a blue mushroom cloud.

'You could've done better,' he says from the bathroom. 'Next week. Read another chapter. Prepare.'

I squint my eyes at his closed bedroom door as if it were a gunslinger challenging me. I know it is locked. I know where he hides the key. On a peeling beige shelf over the kitchen sink, behind a knoll of dusty coffee grinds, there is a track of fingerprints, like a trail in the snow surrounding a cabin, and an upside-down mug. I looked under there once when he was in the bathroom and there it was. I used it once too, though I knew I could pick his bedroom lock in two seconds with my jimmy card. It was the only occasion he left me alone in his apartment, when he'd forgotten to move his car. He made me swear not to touch anything. Not to answer the phone. Or the door. I crossed my heart and didn't even wait till he was done locking the front door to retrieve the key. I purposefully left my fingerprints too, smaller plowed streaks next to his sinkhole lunges.

I picture his plaid comforter, with its leak of cotton stuffing hanging like foam from a dog's mouth, kicked off into a candy-cane-ribbon twist on his futon. I could tell he never converted it back into a couch from the mound of splayed and dusty books that lay beneath it like escaped pine cones in the shag pile of brown rug. I was pleased there were no condoms. I reached into my back pocket, pulled one out. I ripped it open and lay its shed snakeskin under the overhang of the bed, visible to any others sniffing for markings. I threw the condom's gold wrapper under too, closer to the pillow, where in the heat of a passion it might've been disregarded. I tore off a limb of the dying cactus on his nightstand and put it under his pillow.

He never said anything about me having been in his bedroom. He didn't even move the key.

'What are you talkin' about? I did the same work your fuckin' students did, right? You said we would go over my work . . .'

He swings the bathroom door closed, allowing the craggy

hinges to speak for him, but then thinks better of leaving me out of earshot; the squeak of the door reopening is too palpable in its slowed motion, like a three-year-old trying to be sneaky. 'So when are you goin' to look at my work?' I shout out.

The cavernous echo of his pee stream drowns me.

I walk to the window next to his small dining table, covered in more books. I pull back the curtain and stare at the windows across the street. Not one light is on. Everyone is tucked in tight. Like all his students are. The telephone lines are rigid the way they are when iced. His radiator knocks out the Morse code message of warmth, banging its way up. I like the smell of it, like a grimy burning orange.

The toilet flush is followed by the muted thud of its lid slamming down on its padded seat. I flutter the curtain so it is hooked on his rubber plant. I wiggle my hips in front of the darkened windows and wave my hands at my invisible audience.

'Put your clothes on now,' he says from the bathroom with one of those practiced tones that sound like shouts even though the voice is barely raised. I will know I am an adult when I can see through walls.

His vigorous, foamy teeth-scrubbing is punctuated by bullet-like spits. He never notices when I wipe up the white splats of regurgitated paste from the basin. Or if he does he doesn't acknowledge it. I yank up my underwear, my pants.

'Close that curtain!' I turn, he passes out of the bathroom without looking at me. I decide not to close the curtain. I do not have my adult superpowers yet, but I can still be deaf.

As I pull on my shirt I notice the hand. In the corner of his window, barely holding on to the glass, the fingers sliding down. 'Grab it!' I gasp and lunge for it.

'What are you . . . !'

All I can do is follow the kite-loop dance of the leaf falling and know it was a hand. There's no more catching. Once you've let go, you're just a witness.

'You're leaning out too far!'

I am leaning out the window, I don't remember opening it.

My shoulders are seized and pulled, the effect like a seat belt's on impact. I catch my balance and watch as he calmly lowers the window shut and replaces the curtain.

'I told you not to come here high.' His voice is so quiet I can barely make out what he is saying, but the irrevocability of his tone is familiar.

'I'm not.' I smile as sensibly as I can. My eyebrows knit in mimic of his. 'I just was, seein' . . . something.' He walks past me to the cavernous carved doorway of the foyer. His belt is buckled.

I spin to face him, but anchor myself with a hand on his desk.

'OK, OK, so when Brownlow says, "You can be for the good, or you can be for the bad . . ." ' His eyes roll up to examine the dusty light fixture. I feel as if his floor is made of thick cork. I gesticulate wildly with my hands, as if I were winding an old-time car. ' "Or you can be miserably in between . . ." is Dickens saying . . .' I watch his face. Nothing.

'I'm not doing this.' He folds up against a wall. His lack of movement only speeds my hands like gyros.

'We didn't go over everything. How am I gonna pass the fuckin' GED? You came before we got to!'

He sighs, exasperated, and starts to say something, then stops. I sit myself quickly in his desk chair. 'And what if I won't go . . .' I say, rotating slowly, letting the grin spread menacingly over my mouth while I stuff the money in my front pocket. I like the momentary look of panic that stiffens his body, but then he knows that, like a bear not eating dead stuff, I don't like to stay where

I am not wanted. He walks over to my jacket, hands it to me with the same tired sigh.

'Shoes. On.' He rakes my sneakers out to me with the side of his foot. 'Let's not go through this every time. It's getting old.' I take my jacket from the hook of his fingers and pull my sneakers on without undoing them. I follow him toward the door, then remember my books; I turn and move fast for his desk.

'Uh, uh, uh!' he calls as if to a toddler putting a found toy in his mouth.

'My fuckin' books!' I flutter it up toward him. He undoes his front door locks with angry snaps.

I halt on a white square of linoleum, three blacks and two whites away from the door. I put my notebook on top of my head and take slow regal steps, stopping at each square till I am standing on the last one. I turn to face him. 'King me.' I smirk and tip my head so the book slides off. He catches it.

'Yeah.' He tosses the book to me like a basketball pass and starts to shut the door.

'Next week as usual?' I hop back in, onto a white square. He doesn't answer. 'Am I where your students are?'

He is looking over my head, to the window. I feel a longing to swirl the gray-brown curls that wrap the wire of his glasses like grapevines. I remember my mother's thumbs setting waves in my hair. I reach up to touch his hair but he redirects my arm with a kung fu move and lowers it to my side. 'You need to leave.'

I step out into the hall but jar the door with a fast placement of my books in the frame. 'You're not gonna read what I wrote. You didn't ask to keep my notebook. You came faster than usual, you didn't finish reading . . .'

'Shhh!!!' He hushes me with his mouth, taking a sandwich bite of air.

'Yeah . . .' I whisper and crane my head conspiratorially around his hallway at the row of sealed apartment doors. 'Will you . . .'

'I'll read it.' He whispers back. He raises his eyebrows at me and I allow him to slide my notebook from my hands. 'It's very impressive work.' He leans on the door.

I return the pressure to keep it open. 'Better than Jacob, right?'

'Jacob?' His face goes wide, he goes slack on the door.

'You called me Jacob this week. Last week too. Am I, ya know, as smart as him?'

He nods slowly, rubbing his mouth with his wrist; his stubble makes a shuffling-cards sound. 'Yeah.' He moves his weight back on the door.

'That's what I thought.' I wedge my sneaker firmly into the space the books are prying open. White paint chips are still buried in the navy weave of the hallway rug from the last time my foot played doorjamb. He adds more of his weight, but I don't give any sign that it hurts. 'Tell me . . .' I mutter into the outside of the door. There are scratches and dents around the lock like slingshot misses.

'*Shhh!!!* My neighbors!' He gives the door a thrust. I wince but cram my foot further and more paint chips flake away from the doorframe.

'But you read some of what I wrote . . . So is it still . . .' I relax my head against the door, listening for his breath.

'Yes.' He takes in air but it sounds like a balloon deflating. 'Yes it is.' He stops pushing.

Relieved from the vise grip of the door, I prod and tap my foot like an impatient parent. 'So say it.'

'Your work is special,' he says too quickly, and adds in a whisper, 'Better than Jacob.'

'So they say.' I extract my foot and the books just as he reapplies his force. The door slams shut. I hear his muted swearing and emphatic pleas to get before his nosy neighbors call the police. I loiter just long enough to bug him, waving merrily at the small circular fish hole in the door opposite his. Its hatch dances back and forth with metallic clanks from inside. I don't wait for the elevator just in case the cops are fast tonight, though I know it is too cold for them to be outside, just sitting in their cars. The stairs are chilly and I wish I'd stolen his scarf.

I get outside and watch my breath fan out and reflect the constant yellow flashing of the traffic light. It is quiet like it snowed, but it never really snows in San Francisco. It never sticks. Snow would be too much of a relief, too soft, too coating.

I tuck the books inside my jacket and jam my hands in my jeans pockets. The money feels gritty and I am warmed by all its possibilities. I head to the boarded-up shop with the deep entranceway piled with bodies snuggled close like a fox den. Someone will be awake. Someone will have something warm to sell. I walk faster while replaying the last of the conversation. I mix it up with the other times he's said it. He used to say it all the time. I make it like that. He probably just takes it for granted that I know. Know what I really am. Like what he said.

On the Waterfront

We watched 'em from the safe sidewalks around Old First Church on Van Ness as they'd queue up outside, nervously bouncing, playing with their hair, trying to hide their braces but still proudly displaying their varsity football and cheerleading sweatshirts. They'd tap their feet excitedly to the rock 'n' roll blasting over the loudspeakers out onto the street. Sometimes we'd cross over to purposely parade past them. We'd turn our boombox way up and blast homemade punk tapes, our faces bared in sneers as they whispered and laughed at our gashed clothes. We'd hock up and spit a colorful mass too close to where they stood in line. 'Go home to Kansas!' Crayon would always shout, butting his multi-spiked mohawk at the dudes in frat jackets—who in return barked their advice that we bathe posthaste. As soon as the bouncer would joust toward us, we'd dash back to the neutral territory across the street.

And just as hyenas attack the most vulnerable with psychic precision, without ever verbalizing our strategy we'd charge past Hard Rock. That's when they'd walk out, swinging their shopping bags ballooned with souvenir sundae glasses and logo T-shirts to add to their collection, proclaiming to which Hard

Rock Cafes they'd completed their pilgrimage. This was their hegira to Mecca from Middle America.

After their meals they'd loiter outside, palpably laid-back, unabashedly air-guitaring and karaoking to Van Halen. It was a mystery to us, whatever it was that caused such a transformation from the stiff geeks waiting in line to the relaxed, sated vibe they exuded walking out—most were too young to be served alcohol, so we knew that unlike us, they weren't high. But the power had shifted. As they streamed past us to catch a cab back to their hotels, we'd lean toward them like trick poodles, licking our lips, leadingly inquiring if they could really fit those leftovers in their hotel fridge. It was hard not to admit how much we longed for the boringness of a home—or the ability to find elation in being a pane of glass away from an outfit that once belonged to Jimi Hendrix. Even the hardcore gutter punks who would never enter a youth shelter, no matter how wet and freezing the night, would come sniffing around for a bag of leftovers.

Once a year, however, we got our time inside. The Hard Rock Cafe feeds everyone who wants a Thanksgiving dinner with all the trimmings. All the Polk Street kids go, and no waiter ever says shit when we appear for seconds later in the day. There's a certain power that comes with sitting in those booths, armed with the comfort of not only being a customer but also of having an emotional connection to the culture—to memorabilia, to the past, to what we street kids try so hard to erase. We felt unease as we sat there, even though we knew we wouldn't be hit with a bill. We riffed on the Hard Rock name, telling ourselves how the other Hard Rock that would feed us is Alcatraz, if they were still open for business. We made jokes about how goofy it was, this crap in cases, this useless past on display. That was our parents' music blasting out of those speakers—what they'd find valuable, what they'd treasure, what they wouldn't throw out, unlike their children.

There are places in the city I wander through to feel a part of. I walk the strip along Jefferson down from Polk, to the Yellow Brick Road of silver spray-painted men that come alive robotically for a dollar, the bushman who lies in waiting to scare those meandering past. I follow behind families, and my skimpy hustler clothes match their inappropriate-to-our-weather tourist clothes. No one looks at me funny. I could be the insolent teenager of the Midwestern clan I am trailing. I tromp along the pier as they lean against the railings to be entertained by the sea lions. I lag at just the right pace as any embarrassed teen would with parents decked out in identical Alcatraz Escapee T-shirts, as they walk through an underpass leading to Pier 39.

Whenever I'm at Pier 39, it always feels as if I've entered the portal to Oz. It's a boardwalk, minus the lost menace of beachfront amusement parks or the mysterious manhandling bustle of carnivals. Despite the ubiquitous souvenir shops, there's a timeless sweetness to the place. I sit on a bench to take in the free juggling shows. I wait in line for the carousel with my unaware adopted family, and it isn't until I am asked for my ticket that I'm shocked into realizing the family I've adopted hasn't bought me one. I follow them into the arcade, to the ice-cream shop, to the otherworldliness of the Aquarium of the Bay. Every now and then they notice me shadowing them, and the father asks me loudly if I have a problem, or the mother nods quietly and buys me a cone with the rest of her brood.

I felt an unexpected excitement when I saw that the Hard Rock on Van Ness was moving to Pier 39. I go with my friends who are my family, and we ride the newly refurbished carousel and play skee-ball in the redone arcade. With hesitancy I enter the new Hard Rock—closer now to the Rock, as we once joked.

The waiters welcome me with the same affability they had when I came to eat for free on Thanksgiving, but I know they don't remember me. I relax into the world of comfort, and somehow I can appreciate the consequence of memorabilia in the stories we tell. I cry as I stand in front of Kurt Cobain's guitar while eating my sundae in the Hard Rock glass I will take home. I will wear my Alcatraz T-shirt. I know now what all these things mean. And as I watch the family that's not really my own pass through the turnstile for the Turbo Ride, I will whisper, 'Remember me.'

Stuff

I am high on an arrangement of cleaning solvents. All five of us are. We pooled our money to get a hotel room. It is a rare aligning of the supersensible regions when enough of us have the money and are willing to pass up buying a bag of heroin and chip in for a hotel room instead. Usually the concord has been brought about by a freezing wet spell that just won't let up, coinciding with a dearth of suitable street drugs.

Crayon is the only one who looks 18, is in possession of a credible driver's license and has the prized credit card a trick let him keep. It has a $100 spending limit on it, just enough to get us into this hotel room. It ain't fancy—they wouldn't think of trusting the folks who usually stay here with an honor bar, much less a bunch of scraggly street urchins like us. But it does have a 13-inch TV with HBO. After the one cleaning staff hauls off, Serenity uses Crayon's maxed-out credit card to jimmy into the supply closet. There, sitting in plastic buckets on the pressed wood shelves like croutons at Sizzler, are the cleaning solvents.

We sit on the floor, small brown paper bags sealed to our facial orifices as if we are in an airplane that did indeed run into a severe altitude problem.

We mean to mine this room for all the opulence it has to offer. All the bleach-scented threadbare towels, stained inflexible sheets, even the cellophane-entombed plastic cups, will come with us after we check out. We each, in turn, will push in the little silver lock in the doorknob of the bathroom door and take extensively long hot showers, which we aren't able to take at the youth shelters. 'Watch out world, I am an adolescent and there is a lock on this shower door!' is a phrase that is not bandied about in shelters. But, for now, we switch on the bolted-down TV, using the fastened-down remote, and go right away to HBO, for this, too, is a paid-for luxury, and we will use all of it—even if what we really crave the most is to collapse on a bed that is ours for the night, without any grownup rules or regulations, no fear of cops or social workers. For we all know that swindle. Sleep is the same as shooting drugs, as soon as you inject it, you nod, and next thing you know, it's over and you are out in the cold wet world again. Though a deep slumber is what we may really require, it's too painful to have this glorious opportunity wasted by being unconscious. We sit congregated around our TV. George Carlin is doing his 'A Place For My Stuff' routine. It's all about folks' stuff, how we all need to store our stuff, our lives are about accumulating stuff, then ya gotta get a bigger house to put all your stuff in.

I've heard it before; my mother had a trucker boyfriend who played Carlin tapes in his 18-wheeler as he drove. As Carlin spoke his outrage at our need to keep and store our stuff, the trucker announced with pride, 'I own all my dang stuff in this here truck!' My mother did not like being categorized as his 'owned stuff,' and at the very next truck stop, she took our bag of stuff, and we became minus items on his stuff list.

My sinuses feel Brillo-padded by the inhaled oven cleaner. I look though a pixilated haze at our backpacks spread out behind us. No one is very far from his stuff—by habit we've arranged it so if we pass out, we'll land on our stuff, we'll wake if anyone tries to steal any of our stuff. I watch Gotti rise for her turn to use the bathroom and realize none of us are insulted that she takes all her stuff with her. We all do the same. Carlin is saying, 'That's all you need in life, a little place for your stuff. That's all your house is: a place to keep your stuff. If you didn't have so much stuff, you wouldn't need a house. You could just walk around all the time.'

And man, I think, not having a house, living on the street, you kinda *become* stuff. You're the stuff folks have to walk over, you're stuff they have to deal with, have to move past without being guilted into digging out some change. And our stuff is the homeless problem stuff. Some shelters let you keep some stuff there, but they go through it. They throw some of your stuff out if they want. Cops always want to take your stuff. Believe me, privacy is not for the homeless.

But I have a secret.

There are lockers at the Transbay terminals. There are rows of wood benches, church pews, usually filled with homeless people sleeping off something. But at night, a lot of them never make it to a bench and travelers play body hopscotch to get to their Amtrak trains. I have a key with a plastic orange square on it, the color of a prison jumpsuit. I keep the key tied to my waist, so if anyone took my other stuff, they wouldn't get my key. In the beginning I moved my stuff to a new locker every day. They had time limits on storing stuff, and folks watched. Homeless folks watched, the occasional guard, and if it was too obvious you were storing your stuff, someone would bust in your locker and empty it for you.

One bitter cold day when there had been no convergence of money, I woke up in a shelter and could not swallow. I got up and I fell down. And then I woke up at General Hospital. And I tried to explain I had to get my stuff. I ripped at the tubes that ran into my arms until they had to tie my hands down. I screamed at them, I had to get my stuff!

'Your stuff will wait,' a doctor told me and inserted some stuff into my IV that made me not care about my stuff any more.

When I was released with a parting bag of stuff I was to keep swallowing, I headed to the Transbay. I knew my stuff wasn't going to be there. I knew I shouldn't even bother going.

George Carlin is saying, 'And when you leave your house, you gotta lock it up. Wouldn't want somebody to come by and take some of your stuff.'

I step over the bodies layered in their blacks and grays like a topography map on my way to my locker. It is still closed. My heart pounds. I unfurl the string holding my key from around my waist like a train engineer. I am on one of those game shows, I am seeing if my key fits, what stuff have I won? I slide it in, and I flick my wrist. It does not move. I've seen them, they come in their uniforms, they come and with a quick tug with shiny tools, they pull out the whole cylinder, change the lock, haul out the stuff inside. A new orange key is inserted, waiting for a proper owner. This one's new key is gone, so I know someone else's stuff is in there. Probably someone with a house who only stores peripheral stuff in the Transbay lockers. Someone who lives by Carlin's words, 'That's what your house is, a place to keep your stuff while you go out and get . . . more stuff!' I knock my head against the locker until I feel a hand on my shoulder. I spin around and the short woman in front of me holds out her heavy canvas-gloved hands.

'Whoa . . .' she says and makes a grip of her shielded fingers as if she were pulling back on reins. 'Whoa there.'

I know she is the one that confiscates stuff. I've seen her, gingerly emptying the lockers into garbage bags.

'Fuck off!' I shout into her face. I want to spit, but I also don't want to go to juvie, and I note in the corner of my eye that security is heading over at a rather non-leisurely pace. So I duck out of her reach and begin to sprint for the exit. 'Wait!' she yells out to me. I turn and give her the finger. I won't turn and show her my face, she saw it once, I won't give her the satisfaction of seeing it again. I wipe fast at my eyes.

'I have your stuff!' she calls out. I keep moving till the words sink in. I spin around. The guard is now behind her. Without looking at him she gives him a fast, low wave, as if she were shaking bangles. He steps back reluctantly. 'I have your stuff,' she repeats quietly. Some of the bums have hoisted themselves into a better position to observe the action. The commuters walk by with their hurried clip.

I clear my throat. It still hurts when I swallow and I think without the force of rage, it might not be able to produce words. I feel like the raccoons we watch them trap in the park at dawn. 'Come on baby . . . got some tasty stuff for you . . . come and get it . . .'

'Where . . . where is it?' My voice cracks. I tighten my grip on my plastic hospital bag that reads 'Personal Belongings' in bright blue.

She starts to walk toward me, I step back. She turns toward the guard behind her and says some words I can't hear. He nods and we both watch him walk away. She waves me over. I estimate the guard's distance versus mine. I judge it a mathematical equation that works out in my favor, so I stiffen my body and cautiously move toward the wall of lockers. She is holding something in her hand and at first I think she is going to play a game of guess which hand with me, but as I approach, she turns over her palm to display a key. This one has a red plastic square, the color of blood in a specimen tube.

'Where's my stuff?' I whisper to her, my eyes on the key resting in the middle of the blackened suede-like cloth of her glove.

'It's in the lower locker, at the end,' she points with her chin. 'Why you gotta make a scene? Take this.'

She holds the key out further and I peck it out fast, the way I've seen some of the park raccoons that have been around for a while do—they nab out the food from the side, without getting into the trap. 'What, you think I'm playing with you? I could get fired for this!' She frowns at me then follows it with a fast wink, which makes me confused as to how to answer. She reads my face and takes a quick breath. 'That's your key. Don't lose it. It won't need no money.' She turns and, just like that, walks away.

I watch her head through a huge, thick door marked for PERSONNEL ONLY. I examine the key and look around. The guard is busy nudging a seemingly lifeless body with his foot. I head straight to the bottom locker she pointed to and squat right in front of it. I don't know what I expect. I look around and no one is watching any more. All the homeless are prone again. The commuters are still rushing past me in a blur. I try to detach myself as I fit the key in, the way I do when the men hand me my money and start to undo my pants. The lock clicks, making little gulping noises, and with a faint metallic gasp, it opens for me. I sit in front of the locker and stare at the contents. There are all my notebooks, stacked neatly and tied with twine like how schoolboys carried their books in the olden days.

'I like your stuff,' the Transbay maintenance woman says from behind me. I don't respond. I just close the door of my locker and tie the key back around my waist.

She doesn't stop; the soft scuffle of her shoes travels past me. I lean back to watch her till she recedes into one of the cavernous rooms of the terminal. I slide my notebooks halfway out of the locker to shove into my Personal Belongings bag. I sit and stare at them frozen, as if I just ID'd a body in the morgue. I trace my fingertips along the careful bows she made on top of them. I turn and can see her vague form stuffing newspaper from the benches into the trash. I reach into my plastic bag and pull out two pages of stuff I wrote in the hospital and place it on top of the pile. I push it back in the locker, wrap the key round my ankle and slam the door. 'Don't touch my fuckin' stuff,' I whisper toward her, grab my bag and leave.

And now, after I've gotten clean and I have a bed to sleep in every night, and some of the stuff in the locker's actually been published, I keep meaning to go back. To tell her. To give her the letter I've typed. And somehow it's years before I do make it back there. I feel as obscured as I always did, among all those headed off, hurrying with purpose, stuff to do. I enter the overly lit building.

But the lockers are gone. I knock on the PERSONNEL ONLY door. I am told the lockers were torn out a year ago. The homeless are chased out now too. The terminal is not open all night any more. I describe her, but the personnel only shrug—everyone I ask, he shrugs. I go to where the lockers once were, now just a wider corridor. And like laying flowers at a plowed-over grave, I let fall my note to her. Telling her how my stuff is going to be published. Saying all I was unable to. I watch as the feet rumble by, trampling my note. Turning it black with footprints. As I walk out a Transbay employee is herding out a homeless woman. She reaches for her stuff from the worker, but he smiles brutally and tells her, 'This stuff is confiscated.' I imagine grabbing the bag from him and running with her into the street, but I keep walking. I keep walking and wish I had that key to give her.

Acknowledgments

My sincerest gratitude to all of the following:

My sisters of 465 Friendly Home for Girls, Akerman LLP, Irwin and Evelyn Albert and family, Jo-Jo Albert, Asia Argento, the Authors Guild and Jan Constantine, Amy Baker and Harper Perennial, Adrian Bartol, Julia Bernhardt, M.J. Bogatin, Will Brandt, Kurt Brungardt, Jose Luis Carreon-Macedo and Simple Cloud Works, Christelle de Castro, Lucas Celler, Godfrey Cheshire, Bill Clegg and the Clegg Agency, William Corgan, Deadwood Season 3, Justin Desmangles, Cheryl Edison, Judy Farkas, Grant Faulkner, Gina Forsythe, Leon Friedman, Uwe Gabel, Mary Gaitskill, Henny Garfunkel, Panagiotis Gianopoulos, Jane Gilday, Dr. Richard Glogau, Dr. Erica T. Goode, Carol Haas, Miranda Albert Haines, Chris Hanley and Muse Productions, Fayette Hauser, Laila Hayani, Sean Howell, Aïda Jones, Martha Keith, Todd Kessler, Noah Khoshbin, Julia Kim, Dr. Kevin Knopf, Dr. Josh Korman, Gretchen Koss, Katia Kulawick Assante, Kimberly Lau, Bruce LeRoy, Marie LeRoy (Vitalie), Jasmin Lim, Gary Lippman and Vera Szombathelyi, Paula Malcomson, Shirley Manson and Garbage, Maria Di Maruka, Tracy Marx, Beverly Mesch, David and Rita Milch and family, Andrew T. Miltenberg and Nesenoff Miltenberg Goddard Laskowitz, LLP,

Nancy Murdock, Dan F. Nicoletta, Lewis Nordan, Stella Okolue and the staff of 465 Friendly Home, Sharon Olds, Jess Owens and Jennifer Parkes and family, Dr. Terrence Owens, Levi Palmer, Diane Pernet and A Shaded View On Fashion, Barbara Petratos, Mike Potter, Carmelo Puglisi, Christine Rahimi, Nathaniel Rich, Karen Rinaldi, Noreen Ringlein, Lucinda Riva, Rudy Rivera, Roaring Mouse Cycles, Dr. Bruce Roberts and LightHearted Medicine, Mick Rock, Rock Point School, Joel Rose, Henry Rosenthal, Albert Sanchez, Karen Schulkin, Katrin Schumann, Johnny Silver, Smashing Pumpkins and Billy Corgan, Tom Spanbauer, Art Spiegelman, Michael Spring, Jerry Stahl, Jeff and Joan Stanford and family, The Stanford Inn Mendocino, Lauren Stauber, John Strausbaugh, Patti Sullivan and Jill Harris, Catherine Texier, Thomas Tillinghast and his vicious dogs, Joslin Van Arsdale, Gus Van Sant, Suzanne Vega, Eric S. Weinstein, Robert Wilson.

Special thanks to Nicole V. Gagné.

Love and gratitude to Donald David.

All my heart to Trevor Knoop.

ALSO BY JT LeROY

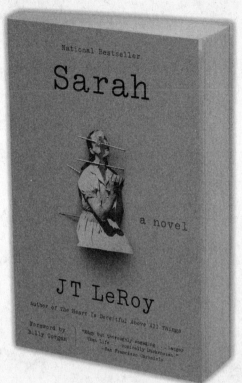

SARAH
A Novel
Available in Paperback and Ebook
Foreword by Billy Corgan

"A deft and imaginative...novel." —*New York Times Book Review*

Sarah never admits that she's his mother, but the beautiful boy has watched her survive as a "lot lizard": a prostitute working the West Virginia truck stops. Desperate to win her love, he decides to surpass her as the best and most famous lot lizard ever. With his own leather mini-skirt and a makeup bag that closes with Velcro, the young "Cherry Vanilla" embarks on a journey through the Appalachian wilds, dining on transcendental cuisine, supplicating to the mystical Jackalope, encountering the most terrifying of pimps, walking on water, being venerated as an innocent girl saint—and then being denounced as the devil.